THROUGH
the pain

THROUGH *the pain*

For all Content Inquiries, please visit my website:

Dedication

For those whose childhoods were ripped away too soon...

Prologue

He calls himself the Bishop and he's a mountain of a man. The palm of his hand could easily engulf my face. *That's* how big he is. Stepping into the cage, my heart beats along with the bass of the music, only heightening the adrenaline coursing through my veins. Winning this fight would put four grand in my pocket. That's the mortgage and groceries this month with extra for savings.

He snaps his head to the side to crack the thick column of his neck, the sound circling around me over the thump of the music. The crowd roars with the intensity of the energy inside the basement of this compound as the smell of sweat and beer soaks the air. I'm on a winning streak, and so is he. This is our first match against each other, and even though I knew it would eventually happen, I was surprised when I heard about the pairing.

"Tonight is a big one," the emcee calls into the mic from the booth at the far end of the room, amping up the crowd more. "Are you all ready for this?"

I barely have time to turn and look at my opponent before his feet are thundering across the mat, jarring me into action just before his fist meets my nose. I fall to my knees as the audience loses their shit and then punch him in the right knee, quickly rolling out of the way. There's only one way to crumble a mountain and that's to destroy it from the base up.

The cage meets my back as I push up and jump to my feet, keeping my eyes on him as he slowly turns to find me over his shoulder before rising from his knees. He grins wide when he sees me tucked in a corner and it takes everything in me not to smile back. It's better if I play the part of a distressed teen fighting a grown-ass man. Schematics.

The Bishop stalks toward me with his fists curled at his sides, slightly favoring that knee I hit, and a vibration starts in my core. It's been there and waiting patiently to be called upon, my constant companion, but the rage is only simmering right now. I need to let him get in a good hit to really get it boiling. No pressure though. It's not like his fist could *break my whole fucking face.*

I flick my eyes first to the right and then to the left, giving him the impression I'm panicking and looking for a way out as I bring my fists up in front of my face. His chuckle nearly has me breaking my role and laughing in his face. He may be big, and he sure is able to fucking snap me in two with his bare hands, but I'm not scared.

If anything, I'm fucking excited.

The Bishop lunges forward to grab a hold of me, but I push back against the cage, letting the metal absorb my weight, and then I spring forward, jamming my knee into his groin. He bends over with a yell to cup his balls and in the same motion, the same knee connects with his nose. He flies backward, his back hitting the mat with a *thud,* and then I'm on him. Two sharp jabs to the throat and another to his broken nose has his eyes rolling back into his head as he tries to choke in air.

I roll off of him as he slowly moves up to his knees, his face wincing from the pain and his upper body swaying with his unsteadiness. I wanted to drag this out longer, enjoy the fight a bit, but something isn't feeling right tonight and I'm anxious to get home. I hop and swing my right leg out, letting my foot connect with his cheek in a hard, roundhouse kick.

He hits the mat one final time, and the place erupts in a multitude of screams and boos. Regardless of what anyone else is feeling about the match, I can feel how heavy my pocket is about to be with four grand sitting in it.

The front of my house is engulfed in flames. I stand transfixed in my front yard as I watch the orange and red blaze lick toward the starless night sky. My mother is home… my mother! I break free from the hold the inferno has over me and run for my front door, my mind scrambling to absorb everything that's happening. The heat is emanating from the polished wood surface, radiating in thick waves and seeping through my clothes. I can hear the fire crackling on the other side of the door, blocking off any way of getting through, and my heart pounds as I spin around.

I run along the side of the house and hop the gate into my backyard, my shoes sinking into the mud. Smoke billows out of the rear screen door, but the fire hasn't reached its way back here yet. I pull the neck of my hoodie over my mouth and nose, then rush headfirst through the fumes, my hand stinging where I gripped the handle of the door.

"Mom?" I yell out, my voice cracking with the acrid smolder. There's no answer. "Mom!" My chest begins to hurt with the pounding of my heart and my eyes sting from the thick smoke.

Our bungalow is a hot box, and everything we took pride in is burning to the ground. Our very first house we worked so hard for, putting our sweat and blood into, is turning into ash. My heart breaks knowing it's all destroyed, but my mother is more important. I look left to the hallway that leads to the kitchen and see flames licking their way toward me along the ceiling. Then I look to the right, down the other hallway leading to our bedrooms, seeing the pictures of me as a baby and family photos with my mom smoldering and melting away. The floral wallpaper I despised, but helped my mom put up, is curling and aflame, the flakes of ash floating around me.

Where the fuck is she?!

I think I hear a faint voice coming from the kitchen, making me rush to my left. Heat spreads along the parts of my exposed face, stinging the sensitive flesh. The smoke gets thicker, and my lungs are screaming with every smoke-filled breath I take.

"Mom!"

I crouch down to my hands and knees where the smoke is thinner and try to make my way to the kitchen. The black-and-white checkered linoleum floors are turning brown and bubbling in front of my eyes. "Mom!" My voice is hoarse and my throat feels like it's on fire, making my eyes water as tears run down my cheeks in steady streams.

I have to get to her. She's all I have, my only family. If she dies, I might as well die too. She's the only one who can grip the darkness inside of me and hold it back. Without her, I will lose myself, becoming nothing more than the monster I am constantly at war with.

I crawl along the tiled floor, but my legs and arms are heavy, their movements stiff and slow. The tile in the hallway grows hotter and I look toward the ceiling to see flames eating away drywall, exposing insulation and wood beams. Still, I push forward. I'm halfway to the kitchen when I can no longer keep my eyes open, the sting from the smoke and heat proving to be too much. My breaths are coming in quick pants, and I feel light-headed, my thoughts becoming fuzzy as I try to remain focused.

I struggle to open my eyes and see a wall of flame, watching as everything goes dark.

Regardless of the fire blazing around me, I let it take me.

"Ember!!" I hear my best friend, Tommy, bellowing

over the cracking of the flames. "Ember, please! Oh God! I was too late. Help!!!" I'm lying on a hard surface and a cool breeze runs along my scorched face. I try to lift my head but it's just so heavy, and I open my mouth to answer him but no sound comes out. My lungs and throat scorch like the fire is raging inside of me, trying to force its way out. I push to open my eyes, to tell him I'm here, but they won't cooperate.

Fuck, I'm just so tired.

"Emberlise, baby, look at me." It's my mother. I blink a few times to clear the fog to find her standing in front of me with a serene smile on her face and her white-blonde hair blowing in the wind. "You're going to be okay, baby."

"Mom? Are you okay?" I ask her, my body feeling light. She continues to smile as she watches me. "Good. I'm so tired."

"Rest, baby, I'll be here." I nod, then let the darkness take me again.

Chapter One

A loud, insistent beeping sound pulls me out of my sleep. I've never been a deep sleeper, and the only times I have slept like this was when I passed out from exhaustion or too much alcohol. What the hell did I drink last night?

I mumble something and reach out to slap at my cell phone on my side table, my eyes refusing to open. Fuck school today. I'll tell Mom I got my rag. My hand hits a bar and I feel a tearing pain, making me hiss.

"Ember?" My eyes fly open when I hear Tommy's frantic voice.

"Tommy?" I croak out. "Fuck."

My throat feels like sandpaper and all I see is a plain, white-tiled ceiling. I turn my head toward the beeping sound and see a hospital monitor, then let out a groan as all the memories flood my brain from the night before. My house burning and me trying to get to my mother… my mother! I try to lift my head from the pillow, but the room spins on its axis, driving me back down.

"Hey, Blur, look at me," Tommy murmurs, using the

nickname he gave me over ten years ago. I slowly turn at the sound of his voice and see his dark brown, almost black, eyes wide and staring at me on the other side of my bed. He's sitting in a chair, his long legs nearly folded in half. "How are you feeling?"

"Mom…" *Fuck, it hurts to speak.* My hand grips the thin column of my throat as I wince through a swallow.

"Hey, it's okay. I called the nurse, and she's going to come check on you." He brushes some hair off my face, my brow tensing as I look at him. This is unlike Tommy. He's never affectionate. I'd get a half hug or a hair ruffle when I was feeling out of sorts, but never tenderness.

Something is wrong.

"Water," I growl, the pain becoming unbearable the longer I try to speak.

My dry throat is making speaking feel like death and I need to be able to speak to find out what's going on. Tommy scrambles to his feet to grab a cup filled with ice chips, then gives me an apologetic look as he places an ice chip in my mouth. "They said to only give you this."

"My mom?" I ask in a hoarse whisper, the ice melting in my mouth. I sound like I smoked a whole carton of cigarettes, one right after the other. Although, the ice has helped a little.

"Just wait for the doctor, Ember." Sadness bleeds into his tone and his face is a mask of agony, leaving me with knots in my stomach. I turn away from him to keep myself from exploding.

It's bad, it's terrible. I can feel it. I tremble, feeling the fear building and sliding down my limbs, which only fuels my anger. I hate feeling afraid. My chest still burns, like it's on fire as it spreads up my throat and I'm thankful when I lose consciousness again.

"When will she wake up?" A woman's voice breaks through the blissful silence. Irritation coats over me as my sleep is disturbed until everything slowly comes back to me. Who's that in my room?

"Her body has been through serious trauma, and she has severe smoke inhalation. Her coming in and out of consciousness will be normal as her body rests and heals." He sounds like a doctor and I wish I could grill him right now, but it's impossible to even get my eyes to open let alone words to come out of my mouth.

"I can't believe this is how I'm meeting my niece. Damn you, Rebecca." Niece? Who is this woman and why is she talking about my mother? The beeping of the heart monitor next to my bed picks up speed as my chest begins to tighten.

Quiet sobs filter through my numbing state and I hear another male's calming murmurs. Who are they? My mind is slow to process everything I'm hearing and when I try to open my mouth to speak, nothing happens.

The sound of beeping permeates the fog once again. As I come back to consciousness, my head feels clearer and my chest has a dull ache compared to the roaring heat I felt before. My throat is still dry, but the pain is beginning to subside. I open my eyes and see the same ceiling as before, then turn to the right and find Tommy fast asleep in the armchair with his arms and legs thrown out wide.

"Tommy…" I strain to speak, but he stirs as his eyes open slowly.

"Ember?" He rubs his face and sits up. "Here, you must be thirsty." He brings me a cup of water, touching the straw to my mouth. An upgrade from ice chips, thankfully. "Drink slowly." His voice is still groggy from sleep and his hair is tousled as if he's been running his hands through it.

The cool water feels good against my parched throat,

soothing away the pain. I close my eyes and concentrate on my breathing, a technique I've mastered over the years when I feel myself starting to lose control. Once I'm done, I give Tommy a look, relaying that I need some fucking answers.

"Blur, you're so fucking strong. You can do this. You've taken down men twice your size. I watched you fight two men and look for more. Just breathe it out." It's the usual talk he gives me when he feels like I'm teetering on the sharp edge of my sanity. It's a dangerous slope to be on, and once I tip over, it's so hard to haul myself back up.

"That last cage fight, the one with the Bishop," I begin. "There was something off about it. I could feel the tension in the room."

"Raphael is out of jail. He showed face at that fight, and then you decimated his best fighter." His grin lights up at the memory. "Like I said, you're so fucking strong."

Raphael is the kingpin of the Eastside Rampage, a gang that supplies the Bronx with drugs, guns, and illegal fights. He was put away for fifteen years on trafficking, racketeering, and money laundering charges. Tommy says they were never sure who the informant was, but to be assured Raphael has a vendetta and a score to settle.

Tommy is right. I'm strong and I'm a fighter. I've trained for years to be this strong and the anger that feeds this strength is a constant struggle to control. It must come from the father I never knew because my mother is as sweet as pie. Couldn't even hurt a fly.

My eyes widen, and I search Tommy's face at the thought of Mom. "My mother… tell me now."

His face contorts with pure agony and he opens his mouth to speak just as the door to my hospital room swings inward, and in walks a woman who looks too much like my mother to be real.

My mouth opens and shuts as I try to figure out what to say. She saves me the effort, though. "Hello, Emberlise. I'm your

Aunt Debra. I'm your mother's sister… Younger sister, by a few years…" She's rambling, just like my mother does when she gets nervous. "I didn't know you existed… I knew nothing. I tried to find her for years, but she disappeared."

"What are y—" I croak out, but she cuts me off.

"Sorry. We shouldn't start off like this. I'm just really glad you're okay and to have found you. Even under these circumstances." She comes to stand at the end of my hospital bed, placing her hands on the railing. Her face is filled with remorse and her eyes are glossy with unshed tears. She's wearing a pantsuit, the creases perfectly ironed, and her blouse a champagne color which sets off the tone of her skin.

What circumstances? Before I can voice my question, Tommy stands up. "I've got to get home. Jason is there alone… You know how he gets," he says, his eyes not quite meeting mine. "I'll call you tomorrow before you're released." Tommy's fifteen-year-old foster brother, Jason, is a train wreck.

"Wait," I demand. "I need you to tell me—"

I'm cut off again and I narrow my eyes on my supposed aunt. "It's okay, Tommy, I will take it from here." Anger rushes through me like a knife, the edge sharp and deadly. She may claim to be family, but I don't know her, and I don't appreciate her talking over me.

Tommy nods and leans down to kiss my forehead. Another sign of affection telling me something is definitely wrong. "I promise I'll call tomorrow." Then he's gone.

"Why are you here? Where is my mother?" I ask her. Fuck, she looks so familiar but foreign. It makes me feel nostalgic but apprehensive at the same time.

She moves slowly and sits in the chair Tommy vacated, her posture straight and her shoulders tense. "Your mother had me listed as yours and her next of kin." Tears roll down her cheeks as she hiccups into her hand. "I didn't even know you existed. I spent a few years after she left I–looking for her, b–but I was young. After those few years of nothing, I became a–angry.

I just stopped looking, but I thought about her often. I m–missed her, but I was so angry."

"Where is my mother?" I demand again slowly as I lean up to rest against the headboard of the bed.

"Honey, I'm so sorry. She's not here. Oh God, I don't even know how to do this!" She's sobbing openly now. My heart crashes into my stomach at her words and my mouth dries with fear.

Not here? Like not here in this hospital? Why not? Where did they send her?

"If she's not here, where is she?" I ask slowly, enunciating each word. It's like she should be lying in this bed instead of me.

"Oh, God," she groans through her hands. "It's not good, Emberlise." She's using my full name, looking distraught and avoiding my eyes.

That's when I know.

My mother didn't make it.

I hear a high-pitched scream and realize it's coming from me, my whole body erupting with pain as I scream out all the air in my lungs.

"I'm so sorry!" this woman cries out as she grabs my hand, her voice shrill with panic, but my fingers refuse to tighten around hers. "We'll get through this together. You're not alone."

I've never been so alone.

My mother was all I had. Now it's just me and the darkness. I scream again as the nurse rushes into the room, her face filled with worry. "Okay, dear," she says soothingly. "You are one strong girl." I wish everyone would just stop saying that to me.

I watch as she injects something into my IV and my eyes instantly become heavy. Great, she's drugging me. "No… drugs… I… hate this… feel…"

"Just to help you sleep, dear. No matter how strong you are, your body needs rest."

Her voice fades along with the sound of my mother's sister's sobbing and I welcome the void because it's easier than reality.

The next day, I'm released into the custody of my Aunt Debra and Uncle Scott Williams. They're the typical cookie-cutter married couple, in love with stars in their eyes, and they look at me like they might've won the lottery, regardless of how they gained custody of me.

They don't know shit.

The hotel bathroom's mirror reflects a girl I don't recognize. The mahogany hair reaching the middle of my back is limp and dull, my usually warm olive skin is looking slightly green, and my pale turquoise eyes—my mother's eyes—look back at me lifelessly. Most of my features belong to my mother, like my eye color, pert nose, and full cupid bow lips, but my skin tone, hair, almond-shaped eyes, and beauty mark under my right eye belong to the man who sired me. That's what I assume anyway since I've never met the man.

My body feels completely worn out, and it hurts to expand my chest for a deep breath. I place my hand over my left breast and feel my thundering heartbeat, a constant reminder that I survived when she didn't. I've lost weight since being in the hospital and the stress of what's happened. I usually pride myself on keeping my body toned with very little body fat because of what I choose to do to make money, but I can see I've lost some muscle mass. At five foot eight inches, I'm a little more than average height for a female and where most girls are watching what they gain, I'm picky about what I lose.

All I want to do is curl up on the hotel chair and cry for days, but my body and mind are on high alert. I don't know these people who are calling themselves family, this room is unfamiliar, and my future is unclear. So I force myself into survival mode and shove my grief down, tucking it away in a pocket I can revisit later.

The sounds of humming penetrate the thin walls, reminding me I'm not here alone. I throw my hair up into a messy bun and splash water on my face before leaning toward the mirror once more. The water droplets run rivulets along my cheeks to finally drip from my jaw, the muscles there tense from days of holding in everything. This situation with my new family is going to take some getting used to.

I exit the bathroom to find my Uncle Scott sitting at the end of one of the two double beds in the room, the TV remote in his hand and his eyes on me. The chair by the window beckons me and I sink into its plush cushion. I see a bus below dropping a group of people off at the bus stop as they scatter around to their jobs—or if they are anything like my mother was—their second job of the day already. There's a gaping hole in my heart and every time I think about her, I have a hard time breathing.

Like right now.

"Hey, Emberlise. In through your nose and out through your mouth," my shiny new uncle says soothingly while patting my back awkwardly, making me tense further. The foreign touch makes my skin crawl, but I endure it to avoid being difficult. They're all that's separating me from foster care and overrun group homes.

"Ember," I correct him once I catch my breath and press a hand to my pounding heart. "You can call me Ember."

"Ember it is." I finally take a look at him and the room we're currently staying in. His clothes are all designer and pressed. His coiffed blond hair shines under the dull lamps and his friendly, brown eyes twinkle with something that looks a lot like hope.

We're sitting in a fancy room in a pretty expensive hotel while my aunt settles my mother's estate. How rich are these people? They've already replaced my entire wardrobe back at their house and my aunt says you can never have too many shoes. Sounds spoiled and pretentious, nothing like the morals instilled in me, and it does nothing to ease the anxiety pulsing through me.

I just want my mother. No amount of money, shoes, or clothing will ever replace her.

Tommy called today as promised. He reminded me of a few engagements I had planned before my whole world came crashing down, and he also brought up a good point. Where do these people live? And where will I be living? He doesn't think it's New York because my aunt said my mother disappeared from home. So, where the fuck is my home now?

The hotel door opens and my aunt comes in looking tired and sad. It's easy for me to fathom how she's feeling. Today they concluded the formal investigation into the cause of the fire… gas leak. It was an old house and the gas lines hadn't been inspected in years. To think we saved and worked so hard for that place and just like that, it destroyed my family. We should've just stayed in the projects. At least there the danger is in your face and not hidden behind fancy wallpaper and tiled floors.

My mother was all I had, but I certainly wasn't all she had. This woman clearly loved her and she's feeling her loss as well. I feel a familiar burn in my stomach when I think about the family my mother had hidden from me and I swallow down the anger as betrayal washes through me.

For my entire childhood, I was practically alone. I never blamed my mother because I knew without her having two jobs, we'd be homeless, and trust me, we lived nowhere fancy. The front of our first apartment in the projects always had someone sleeping on the sidewalk, rodents ran over our feet in the hallways, and I've opened cabinets to find roaches feasting on our food. So I knew how easy it would be for us to go from a one-room apartment to the sidewalk too, but we clearly had family, who, by the looks of it, could have helped us.

Breathe, Ember.

"I wish I knew you existed." My aunt's voice cracks with emotion as she sits on the bed beside her husband. "I feel like I'm looking at someone I'm familiar with, yet I know nothing." They clasp hands as he leans in and kisses her temple.

I think about what she said and realize that I can tell them a few things. Doing so could be a distraction from the battle of emotions inside of me too. "When I was five, my mother decided to put me in some ballet classes at the community center. It was a free program and certainly helped a lot of the less fortunate children. I went for maybe two and a half lessons. Wasn't my thing. It was in the middle of that third class when I came upon the gym in the same building. I looked inside the window and watched mostly grown men fighting. To me, that was a dance. They looked like they were dancing." I'm not sure why I'm telling them this story, but if they want to get to know me, this is the best place to start. So I continue while keeping my eyes on them. "There I was, five years old, entering the gym full of adults. Imagine it. I had on some thrift store, pink tutu my mother found and I was standing in the middle of a room full of grown men sweating and grappling." My aunt softly chuckles and my uncle's eyes are full of humor. "I put my hands on my waist and declared to them all that I would be taking that dancing class from now on. Most of them looked at me in my tutu and outright laughed, but there was one guy, his name is Juan, he came right up to me. He bent down to my level and said, 'If you're serious, I expect you here every Monday, Wednesday, and Saturday.' I was so excited." At the memory, a small smile plays on my mouth and I begin to twist my fingers into the hem of my shirt. "When my mom picked me up, I told her I quit ballet but found another dance class I liked. She was always exhausted, so my declaration was only half listened to. She patted my head and mumbled, 'Sure, honey.' So, for the next few years, that's what I did. I trained in MMA and I became good. Juan is an amazing teacher and he's my coach now. He didn't teach me like he did most of his students, obviously. I'm a girl and it's different. I will be the first to admit that, but I have my own strengths *because* I'm a girl. I'm quicker than most men and women my size and I use that to my advantage. It's kind of what I'm known for, and my ring name is Blur."

"That sounds like a comic book character. Are you a vigilante?" my uncle asks with one eyebrow raised in speculation while my aunt just turns a little green in the face.

That's fucking funny. They have no idea what I've been doing to survive these streets.

"No, I compete here in New York. Sometimes legally and other times not so much, but the payout is great and it supports us. So my mother only has one job instead of two or three."

My aunt gasps and I don't know if it's about the illegal fighting or the fact that someone had two or three jobs to survive. Both of their eyes stay trained on me though, neither moving an inch on the bed.

"You fight in rings?" she whispers, her hand inching up to press against her chest as the other stays fisted in her lap.

"Or parking lots." I shrug. "I've been lucky with my winning streak, but there have been times I've lost… badly. That's how I learned an important lesson. Get knocked down, but make sure you get back up. Then you learn how the hell you got down in the first place and never make that mistake again."

"Wow," my uncle breathes out before turning to look at Aunt Debbie. "That's impressive." He sounds impressed while my aunt looks worried.

"I'll be honest," my aunt says as she slowly shakes her head. "I don't like it, but I'm curious to see you fight."

"I'm glad you said that since I have a fight tomorrow night." Uncle Scott snaps back around to stare at me as the color drains from Aunt Debbie's face.

"What?" they both ask in unison.

"Totally legal. It will help center me and get my mind off things. Would you like to come with me to meet my coach today?" If they say no, I will sneak out and call it quits on this new family, but I hope that they don't because I want them to know me and accept me for who I am.

"Yes, we would," my uncle answers, looking at my aunt

again. "Right, Debbie?"

"Okay," she agrees, throwing her hands up in the air in defeat.

Chapter Two

My coach, Juan, looks confused as I walk into his office
with my aunt and uncle in tow. His graying hair is combed back
over his head and held in place with pomade to hide his bald
spot. He's wearing an all-white tracksuit today with his worn
tennis shoes. It feels like any other day, but it's not and the
sight threatens to spill the grief I've so carefully tucked away.
I breathe in deep, pushing down the rising wave before I sink
beneath it.

"Ember, I didn't expect you here today," he says, placing
a hand on my shoulder as his eyes soften. "I'm really sorry about
what happened." I shrug out from under his hand and step back
because the touch is too comforting, and if I fall under the weight
of his sympathy, I will sink and never come back up for air.

"I need to fight, Juan." He covers his forehead with
his hand, his palm dragging down over his face to his chin
as I dismiss his sympathies. "It'll help." With a look over my
shoulder, I find my aunt and uncle watching us closely as they
huddle near the door where I asked them to wait. They stick
out like a sore thumb here in their fancy clothing and groomed
features and my aunt is feeling it as she clutches her purse to her
chest while looking suspiciously around the room.

I look back at Juan to find him watching me with a crease between his brows, his hands back on his waist. He knows exactly what I'm referring to, and he knows it will help because he's trained me since I was a young girl.

"Or you will make a mistake and get seriously injured because of what you're going through," he retorts, then flicks his gaze behind me. "Who are they?" He sounds cautious as he eyes my new guardians.

"This is my mother's sister, Debra, and her husband, Scott. My new guardians. I told them everything and they… ah… want to see me fight." I cringe as I say the words, knowing that the way they look doesn't add up to what I'm asking for.

Juan proves me right when his eyebrows shoot up and his hands drop from his waist with his surprise. "Seriously?"

"Yes. So let's go hit the mats and get some practice in before tomorrow." I nod and begin to pull off my hoodie, grabbing the roll of tape from the pocket. Though I shove it back in when the bright pink color has my throat sealing. "Pass me the tape." I point to the black roll on his desk. It's the complete opposite of the one my mother gave me, and right now, I can't bear to see anything that reminds me of her.

He looks like he wants to argue more, but Juan knows me better than anyone else—next to Tommy anyway—and arguing would be futile. If I don't fight, I may explode and lose the only family I have left. The only people willing to care for me. I beg Juan to understand with my eyes, showing him the consequences without saying a single word. Not that I have to, he knows as well as I do what could happen if I don't let this suffocating energy free. He tosses me the tape with a nod and I exhale the breath I didn't realize I was holding.

I'm supposed to be fighting a UFC prospect tomorrow. This fight has been in the plans for nearly six months and it was always meant to be a chance to penetrate the legal fight circuit when I come of age. She has six inches on me, is about seventy pounds heavier, and is three years older. I'm not worried about her size or age, I've taken down bigger and older, it's the potential this fight holds. I fear not being good enough or failing, especially now when I need something to fall back on if my new family decides to dump me because our lifestyles are clearly polar opposites.

My fights give me the outlet I need to release the aggression inside me, whether they be legal fights with females in my weight class or illegal with both male and female of any weight class. Sometimes I do a little work for the local gang and help them with the members needing to be put in their place, but Juan pretends not to know that because he says ignorance is bliss.

Since my opponent is larger than me, Juan suggested working on submission holds instead of a knockout. It's standard practice to do that. A submission hold done right could take down anyone. Little does he know I've had my fair share of knocking people out, but I humor him. Besides, I love submission holds.

We practice the toehold first. This one can be extremely painful if executed correctly. By cranking the ankle and putting pressure on the foot just right, you can break small joints if the opponent doesn't tap out. So Juan does some evasive moves while I quickly take him down into the hold. By the tenth time, he's taken out and I'm declared a pro with the toehold. I'm shocked when I turn to look outside of the ring and find my aunt and uncle still seated on the sidelines watching.

Next up, we work on the triangle choke. This one is simpler since I'm not scrambling to grab legs or feet. It's an upper body move, which leaves the opponent strangled between their own shoulder and my arm. Since this woman tomorrow will be taller than me, I'd have to bring her to her knees first.

Then we finish off with some neck cranks and armbars. I can feel my body flowing into each move like water. That's why, at the tender age of five, I thought this was dancing. I'm a mess of sweat when we're done but Juan knows me well, and I'm always amped after grappling.

"Go take thirty and run it off. I want to have a chat with your aunt and uncle." He's panting hard as the sweat drips from his brows, but his eyes are hard, daring me to argue. He wants to feel out the new parents and it assures me to know I have more family than I thought.

"Yes, coach," I reply as I jog over to the treadmill. I set it to a medium jog and watch the three of them converse through the mirror in front of me. My aunt now has a permanently shocked look on her face and my uncle looks like he might grill Juan. I grin to myself, knowing Juan is one tough SOB. If he's being grilled, I'm sure he's giving it right back.

I finish my run at fifteen minutes instead of thirty and head over toward Juan. He stops his lesson with another fighter at the punching bags and pulls me aside, a forlorn expression on his face. I watched the new guardians step outside a few minutes ago, both of them a little pale in the face after watching what, I suspect, they thought was their new pretty niece fighting a grown man.

"What were they saying to you?" I ask him as I take a towel off a nearby cart to wipe my face and chest.

"They wanted to know about your life here, Ember. I told them what I could, but I didn't lie. I also told them I suspected you were involved with some shady shit and if they can take you away from here, it would be for the best." He looks grim and his voice matches, but I can see it's hurting him to say it.

"What? Why the fuck would you say that, Juan?" I feel my face heat as I whip the towel into a nearby bin, my body coiled with anger. "Our training would stop and you wouldn't see me anymore!" He can't see what I'm feeling on the inside, but it's as if I'm being ripped apart. I'm losing someone else.

"That breaks my heart, it really does, but you deserve a better life, and those people look like they can give that to you." His eyes gather moisture as his voice shakes. I can see the sincerity in his gaze and it only makes me want to scream in frustration. "If I had the means to give you better, I would fight it, but this is your best shot."

"I can't believe you're saying this." A tear slips down

my face and I angrily brush it off as I avert my gaze. I refuse to cave and give up even if my entire world is burning to the ground. I'm not a quitter.

"Look around you, Ember. This place is falling apart. The children that come here have nothing and this neighborhood is teeming with gangs. You are so far in with the East Rampage, it's only a matter of time before something bad happens to you. Your mother would want better, and God rest her soul, but she worked way too much to keep tabs on you. These people can provide proper schooling because I know how smart you are, and they can help further your acting with the right opportunities." My chin falls to my chest as I drag in a breath, my eyes staring at the ripped canvas on Juan's shoe.

Right, my acting. The thing my mother absolutely loved watching me do. She hated the fighting but took on an extra part-time job just so we could afford summer acting camp and extra acting classes. I love acting too, but deep inside I know what I'm fantastic at. Fighting is my passion and I'm better at it than acting, whether people believe in me or not.

"Come here, kid." Juan pulls me in for a hug, his woodsy scent enveloping me. I fight the sob swelling inside of me as I soak in his warmth, knowing this may be the last time I see him. Living here and training in this gym is no longer an option for me. "This is for the best. Think of your mother and how much she'd want this for you." I nod and return his hug. There's something inside of me brewing with questions I fear the answers to. If my mother had this family so willing to help her, why did we struggle so much? Why was I forced to do the things I did to help us make ends meet? It's hard to dwell on those thoughts though because they feed the swelling anger inside me, and I don't want to ruin the little control I've been barely holding on to.

After letting Juan go, I head to the showers in the back, passing by familiar people congratulating and professing sympathies all in one. I acknowledge them with a dip of my head and continue moving and compressing the grief. There will be time to face it later because I need to concentrate on my fight first. It will be held here tomorrow night and it's not some star-studded event. My opponent, Carly Hader, has heard some rumblings about me through certain circles apparently and has said she wants to 'practice with me.' We're unable to have a legitimate fight because I'm not in the UFC league, but she clearly wants to showcase she can beat me regardless. At least this way Juan can charge admission for a fight, even though we have to technically call it a practice, and yeah, we may be a low-income, Bronx gym with some ratty no-good patrons, but we support our own. There will be many people here tomorrow night to watch the local fighter going up against an undefeated one.

I meet the guardians outside by their parked car and they straighten when they see me. On the way over here, I learned that it's some kind of Mercedes, but I'm not good with cars so I couldn't say what it was beyond the color champagne. Mom and I couldn't afford a car and public transit is readily available here.

"There's Blurry! The current undefeated champ!" my uncle screams out with a gleeful expression, his hands in the air. This pulls a chuckle from me, even if it makes my aunt cringe. Juan, of course, must've told them that. "Let's get some chow! You must be hungry after all that." He throws some punches into the air between us, making me laugh again.

"Oh God," I moan and swat his fists away. "It's Blur! Are you guys hungry? I can take you to some pretty sweet Chinese takeout if that's something you like?"

"Is it all-you-can-eat?" Uncle Scott's eyes shine with interest as my aunt groans, her mouth tipping up into a smile.

"He's a machine," she says with obvious affection before rubbing his stomach. "You'll learn soon enough."

"Yeah, there is one around here. I've got to keep it light, though. Can't over carb before a fight." I shift from one foot to the other, waiting to see how they react to the thought of me fighting again.

"That's all good. You eat the veggies and I'll take care of the rest." Uncle Scott grins while patting his flat stomach.

My uncle is on his third plate when I nervously decide to broach the subject of where I'll be living. "So, you now have custody of a sixteen-year-old, congrats, by the way. Where will I be living? Do I have cousins?" Once the questions start, there's no end, but I force myself to stop at two so I can at least hear the answers to the most pressing ones.

"Right. We were trying to figure out when the best time to talk about that would be," my aunt begins. She drops the fork to her plate and steeples her fingers under her chin as her throat works on a swallow. "We actually live in Ontario, Canada." Shock settles over me as I swallow down my food, placing my fork on the table. Canada? I know it's not on the other side of the world, but that's an entirely different country! "I know. It will be a change. We live in a small town called Whitsborough, which is about forty-five minutes outside of Toronto," she continues. "All great shopping and city living is close by!" The worry shines from her eyes as she stares at me, hoping I'll reflect some of the excitement she's forcing in her words.

Shopping? I don't give a fuck about shopping. I'm going to be a Canadian. Forty-five minutes from the city? So, like in the country? Will I live in a log cabin?! I begin to hyperventilate as my chest ceases from lack of oxygen. Annoyingly, this is becoming a common occurrence in front of them.

"In through the nose, Blurry, and out through your mouth," my uncle soothes as he leans over to rub my back. My fingers dig into the wooden tabletop as I suck in a breath. "There you go."

"Ember, it'll be okay. Your coach told us about your acting and he says you're good. The high school near us focuses on the arts. You could go there and get extra training…" Her voice begins to sound like it's underwater, and the only thing resonating with me is the fact that I will truly be leaving my mother's memory and our life behind.

In the grand scheme of things, I know these are all good things. Mom and I lived in a rough neighborhood and I didn't get all the privileges some children have. Yes, there was a time when I wanted to be an actor, but it was only so I could provide for my mother and me. It was the one thing that put pride in my mother's eyes when she spoke about me. The fighting made her anxious, but she never took it away because it calmed the constant hurricane inside of me. Plus, I like to fight. Will I have to give it up for some little town in Canada?

Once I get my breathing under control, I clear my throat and release the table. "It's not… like a log cabin in the middle of the woods though, right?" I ask with trepidation as my aunt and uncle give each other a look, his hand moving from my back to his full stomach.

"No, no!" my uncle teases as he leans back in his chair. "It's actually an igloo."

My periphery darkens with anxiety as my vision zones in on my uncle, my breath threatening to cease once again in my chest. "Is it snowy all year?" I nearly choke on air and stare at them both in shock when they start laughing heartily at my ignorance as I tamp down the anger threatening to surface. My body tenses as I stare at them, both of them knowing I have never been out of New York. How would I know what it's like in fucking *Canada*?

"The weather is pretty much how it is here. We're only like eight hours' drive away," Aunt Debra says, still chuckling.

"Oh, okay, that's not so bad." I deflate with relief, but it doesn't calm the nerves swirling inside of me. I'll still be leaving my life and the country I've grown up in.

"No, you could still come visit friends on some weekends." She tries to soothe the tumultuous energy I know I'm exuding, but it does little to help. I don't like being thrusted into a situation I'm not prepared for. How does one prepare for losing their only family and then moving to Canada?

"You spoke to Juan, and I know he told you what I've been messed up with here. The only friend I have is Tommy," I tell her, my voice dropping as I toy with the food on my plate, my eyes avoiding them. I'm not ashamed of having no friends from school or otherwise. It's because I had to work during every bit of spare time. Friends tend to take up a lot of energy and I had none to give.

"He also runs with this dangerous crowd?" my uncle interjects, his tone filled with curiosity.

I nod and continue to finish my meal, each bite tasting like nothing. I will not speak any further about Tommy's gang affiliation. It's not my place and these are not his guardians. Tommy's only family has been the Eastside Rampage, me, and his younger foster brother. His mother was a crackhead who overdosed when he was twelve and he doesn't know who his father is. This is why it's important we keep in touch. I make a mental note to text him to confirm he's coming to my fight. Otherwise, I may not get another chance to see him before I leave the country.

Later that night when we get back to the hotel, I send the text to Tommy. I also remind myself to talk to the new guardians about cousins that seemed to be skipped over during dinner. Then I crawl up into bed and attempt to sleep while trying to keep the image of my mother fresh in my mind.

My life is about to change and all I can imagine is how badly I'm about to fuck it all up.

When I arrive at the gym the next morning, I find Juan ready and waiting for me by the ring. My aunt and uncle sit in the chairs lined up around it and they watch quietly as I run through moves with Juan. Once we're done, he admits to signing an agreement guaranteeing I wouldn't knock Carly out and not hit her face, something to do with her public image. As much as I want to knock her out for making me sign it, I'd rather beat her in the ring instead.

Two hours later, she shows up with her entourage, her shiny, blonde hair in a French braid as she saunters into the ring. The place is packed and as I look around, it warms me to see it's mostly my people. The seats are filled with other gym members, some kids from my high school, and Tommy. I never really took the time to get to know most of them, but the sight stirs the emotions I've been burying deep. The thought of being uprooted and thrown into a new situation has my anger bubbling, but anger is an emotion I can work with right now.

Most of the fight was spent with us dancing around each other since I couldn't touch her face and she was too afraid to get close. I ended up getting her in the toehold fairly early and she tapped out, but not before she left me with a shiner, which pisses me off to no end. Though I left three grand richer.

Tommy assured me after my fight that he would keep in touch with Skype sessions. I will miss him and New York, even if it wasn't the safest place for me. He told me the gang was already trying to figure out who their next 'collector' would be, but I wasn't sad to be leaving that behind. Being a collector for the Rampage meant fetching money owed or beating the ones who couldn't pay and that was an aspect of fighting I didn't enjoy.

Now I'm standing in front of my new family's Mercedes outside of our hotel, looking around and soaking up the last of New York I'll see in a while. I hug my mother's ashes to my chest and inhale the pollution I'm so used to. My aunt picked them up this morning from the funeral home. We're foregoing a funeral because there's no one here worth celebrating her life with. My new guardians have assured me if I want a funeral, we can have one in Whitsborough. I guess there are many people there who loved her. The thought of having a funeral makes my stomach tighten with anxiety though. I'm not ready to finalize her death yet. Despite having an urn full of ashes, I still feel like I'm leaving her spirit behind.

"Hey, Ember?" I turn to look at my uncle as he approaches me, his tawny hair blowing in the wind and his eyes soft with concern. "She's with you always. She's watching us now, and I bet she's wanting to kick my ass for letting you get that black eye."

I laugh out loud at that. He sure knows how to brighten up a mood. "Bro, I've had worse."

"Bro?! I'm Unc to you!" he exclaims while throwing up some weird-ass hand signs. "Wait… What do you mean by worse?" He gives me a goofy grin as he continues to wave his hand signs in the air.

I snort and get into the car, shaking my head at how genuinely good they are. My aunt is sitting in the front and she turns to give me a soft smile, the unshed tears in her eyes sparkling. They mirror what I was feeling about my mother earlier and I have to look away to keep my composure. After placing the urn on the seat beside me, I end up dozing off and waking up about three hours later. My aunt is now driving while my uncle snores softly beside her.

"Need a restroom?" she whispers from the front, her eyes meeting mine in the rearview.

"Sure," I reply with a shrug. "I'm also hungry."

"Burgers it is," she says with a small smile. "We'll let him nap while we go inside for a bite."

We find a twenty-four-hour burger joint, and I use the restroom while she orders my chicken burger combo, then we find a small booth at the back of the restaurant and I dig into the food, my stomach growling with hunger.

"I know you asked about cousins and we really didn't settle on that topic," she mumbles around a bite of her salad. Oh, thank God I don't have to bring it up again. Biting into my burger, I nod and she continues, "The thing is, there are no cousins." Placing her fork down, she looks off to her right, sadness clouding her features. "I'm unable to have children."

"Oh." I swallow down my food and wince at the lack of words to say. What do you say to that though? It's sad that someone as sweet and kind as Aunt Debra can't have children. It's those types of people who deserve them.

"We were planning to try medical measures, but I have a volatile uterus and would require a few procedures ahead of time. Scott just didn't like the risks involved. So now we are discussing adoption." After we finish our meals, she rips apart the napkin on her tray as she tells me something so personal that when her eyes meet mine, it's not pain I see, but hope. "I know what happened to my sister was a tragedy and my heart will never be the same, but I'm glad you're here. I'm not replacing your mom, but I will mother you to the best of my ability... if you'll let me." Her longing tone has my heart softening, the warmth she's radiating chipping away at the frost encasing my chest.

"Yeah, sixteen is a little older than what I imagine you were thinking of adopting." I try to shrug it off but my voice catches on the last syllable. The thought of having two people willing to love and care for me almost feels too much. My mother loved me unconditionally and now with the prospect of having two more... it makes me feel like I've won the lottery. After all, everyone wants to have a family who loves them unconditionally.

"True, but I'm totally in sync with angst and puberty." She laughs and I join her until I feel a tear slipping down my cheek, my hand swiping it away quickly. That's been happening too much in front of people lately and it's becoming annoying.

"I'm glad you showed up," I tell her honestly as she reaches across the table to take my hand.

"I'm glad you exist," she whispers back as her fingers tighten around mine.

Chapter Three

"Home sweet home!" Uncle Scott singsongs, the sound crashing through my slumber.

Quickly sitting up, I rub the crust out of my eyes as I crack my neck, stretching out the stiffness. Sleeping curled up in the backseat of a car for three hours causes havoc on the body. I also need a shower, and my stomach makes some atrocious noise, alerting me to the fact that I'm starving. My body is used to eating frequently because, as a fighter, I need the constant calories.

A set of wrought-iron gates open in front of us as I look out the window. Gates? They're like twenty feet tall. Are those cameras? Where the hell am I? We drive along a fifty-foot driveway that leads up to a huge seven-door garage. Who needs a seven-door garage?! We near the top of the driveway and the massive house rises up behind the garage. Okay, now it makes sense. This looks like a twenty-room house. Of course, it needs seven cars.

"This is it." My aunt turns to look at me over the back of the passenger seat, something like embarrassment shining in her eyes. "I know, it's absurd, but it's home."

My jaw feels like it's disconnected and hanging uselessly. This was how the other half of my family were living? They had this while we struggled with rent and food? It's hard not to feel resentful toward them, but I take the time to remind myself that these people didn't know I existed until recently.

We round the top of the driveway and stop in front of the huge double-front doors. I shut my mouth and open the car door, my eyes burning from the lack of blinking. Rubbing my watering eyes, I step out of the car, finally blinking against the breeze, and notice it's chillier here than in New York. My skin breaks out into goose bumps as I slowly spin once on the driveway, taking in the lush trees and large lawns full of grass and flowers. In New York, especially where I'm from, it was mostly concrete and pollution. It's the first positive I can see in this situation and I take it as a win.

"Let's grab the bags and get you inside. We didn't really have time to set you up with a room here since we left so suddenly, but you can pick whichever room you want and we'll make it over to your liking." My aunt interrupts my obvious gawking with a small smile while standing beside me and looking out over the lawn, pride oozing from her features. "I promise it'll feel like home in no time."

"Sure." This doesn't happen often, but I'm speechless. Coming from nothing and thrusted into obvious wealth is going to be a major adjustment. I follow her up to the front door and she puts her thumb—her thumb!—against a touchpad beside the handle. The door beeps and I hear the bolt slide back, the mechanical sound making me feel like I'm living in another dimension.

"Are you Iron Man?" I gasp as my hand hits my chest and I stare at her in shock. "Is this the Bat Cave?"

"Did you own a TV?" Uncle Scott calls out from behind us with a laugh. "Iron Man and Batman did not live together. Not that that would be wrong or anything." A snort flies from my mouth as I turn to look at him dragging the bags from the trunk.

"We'll get you set up with your thumb too," Aunt Debra says as she ignores Uncle Scott and leads me into the foyer. "I also ordered you the newest model iPhone because yours is too old for that app."

The beat of my heart in my ears drowns out my aunt, making her sound as if she's underwater as I look around the foyer. Our old apartment in the projects could fit in this space alone. The floors gleam with what must be a wax shine, and the staircase looks like something out of a Disney movie.

"Thanks, ladies," my uncle huffs as he brings in our bags and drops them dramatically to the floor, then presses his hands against his lower back. "No need to help or anything."

I snort, his sarcasm bringing me out of my stupor. "What? You're telling me you don't have a butler?" I retort. "How do you manage to bring anything in over that threshold?"

"That would just be pretentious—" my aunt starts.

"He lives in the garage! We could never live with the common folk!" Uncle Scott cuts her off, waving his hands in the air with a look of disgust. "Debra! Call Jane! This place needs to be cleaned ASAP! I can smell the three-and-a-half-day-old dust!" He puts his hand to his forehead and pretends to look sick. "Oh, it's making me faint. Is this how poor people feel?" He faces me when asking the question, a gleam of mischief in his eyes.

"Har, har." I roll my eyes but can't help the genuine laugh that leaks out of my mouth. "This is way more than I'm used to. I think your garage was bigger than our entire house."

"The garage is our temple. That's where we go to give thanks," Uncle Scott whispers reverently with his hands steepled and his eyes looking toward the ceiling.

"He filled the garage with old cars," Aunt Debra states, making Uncle Scott drop his arms in mock shock.

"Classics!" he screams as he goes back out to grab more bags.

I look around me once more and let the details of this

place seep in. The marble foyer floor leads to an oak staircase in the center flowing up to the second level. To the right is a large oak door. It's closed, so I don't know what's behind there. To the left is a hallway also clad in marble.

"I'll give you a tour." My aunt smiles as I look around wide-eyed. I automatically remove the flip-flops I have on and leave them by the door, too afraid of making the clean floors filthy.

She leads me to the large oak door on the right first. It's stained the same color as the stairs, a dark wine, and the molding is intricate with swirls and leafy designs. The imposing brass handle looks like something out of the eighteen-hundreds. She opens the door and leads me into an office. There's an enormous oak desk in the center stained the same wine color, and built-in bookcases filled with folders and binders all around.

She walks behind the desk and pushes slightly on the bookcase directly behind it. The shelving swings out to reveal a large screen displaying multiple camera views, the sight shocking me. How bad can it be here in a little town?

"This is your uncle's office. He buys old cars, fixes them up, and sells them to the highest bidder. Mostly men, mind you, who want to look decades younger in some hot rod." She looks at me over her shoulder with a smirk. "Whitsborough is full of them, by the way. This screen here is the central hub for our security cameras. You will also have this connected to your phone." Nodding, I try my best to soak in all the information.

We exit the office and walk straight ahead to the hallway that was on the left when we first came in. My aunt's red-soled shoes are clicking along the marble, the sound rising and bouncing off the twenty-foot space above our heads before we come to a large opening on our right. It's a huge family room with three full-sized, black leather couches and what looks like a one hundred—at least—inch TV.

"This is the den." The den?! My mouth drops open as I look around. This was about the size of our kitchen, family room, and dining room combined.

The champagne-colored carpet is plush, and my toes automatically curl into it as I swallow down a moan. One wall is red brick with an enormous fireplace in the center, and the other walls are a light gray with the couch cushions and throw blanket matching the red. The TV is wall-mounted and there's a stand underneath that's housing every type of console you can think of. I think there's also a Sega in there.

"Cars aren't the only old thing he's into," my aunt says with obvious adoration.

I turn to see a large patio door leading out into a huge backyard as my aunt walks toward it and unlocks the latch. Now, the patio door in my old house was one that ran on a track and slid to the side to open, but this door, this fancy-ass, nine-foot-tall glass door, pushes outward.

Next-level rich.

"We have our barbecue and sitting area over here," she chatters on as she disappears around the side. I quickly follow her out there, my bare feet begging to feel the thick grass.

The grass is as lush as it looks, like a sponge beneath my feet. Is this shit fake? I've only seen grass this green on those mini golf courses, but never have I felt it. There is what looks to be a vegetable garden and other flower beds scattered around the massive space, giving pops of color throughout the green. I follow her along an interlocked stone path toward a sitting area. There are cushioned seating chairs with a fire pit in the center and they barely look used.

"We have our summer barbecues out here. It's chilly now, being April, but by mid to late May it'll become warmer," she explains as I nod in response.

Just when I think I can't be any more overwhelmed with everything, she points to what looks like an industrial incinerator you'd find at the morgue. Don't worry about how I know that, just know I've seen some shit while I was running street missions for the Rampage. When she opens the cover, it reveals a grill and a smoker next to it. She then points toward a large shed. "We have a fridge over there and more seating inside. We call that your uncle's man cave where he and his friends have their man sessions." She gives me a look with a roll of her eyes and it strikes me in the chest how much that looked like my mom's face. My heart sinks as I breathe in through my nose, pushing the feeling away.

"That's pretty sweet," I squeak out as I try to move past the emotion threatening to bring me to my knees.

"Yeah, he enjoys it. Now, if we go around the side of the house, it brings you to the pool, but there's another entrance that brings you directly to it. So let's head back in." She guides me back the way we came and I begin to process her words without the threat of a meltdown. Did she say pool?

Of course there's another backyard entrance. It would be utterly preposterous for this house to only have one. We go back in through the big fancy doors and through the den, then move back farther down the hallway.

It opens up into the biggest kitchen I have ever seen. All the appliances are stainless steel, and the fridge is three times bigger than your average, as is the stove. The floors are all marble and the countertops match. The cabinets are oak and stained the same wine color. The table is identical to any other wooden piece in this house and it could feed twenty people easily. I really like how all the little details bleed throughout the rooms. It makes it feel cozy, even if it is the size of a Motel 6.

"I went to culinary school, so I wanted a large industrial kitchen," Aunt Debbie explains as she looks around the kitchen with pride.

"Are you a chef?" I run my fingers along the marble countertop, marveling over my reflection on its surface.

"No. To be honest, those few years were a waste. I ended up going back to school for interior design. So, this house design is all mine, as well as many others in this area." When I look up at her, I find her with her hands on her hips and a small smile on her mouth. This is all hers and I can see why she would be so proud.

"That's really cool." I nod and then groan inwardly when I sound like a drone in awe. My vocabulary was dropped somewhere at the front gates.

With a small smile, she turns and aims for a set of double oak doors and opens them. Inside is another room with deep cushioned seats and racks. Boots line the floor and the tiles gleam as bright as the rest of the house. Inside this room, there are four other doors.

"This is the mudroom." I make a noise in the back of my throat and she turns to look at me with her brow raised.

"Sorry." I cringe and then give her a shrug. "Nothing about this is muddy."

She looks around the space with a chagrined look and a chuckle before saying, "Yeah, I guess you're right. I'm meticulous about keeping it clean." It's the pride, I get it. Hell, I'm starting to feel it too. With a soft shake of her head, she points to the first door on the left. "Inside there is the laundry room." Then she points to the door beside it. "That's a closet filled with extra towels and bathing suits. Here"—she points to the third door on the right—"is the sauna and hot tub room."

A bit of guilt comes over me when I think about my gym and the fact that we didn't even have a sauna in it. We were lucky to get hot water for showers, and now look where I'm living. Juan was right, this will be a better life for me. I nod and keep my thoughts to myself. I don't want to seem ungrateful because I'm not. My life has changed for the better and I know I'm blessed, regardless of how I came to be here.

She opens another identical backyard door as the last one and we step out onto more interlocking stones. In the center is a beautiful pool with a fountain.

"We just had it opened for the summer," Aunt Debra informs me as she bends at the pool's edge to feel the water. "It's warm."

"It's really beautiful," I breathe out.

She stands back up and then points across to another

shed about twenty feet from the man cave. "All the pool deck furniture is in there, along with pool games and floaters." We go back into the house after I've adequately committed the backyard to memory. I won't lie, I'm feeling overwhelmed and I haven't even finished seeing the first floor.

She leads me back inside and through the kitchen to another hallway where there's a powder room, a formal sitting room, and the formal dining room. Then we come to another set of double doors.

"This is mine and Scott's room. We had two masters made for this house because I've just always wanted to be on the main floor." She opens the doors, and I stand transfixed on the scene in front of me.

The room is stunning, and I finally stumble through the doorway as I follow her around the space. The bed is bigger than a king, it has to be, and the rich crimson blankets stand out against the muted gray walls and carpet. It has its own sitting area and a huge walk-in closet with a vanity. I'm amazed by how much clothing and how many shoes this woman has. Then she shows me her enormous bathroom with the claw-foot tub. Everything just screams wealth and I know it's going to take some getting used to.

"The second master is upstairs with the other guest rooms. I'm hoping that's what you choose." Then we're going back down the hallway and into the kitchen, then down the other hallway with the den which leads back to the grand staircase. Just walking from one end of the house to the other is a workout. I run my hand along the polished banister as we head up the stairs, the rich wine color popping against my skin. There are multiple doors spread across the hallway, one to the right of the stairs and three to the left.

She points to a door on the right. "That's the second master. We'll save it for last." Again, I nod. I'm feeling like that bird sipping water thingy, you know what I'm talking about, but I'm at a loss for how to react otherwise.

We turn to the left and open two of the doors beside

each other, which are plain bedrooms, considering the rest of the house, but still outstanding for me. Each has its own bathroom. *Naturally*, as my aunt put it. The last door on the left opens to a set of ascending stairs, the clean, white aesthetic matching the rest of the house.

"There's a loft space up there. It's large and has some beautiful views. Plus, it's completely soundproof. It's empty because we really couldn't think of what to do with it. I wanted it to be a playroom, eventually." She sighs with sadness, drawing my attention to her forlorn expression.

"It could still be one day," I try to soothe her, but it comes off slightly awkward. Emotional displays and providing comfort make me uneasy.

"It's yours now. You can make your own space or a TV room. A place where you can be with your friends," she suggests as she gives me a watery-eyed smile.

"I couldn't do that." I shake my head as I swallow down my rising panic. I don't want to replace the children she's been longing to have. I don't want her to give up on that dream.

"You're ours, Ember. This is all yours as well." She holds out her hands to encompass everything she's shown me and I feel the shock as she pulls me in for a hug, my hands awkwardly patting her back. "Come on, let's check out the last room." She breaks the hold she has on me and grabs my hand, tugging me to the last and only door to the right of the stairs.

She opens the oak door and again—for like the millionth time—my jaw drops, successfully pulling me out of my earlier panic. This room also has a sitting area. It's a smaller scale than my aunt's room, but still expansive. There's a two-seater sofa in a champagne color and it's an antique style with oak wood detail. There's also a chaise in a dark wine color.

The carpet is plush and pure white, like soft, baby lamb fleece, and beside the chaise is a fireplace with a white marble top that matches the one in the kitchen. The curtains are the same wine color and look like velvet. The bed is king-sized with the same wine-colored blankets and a white fleece throw at the bottom.

"You wouldn't have to keep this theme in here. We could redo it." I turn to look at her only to find her wringing her hands, looking nervous as she watches me. I barely register her words as my mouth hangs open because this room is amazing as is. They've even painted the wall behind the bed the same wine color as an accent. Everything ties together perfectly. "Come check out the closet and bathroom," she encourages as she stands in front of a doorway, her face portraying the nerves she's trying to hide with an excited tone.

She leads me into the closet first. It's so big that I don't know how I will ever fill it up. There are custom shelves on one side and the wall across from it has an open space in the center. She sees me looking at it curiously.

"That's for a vanity. We'll pick one out and have it shipped." She closes the door and I turn to her. Why did she close us in here? "This is the mirror." She presses on the door and it unfolds into a three-way mirror. I gasp as I stare at our reflection, my mind scrambling to keep up with what I'm seeing. "Now you can see every angle of your outfit."

Next, we go into the bathroom and it's basically like hers. It has a claw-foot tub as well, and the shower has so many nozzles along with a digital pad for music setup and heat settings. "Your iPhone will have an iTunes account. You can sync the music both in here and in your bedroom."

"I've never seen this much, let alone have it for myself. This room is impressive," I mutter in awe. "I can't accept all of this without earning it."

"Earning it? Ember, this should've been yours from the day you were born. I am so sorry I didn't know you existed and even more so for the conditions you grew up in. I'm glad to give you all of this now, even if it is a tad too late." She sniffles. "Let's go downstairs and get some food in you. I could hear your stomach this whole time."

"I'm starving." I shrug, glad to skim over the emotional confessions.

We trek it back to the kitchen. Trust me, trek is the proper word. When we enter, I smell something so amazing that my stomach makes a vicious ripping sound as my mouth waters.

"That smells delicious!" I gush as I inhale deeply.

"Cinnabon," my aunt says with a sigh and a grateful smile to her husband.

"I figured I'd grab some grub for my two favorite ladies." My uncle grins, tossing us both a wink. We stand at the island in the middle of the kitchen and dig into the ooey gooey cinnamon rolls, my taste buds dancing with the sweet flavors. "I have a meeting in town today with a potential client," my uncle informs us around a mouthful of pastry. "He's a local rapper looking for a few specific cars for his music video. You wanna come with?" It's clear his nap during the ride here was adequate enough for him to work without rest.

"Me?" I squeak out around a mouthful of food.

"Yeah, I could drop you at the mall or the gym," he encourages as he licks his fingers.

"There's a gym?" My eyes widen and I forget all about the food on my plate. "Do they teach classes?"

"Well, my good friend, Andrew, is the owner and I know for a fact they do yoga and some light aerobics. I have seen none for MMA, though," he replies as he taps his chin in thought. "If it's something you want to do, maybe we could talk to him. I wouldn't want you to give it up completely, but there can't be any more fights in the ring. I almost had a heart attack watching that last one."

He's suggesting I teach. I never really thought of that. He's right, it would keep me up with what I love and I could make some money as well. I refuse to mooch any more than I have to. I'm ready to earn everything they're so selflessly handing over to me.

"We are not saying you have to get a job," my aunt stresses as she bites into her cinnamon bun. "This could be a hobby."

"I'd love to check it out." I nod enthusiastically as I bounce from foot to foot. I'm so excited.

"Great, we leave in ten." Uncle Scott grabs another cinnamon bun and nearly shoves the whole thing in his mouth as I run from the kitchen to my room. I quickly freshen up and change my clothes from the bag my uncle brought to my room, only stopping briefly to fawn once more over the tub. As I leave the room, my eyes fall on my mother's urn sitting on my dresser, the silver shining beneath the bedroom light. Can she see me right now? Is she happy I found my way back to our family? I meet my uncle in the foyer five minutes later and he has on what I would assume is a custom-made suit.

"You look fly, Unc."

"Debbie! You hear that?" he calls out as she hums in response from the kitchen. "I'm fly!"

I can't help but chuckle as I follow him out through the front door. His humor is contagious. We cut right and head for the garage, my stomach swirling with anticipation. I want to check out his old cars.

"Oh! Are we going to church?" I ask sarcastically.

"Yes, honey, we need to baptize you," he deadpans as he presses his thumb to the keypad beside a door. "Do you have a license?"

"I do." I nod. "It's a great form of ID. Not that I used it much. Having a car in New York is a hassle because of traffic, even if you do have the money to afford it."

"You're gonna use it today!" he booms in a mock preacher's voice. I'm chuckling again as he opens the side door and we walk in. This garage might have seven doors, but there are fourteen cars in here. Four-fucking-teen!

"Walk around to see what calls to you," he says as he nudges me forward. The lights flicker on overhead and I'm shocked to find that none of these cars look old. They're shining with fresh coats of wax and gleaming with money. These are expensive cars.

What calls to me? I snort out loud. *Am I getting a wand for Hogwarts?*

"Why did you snort? Don't you know that's unladylike?" He snickers as he walks behind me.

"I snorted because I felt like I was receiving my wand, and do I look like a lady to you?" I give him a grin over my shoulder as I pass a bright green sports car.

He full-out laughs, the sound echoing off the walls. "Just pick a car, Miss Potter."

I look around and a red convertible in the back catches my eye. I walk toward it and see it's a two-door badass mobile. "This one," I say, running my hand along the hood.

"Ah, that's Shelby." Uncle Scott moves to a large board on the wall with keys hanging on hooks. Then he grabs a ring and walks back toward me.

"Shelby?" I ask, crinkling my nose. "That's what the car is called?"

"Yep. 1967 Mustang." He tosses the key ring at me and I rush forward to catch it. "You're driving."

"What? I can't drive this!" I exclaim, already feeling anxious.

"She's yours now. So you better learn." He tucks his hands into his suit pants pockets and leans back on his heels.

"Mine?" All the air rushes from my lungs as I look down at the keys in my hand. I couldn't have heard that right.

"Yeah, you'll need to get around," he states with a roll of his eyes. "Our driver will be busy with other things." His sarcasm is heavy.

"Ha. Ha," I laugh sarcastically. "Okay, I'll drive." I grip the keys in my palm, letting the cold metal seep through my skin and dispel some of my anxiety. As much as I want to pinch myself and hope none of this is a dream, I would trade it all in for a chance to have my mother back.

Chapter Four

The drive in this beauty is so smooth, but she's fast. I have to watch my heavy foot because her speed just creeps up and before I know it, I'm already at double the speed limit.

The entire ride is spent with my uncle educating me on the car. Hearing the way he spits facts, I can tell this really is his passion. 'This girl is a GT500KR', *whatever*. 'She has a V8 engine and can pump out almost 400 horsepower', *again, whatever*. I only know that I love the candy apple red and black leather seats. The convertible is a sweet feature too.

I drop him off at the restaurant where his meeting is, and he gives me the directions to the gym, which thankfully isn't that far. It seems once you're in the main town of Whitsborough, it's pretty compact. The retail stores and restaurants are all along the same street, the storefronts looking old but welcoming. My uncle's friend, Andrew, is expecting me for an impromptu interview and I flip down the visor to give myself another glance before I head over there. It's a relief that I will be able to continue to focus on MMA, if Andrew will have me, and I can avoid the tidal wave of grief that's waiting for me to dive in. Just the thought of fighting the undercurrents of losing my mother has me wanting to give up and just sleep forever. I feel the exhaustion settling deep in my muscles and I wish I could sleep, but I haven't been sleeping more than a few hours at a time, waking up to the smell of char and ash because it's ingrained in my brain.

I pull into the parking lot of the gym and stare at the building in front of me, my eyebrows hitting my hairline when I see the large, floor-to-ceiling windows displaying the assortment of equipment inside. I kept my outfit casual, considering where I am. A loose, gray tank over a sports bra and black yoga pants, but the longer I watch people leaving the gym, the more underdressed I feel. The women walking out are wearing what looks like cashmere, off-the-shoulder sweaters, and leggings made of butter. This gym is nothing like Juan's in New York with its fancy facade and rich patrons. Another glaring difference between the new life I'm living from the old.

With a deep breath, I get out of the car, careful not to slam the door, and make my way to the entrance to step inside. It doesn't smell of sweat and hard work, more like sugar cookies oddly. I walk up to the front desk to see a few candles burning, the source of the sugar cookie scent. It feels more like a spa than a gym. The girl standing behind the counter has her black hair pulled up into a messy bun and her slightly upturned eyes narrow on me as she gives me a slow perusal before cocking an eyebrow. She looks to be about my age.

"I'm here to see Andrew." I plaster a smile on my face even though her mouth doesn't move from the straight line it's in. The name badge on her shirt says Shay.

"And you are?" Her voice is laced with attitude as she leans on the counter.

"Emberlise Craven." My smile only grows wider as I say my name through clenched teeth.

"Weird name," she says as she turns to walk down a narrow corridor behind her. She pokes her head into one of the doors and a few moments later she returns to the desk, cocking another brow.

"You have a twitch or something?" My smile drops as I growl the words, my irritation getting the best of me.

"He'll see you now. Back there, second door to the right." She smirks, looking pleased to finally get a reaction out of me.

I walk by her, raising my own brow in the process. If this is how the girls are going to act in this town, I can already say I won't have many friends. It makes me miss Tommy all that much more.

Twenty minutes later, I'm leaving with a promise that if Andrew can get at least twenty people to sign up for my class, I can teach in two weeks. My blood is pumping and I know I'm wearing the biggest smile as I walk through the gym to look around. There's a pool, a sauna, and even some tanning beds. It really is like one of those rich people's spas instead of a gym where people come to work up a sweat.

I walk by the cardio machines and ellipticals, noticing how clean they are. Then I get to the free weights where I find the desk girl, Shay, standing in front of me with two delicious bodies. They all have their backs to me, but I can see the two guys are fit, tall, and thick. My mouth waters at the sight and I slow down as I stroll by, hoping for a better look.

The one pumping fifty-pound barbells as if they weigh nothing has deep brown skin and a close-cropped haircut. The second one doing deadlifts has golden-brown locs hanging to his mid-back and his skin is like a rich sepia. Is that how they breed the guys around here? What's in the water?

I continue walking by when I hear the chick say, "That's her." A smirk stretches along my lips to learn they were discussing me, making me feel special.

I finally leave the gym and walk toward my pretty new car as the hairs on the back of my neck stand up. I'm being watched. I look over my shoulder and see a figure of a guy through the window. It looks like it could be the one with the locs and I keep my eyes on his form as I get into the car and start it up.

"Ember! Dinner is ready!" I hear my uncle scream from the bottom of the stairs. I groan as I sit up and wipe the drool off my face. As soon as Uncle Scott and I got back home, I dove into bed and passed out. The mattress is like sleeping on a cloud, with no squeaking springs or sinking sections. Visions of my room before it was reduced to ash slip through my mind and instead of guilt, I begin to accept that this is my life now and I need to move on.

My stomach grumbles and wins the battle with my exhaustion, so I get my ass off the clouds and slowly scuff my feet all the way to the kitchen. The smell! The aroma of grilled meat wafts under my nose and my mouth instantly fills with saliva.

"Your uncle made us steaks and I'm just finishing the salad," Aunt Debra says as she turns to smile at me over her shoulder. She's standing at the island, tossing chopped veggies into a bowl.

I make my way to the table and begin to pour the water from the pitcher into the glasses. "It smells so good in here. When Mom and I had steak, she would broil it in the oven. I thought that smelled amazing, but it has nothing on this."

My aunt watches me with a sadness overwhelming her hazel eyes. She probably feels bad about the privilege she had while my mother and I struggled. No matter how much I tell her it's not her fault and my mother made her choices, she will just have to come to that conclusion on her own.

"I received your school transcripts today, Ember. You're a straight-A student." She changes the subject as she brings the salad bowl to the table, then gives me a big smile and rubs my back, the touch reminding me of my mother.

"Yeah, I like school. A good education meant a better life for Mom and me." My words are rushed as I step away to put the pitcher back on the table, trying to avoid the emotion threatening to spill as my chest fills with pride. I worked hard for those grades even though the people around me barely made it to post-secondary. I wanted to prove I could do it despite running with a gang.

"I already sent them off to Precious Blood Academy. I was thinking you could start next Monday. It'll give you the week to get settled in." The first time she brought up Precious Blood, I nearly choked. What kind of name is that for a school? I found out that Precious Blood is a Catholic school which is going to be foreign enough to me, but with a name like that, it just sounds morbid.

"Okay, sounds good." Being in a state of constant change has been wreaking havoc on my nerves. I just need to keep breathing through the adjustments happening around me. "What is the arts program like?" If my new parents don't want me to fight, then I will try to concentrate on what my mother loved to see me do.

"You can choose which art you want to study; visual, vocal, drama, or dance." Her eyes twinkle with enthusiasm as she nods. "Your mother and I also went to Precious Blood. I was more into visual arts, but Rebecca was a singer."

"That's amazing." Something in my chest tightens as a myriad of memories floods through my mind. Mom did love to sing and her voice was like a soothing balm over my tumultuous insides.

"We want you to have the best opportunities," my uncle chimes in as he comes into the kitchen with a platter of meat in his hand.

I can feel that they're genuine people who are feeling blessed to have the chance to be parents to a child. I want so badly to feel good about it, to enjoy everything around me, but I can't help but feel the looming cloud of darkness as it makes its way into my new life.

The week passes me by in a whirlwind of clothes shopping with my aunt and overall bonding with my new family. My closet is bursting at the seams, my stomach is always full, and I want for nothing. Despite all of this, my heart still feels empty. I miss my mother more with each passing day and it feels like nothing will ever fill that void. It only became worse when Aunt Debra pulled out some old family photo albums where I got to see my grandparents and my mother as a child. She grieved for her sister as I continued to bottle everything tight inside, refusing to open the door to my own feelings an inch for fear I would awaken the darkness inside of me.

I had tried many times to broach the subject of my father over the week, but my aunt was adamant she didn't know who he was. Usually, if I pushed for more information, it would have her clamming up and she'd withdraw from me. A similar reaction to my mother's when I would ask her.

Now I'm lying in bed and it's well past midnight. My eyes are trained on the bright moon outside my window because I'm so wired and there's no way I can calm down. Tomorrow is my first day at Precious Blood Academy. Catholic school is going to be a challenge because I have never been religious.

Earlier, when I laid out my uniform, I couldn't believe how nice it was, if not a little stuffy. It's a kilt with dark navy blue and black stripes, a white blouse with a crest embroidered on the chest, and a navy blue tie to bring it all together. Aunt Debra said I needed to add flair to the ensemble with the four-inch Louboutins she bought me.

As designer shoes and worries about my new school hound me, I close my eyes and steadily count backward from one hundred until I finally pass out.

Chapter Five

The bell jingles over my head as I enter the little restaurant and the scent of coffee blasts through my nose. I nearly groan out loud, my mouth filling with saliva as I think of the roasted flavor. According to Aunt Deb, this restaurant has the best coffee in town, and I am not a morning person, so this is a win-win. The place is cozy with couches, tables, and shelves of novels in one section, and dining tables and chairs in another. Pictures of the town are all over the walls and even some little league photos with smiling kids. Adorable… enter eye roll here. Don't judge my attitude, I'm totally nervous. In the Bronx, I attended school with the same people from middle school onwards. I'm not used to meeting new people.

Aunt Deb offered to come with me today, but there's no way in hell I can show up with her like I'm some twelve-year-old. I have to do it by myself, as nervous as I am. I'm running on very little sleep and if I don't consume at least one cup of coffee, I will break both ankles by lunch.

My sky-high heels click along the tile as I approach the line and wait my turn to order this coffee my aunt has raved about. It took some practice and now I'm sure I only stumble every other step or so. That's how it is when you've never worn heels before. The line moves fast and before I know it, I'm at the front. The woman behind the counter is breathtakingly gorgeous with dark, golden-brown skin and hazel eyes. Her curly haircut is short and dyed a bright red, setting off the warm tones of her complexion.

"Hiya, new girl," she says in a breathy voice with a warm, welcoming smile. She leans on the counter and tosses a hand towel over her shoulder.

"How'd you…" I begin, but her raspy laugh has me pausing.

"You have on the school uniform, and I know all the kids. My son attends Precious Blood as well. Also, I must admit I have insider information." I give her a puzzled look, making her laugh as she pushes herself off the counter with a shrug of her shoulders. "Your Aunt Debra is my best friend."

"Ooh… I see." I nod as I take in the woman standing in front of me. Is she really Aunt Deb's best friend? I haven't heard a thing about her in the week I've been with them.

"What can I get you? On the house, of course," she offers with a cheeky wink.

"Large coffee, lots of milk, no sugar, please." My usual order spills from my mouth and the sudden shock of homesickness hits my stomach. Wincing, I bite into my cheek to fight off the memories but fail. I miss the small coffee shop I used to go to every day on my way to school. I miss the crowded streets and the people hustling around me to get to work.

"Coming up!" She slaps the counter with enthusiasm, pulling me from my depressive thoughts.

Not a moment sooner, she hands me a cup of coffee to go, and I hesitate. I really should give her the money. I don't want to owe anyone anything, even if it is only a cup of coffee. I reach into my blazer pocket to take out my wallet when she shakes her head with a *tsk*.

"Take it, trust me. Your Aunt Deb will owe me with town

gossip later." She purses her lips with mischief and I chuckle, feeling a little better than I was a second ago.

"Okay, thank you." Smiling and pulling my hand from my pocket, I turn to leave when I realize I don't even know her name. She's not wearing a name tag and I'm sure I'll be seeing her often. "Sorry, I didn't catch your name."

"Sharla. Gosh, you look so much like your mother," she whispers the last part, causing my heart to stutter in my chest and my mouth to run dry. "Uncanny."

"Yeah, I've heard that a lot." Not wanting to rock the boat in our new relationship, I swallow down the urge to force her to tell me everything she knows about the woman I'm learning I knew nothing about. "You knew my mother?"

"Yeah. We grew up near each other and went to school together. Well, I better get back to work here." She dismisses me as she looks to the line gathering behind me.

"Right, sorry. Thank you again." I hold up the cup and toss her another smile.

"No problem, Emberlise. Have a great first day. If you have any trouble, find Vincent, he's my son. He's in the eleventh grade too." Then she's taking another order.

Maybe this little backward town isn't so bad.

This little, motherfucking, backward town is the worst! Getting to the school is a pain in the ass because it's all rough gravel roads, and the potholes!! I hit one pothole while I was trying to avoid another and I'm sure my Uncle Scott is going to be pissed because I think I hit Shelby's fender thingy. Coffee flew all over my kilt and now I smell like a bag of Arabica dark roast.

Pulling into the school parking lot, I rest my forehead

against the steering wheel. Well, more like smack it against the steering wheel. If the blare of the horn wasn't enough, I think I just made a girl shit herself. I put my hand up and mouth an apology, only to be rewarded with the middle finger and a big fuck you.

Great. This making friend's thing is starting off well.

She's tall with a very short kilt, which must be against school code because with each step she takes, it flashes the bottom of her ass. Long pink hair hangs to her waist in loose curls and it looks bright against her alabaster skin. She has to be a model.

Exiting the car, I grab my backpack from the backseat, hoping the pale girl with blonde hair isn't a vampire waiting for the perfect moment to eat me alive. At least the coffee spill stayed on my kilt—thank god for the dark colors—and not on my white dress shirt, because that would've been annoying.

As I navigate through the parking lot, I sense eyes on me. I've never been the new kid before and it sends anxiety shooting through me. Tommy and I went to every school together, straight from elementary all the way to high school. So this is a fresh experience and a little late in my scholastic career for it to be character-building. With a lift of my chin, I soldier forward with forced confidence, refusing to appear weak.

The front of the school looms in front of me with its older brick structure and a faded sign on the front that says Precious Blood Academy. The place looks very pretentious with its set of dark stained wooden doors, large and intimidating, with a sign that reads 'Any visitors please report to the office.' I'm a visitor. My heart pounds and I begin my regime of counting backward to calm down.

"The doors aren't automatic, new chick. Pull on them," a deep, raspy voice sneers from behind me.

Turning around, I find a group of students standing off to the side and the girl I scared earlier is standing among them. The scowl on her face as she looks at me causes my anger to spark. What the fuck is her problem? Narrowing my eyes, I look her up and down. I'll be damned if I let her ruin my day. My eyes land on a beautiful specimen after skimming over the six others, snagging my attention. His skin is radiant as the sun gleams off its brown surface, golden and rich. Those eyes are the lightest moss green, and his full lips turn up into a cruel-looking grin, causing his dimple to wink at me through his scruffy cheek. Yeah, I'm staring, but come on, do you blame me? His light brown hair hangs in locs down his back and glistens in the sun. I mean, when you stand at well over six feet, the sun has no other choice but to glisten on you, right? That was poetic, huh? Is this the same guy from the gym? The stature is the same and the hair as well.

"Do you speak? Or are you just going to stare at us?" Pink hair chick snarls at me, her fists slamming to her waist.

My shoulders lift as I smirk at them. I don't have the energy to bicker right now and Pink Bitch does not want to test me. I may be new, and I may be quiet right now, but I will slap a girl real quick.

Turning around, I open the wooden door and just because I'm a bitch, I look back at them with a mock-surprised face and point at the door. Then I roll my eyes and head inside. As the door shuts, his cruel, raspy laugh filters through as he says, "Marlana, I think you found your match in bitch."

Following all the signs that point toward the office, I try my best to ignore the staring as though I'm a specimen at the zoo. People are nosy around here. I find the office and step inside just as my stomach begins to burn. A large desk takes up most of the space and a curvy woman is sitting behind it. She's late forties, maybe older, and her hair is lined with gray, pulled back into an unforgiving bun. She has her nose down in a book and has yet to even acknowledge me.

"Hello?" I call out tentatively and clear my throat.

"Oh! Jeez! You startled me. I'm sorry. You're new, correct? Well, this being April and Whitsborough, we don't have many new faces. Sorry, let's see. Emberlise Craven?" she rambles along as she puts down her book and shuffles papers on her desk.

"Yes, that's me." Hooking my thumbs into the straps of my backpack, I look over my shoulder to find a gathering through the glass. I'm almost tempted to run out of here and beg my aunt to let me be homeschooled, but the thought of becoming a burden stops me.

"All right, dear, here is your class schedule and locker info. You have a lock for that on you, correct?" I turn back to face the lady whose eyes flick over my shoulder toward the nosy group of students as she gives me a sympathetic smile.

"Yes, I brought a lock." I take the papers and bite my lip. I really don't want to be here.

"Great!" She claps her hands and sits back in her seat, her eyes roving to the novel on her desk with longing. The door opens behind me, but I don't bother to look. I'd rather not be stared at again. "I'll call down Travis to show you around, as you both have homeroom together and he is just a doll." She's looking down as she picks up the receiver of the phone next to her computer.

"No need, Anna, I'm right here," a deep voice answers from behind me, making the hairs along my neck stand up.

"Oh, Travis! Great! I'm glad you came by. Thank you for that!" Anna, the secretary, enthuses. A little too enthused to be honest.

"It's all good. I don't mind helping." I finally turn around and look into a set of jade-colored eyes, the color so green it looks unnatural. His sandy blond hair is cut close on the sides and fades up into a length to grip nicely while his head is between your legs. Finger-gripping strands. Appreciating a stranger's hair as I imagine him in sexual positions is at least dulling a bit of my nervousness.

"We really appreciate it. Travis here is a baseball prospect, and we are so proud of him," Anna continues to gush, hauling me out of my own fantasy to face her again. By the way she's squirming, I'm sure she's also gushing in her panties.

Gross, Ember.

"All right, if we stand here all day, Anna will put a permanent blush on my face." His voice is laced with humor and maybe a bit of arrogance.

"I bet," I mumble with a snort.

"Oh, shoot! You better move along if you want to show her the locker and make it to homeroom on time." Anna claps her hands again then waves us off with a shooing motion, her eyes back to that romance novel with Fabio on the cover. I'm pretty sure my mother had the same one. It became nothing more than ashes when our house burned down though.

"You have everything you need, Emberlise?" Travis asks me sweetly, his question forcing my melancholy away and bringing me back into the present.

"Ember. Just call me Ember," I correct him with a nod.

"Gotcha, Ember. Nice name, by the way," he says, tugging my bag off my shoulder. "I can take this for you. It may be light now but soon enough, Precious Blood will have your back breaking with school books."

Anna chuckles at his statement and goes back to her book, effectively dismissing us.

Travis opens the door for me and we exit into the busy hallway full of students. As soon as we step out, everyone is staring again and it's so quiet you could hear a pin drop. I swallow down the urge to grab back my bag from Travis' hand and dart out the way I came in. It's going to be tough to make it through the year being stared at like a caged animal on display.

"We don't have many new people here in Whitsborough, so you're a bit of a spectacle," Travis says to me quietly with an apologetic smile. Then he leads me down a hallway as he slings my bag over his shoulder.

"I kind of figured that out earlier." I glare at some students as we pass, my hands itching to slap a few faces.

"Probably not the best feeling, being ogled on your first day." He gives me a smirk over his shoulder, those pretty green eyes of his twinkling.

"It's different…" I roll my eyes as another student trips over his feet as I walk by.

"Here's your locker and it looks like you're right beside Marlana." Following Travis' line of sight, I find the pink-headed girl from earlier. She's leaning against the locker next to mine, holding a textbook to her chest with a scowl lining her features.

"Sure," I reply with a shrug as I take in a deep breath. Fighting on the first day of school will for sure have my new parents putting me up for adoption.

"Are you a designated babysitter, Travis?" Marlana asks with a grimace toward me. Her pink hair isn't looking as cute as I originally thought when paired with that face. My hand curls into a fist as I step closer, my blood singing for violence through my veins. Fuck it, let's hope I'm adopted to a family far away from Whitsborough.

"Nope," he answers, his hand landing on my shoulder. "I volunteered to show Ember around. I was hoping to give her a good first impression." He gives her a pointed look, but it's lost on the girl who's set on hating me for no reason.

"Aren't you just a saint," Marlana snickers, her upper lip curling into a sneer.

"Oh, Jesus, relax," I retort as I reach forward to grasp the handle of my locker when Travis' gasp halts my movement.

"This is a Catholic school and that's blasphemy," he whispers with a look of outrage on his face.

My cheeks heat and I probably look like a ripe tomato as I glance around to check if anyone else is listening. People are staring, but it's no different from earlier. Travis and Pink Head begin to laugh as he leans against the locker on the other side of mine.

"I'm playing. Relax, Ember." He playfully swats my

arm. I shrug and give him a half-smile. His playful nature reminds me a bit of Tommy and the thought has a wave of homesickness ripping through my chest.

"You should come to more parties, Travis. We could really get to know each other better," Marlana purrs and brings me out of my weak moment. I take this opportunity to open my new locker door, blocking Pink Head's face from view and mock puke inside. Travis laughs louder at my actions as I grab my bag from him.

"Hey! What the hell are you doing?!" Pink Head screeches from the other side.

I close the door slightly until she's back in view. "This is a Catholic school, Bubble Gum Head, you shouldn't speak of,"—I lean in closer to her—"Hell." A few students look over at us curiously as we continue to make a scene in the hall. So much for avoiding being stared at.

This only causes Travis to laugh louder, bent over at the waist, and Bubble Gum's face is the color of a red Jolly Rancher. I must be low on blood sugar if candy is all I'm thinking about. It might be the lack of appetite to eat breakfast this morning combined with half a cup of coffee.

"You better watch your ass," she snarls, getting into my face. I made it fifteen minutes without a fight, so in my books, that's pretty good considering this hoe's attitude.

"I would take a few steps back, Pepto. I haven't had a good fight since I moved here and you're about to break my record," I warn, my words spoken menacingly low.

She visibly swallows but stands her ground. Nice, the bitch has some backbone.

"What's going on?" A deep raspy voice sounds behind me. I turn and lock eyes with the guy from this morning, his green irises hard and cruel.

"Just dealing with trash. Anyway, are you coming over tonight, Vin?" Marlana asks with a seductive lilt, her threatening me long forgotten. "You ditched out on me yesterday."

"Yesterday I had a rehearsal with the guys. You know how it is, Mar. Bros over hoes," he answers with a cocky lift of his lips, his dimple prominent in his left cheek. Did I mention how much I love dimples?

To my surprise, Pink Hair laughs, her hand landing on his chest. Is she insane? He just called her ass a hoe, and yeah, maybe she is, I don't know her, but I'm pretty sure that was a straight-up insult.

"Yeah, I was just disappointed we didn't do that thing we tried last weekend again. You know, the thing you really liked?" she mock whispers, but everyone can hear her. Yep, total hoe.

"All right then," Travis interjects. "I need to get you to homeroom, Ember, or you're going to be late on the first day." Travis' hand lands on my lower back as he tries to steer me away from the scene.

"Run along, fresh meat." Pepto shoos me away as she steps possessively in front of her man.

"See you around, skank," I throw back as I'm closing my locker and grabbing my bag.

"Watch it, bitch," she grits out from between her clenched teeth.

Turning suddenly, I stare her down as my heart pounds in my ears. I don't care where I am or who's watching because this bitch is about to bleed. The thought of blood makes my heart rate increase and that familiar pull deep in my gut appears like a sweet melody of violence, luring me inside its trap. She hurriedly grabs her bag and turns in the opposite direction, her man watching her go with a raised brow.

The warning bell rings and we have six minutes to get to class. Travis' hand presses into my back once more as he guides us down the hall, giving me the space to breathe and hoping I can regulate my anger before we reach the classroom. Thankfully, I haven't scared him off yet because I could really use a friend inside these halls.

"Here we are, room twelve in the H Hall. We have Mrs.

G for Religion. She's a Jesus fanatic, so mind your language and praise the Lord." Travis closes his eyes and steeples his hands under his chin, cracking one eye to take in my questioning look. It breaks the tension and I chuckle at his lopsided smile.

An exaggerated snort sounds from behind me and I turn around to stare into the same set of moss-green eyes I've been finding often this morning. Looks like Vin followed us here. With him this close, I can soak in his features without looking obsessed. His lips are deliciously full and plump, his nose is prominent but perfect for his face, and his square jaw cuts sharply. Holy smokes, are all the guys in this school so pretty? He's slightly taller than Travis but has the same body build. Athletic without too much bulk. Just the right amount of lean.

"Look like the golden boy of Whitsborough got his claws into you. Watch out for this one, new girl. His privilege puts him well above the rest of us," Vin sneers toward Travis, his eyes lighting with pure hatred. I am well-acquainted with that look; I've seen it many times when I was collecting debts for the Rampage.

"This is Vincent," Travis introduces, his eyes on the tiled floor and his voice not reflecting an ounce of the hatred he's receiving. My heart suddenly weighs heavy for the first person to befriend me. If I find out Vin is bullying him, his nose will be molding to the shape of my fist.

"Trust me,"—I turn back to Vin with a sneer of my own—"I don't mind a bit of privilege above me if it looks like that." I gesture to Travis. "Are you following us, Vincent?"

"It's Vin. I don't think we were properly introduced." He holds out his hand, the long fingers sporting callouses I assume are from the gym.

"I'm Ember," I reply and ignore his hand. "Golden boy and I are going to be late if you keep us out here any longer." I slip my arm into Travis' and smile when he looks at me, traces of sadness still lingering in his green eyes.

"Nice meeting you, Em." My gaze flicks back to Vin and his cruel grin as he drops his hand, his eyes angrily flashing to

Travis.

"It's Ember," I retort, my anger swelling once again.

Vin shakes his head with a grin and starts off down the hall, his swagger exaggerated as girls follow him with their eyes. Not that I blame them.

"You can sit by me, if you like." Pulling my eyes from Vin's back, I nod at Travis.

"Thank you." I squeeze his arm tighter. There's something about this boy that makes my protective nature rise with intensity. His reactions tell me he doesn't usually have someone looking out for him.

When we step into the classroom, Travis begins to guide me toward the back. Those last two rows are usually coveted by most students, but I've always enjoyed sitting at the front more. It's the perfect place to become familiar with your teachers, and I strive to succeed in anything I put my mind to. I also wouldn't want to miss anything by sitting in the back.

"Hey, Travis? I'm used to sitting in the front. Is it okay if we part ways here?" I pull on his arm to stop him, my hand wrapping around the bunching muscle under his dress shirt.

"No problem." He squeezes my hand with his own. "There are a few open seats at the front. I'll come sit with you." He looks down into my face as his eyes rove over my features, the scrutiny making me blush. This wasn't the type of attention I would receive back home. It was no secret that I was the rough girl who liked to fight and run the streets, so romance was never really a factor in my short relationships. I can't deny the attraction growing for him and it's also reflected in his eyes, but I'm not ready to start something when I already have so much to unpack in the emotions department. Besides, I would much rather have a friend than a fling.

"You're the best." I smile and avoid the heated look in his eyes.

We move to the front row, and I notice a girl with maroon-dyed hair pulled back into two Dutch braids down the sides. She has on a pair of thick, black-framed reading glasses, and her ears are decorated with multiple piercings. Not to mention the tattoo peeking out of her uniform shirt collar at the back of her neck, making me like her already.

"Hi, is this desk taken?" I put my hand on the back of the chair as Travis' heat stays at my back. When the girl turns to look up at me, I'm stunned at how beautiful she is.

"Nope. You can have it. You're the new girl?" She has the hint of a grin on her full mouth as her chocolate brown eyes move over me with humor. She doesn't have any makeup on her face and I'm in awe of how flawless her olive-toned skin is.

"Yeah, that's me. I'm Ember." I hold out my hand to her, hoping I can add her to the very short list of friends I have.

"Hi, Ember, I'm Adrianna." She grips my hand, showcasing a little tattoo between her thumb and forefinger in the shape of a spade. She's already the coolest chick I know.

Her eyes widen a bit as she takes in Travis standing behind me, her cheeks coating with color as her mouth drops open. I get it, I think I had the same reaction.

"Hey, Adri," he breathes out, and my brows crash together at the forlorn sound of his voice.

"Hey," she quickly replies, turning her face and looking straight ahead. Her spine is stiff as I slip into the seat next to hers and then Travis does the same next to mine, but Adrianna doesn't turn her attention away from the blank chalkboard.

The teacher arrives at that moment, her presence replacing the tension I have somehow put myself in the center of. She's older, maybe nearing her fifties, and her skin is glowing with whatever highlighter she uses. Or the grace of God perhaps. She's dressed in a pencil skirt and jacket with her gray hair up in a bun. Mrs. G has a pleasant face and a sweet smile as she stands in the center of the blackboard.

"Hello, children of God. How was your weekend?" she asks, her voice like soothing honey as she clasps her hands to her chest. Everyone answers in a chorus of *fines* and *goods*. "Praise be to God," she coos and tips her face to the ceiling. I'm in a classroom of hippies and about to be served a special Kool-Aid. No joke. I glance around nervously to check if everyone else is thinking the same thing, finding their faces masked in boredom. "Let's say our morning prayer. Travis, it's nice to see your face up here at the front today. You can start us in prayer." She drops her chin to give him a serene smile, the look only heightening my anxiety.

"Okay, Mrs. G." Travis stands and bows his head as I take in the classroom around me, everyone bowing their heads with him. If a pitcher of Kool-Aid shows up, I'm not drinking any of it. I'll claim an allergy. "In the name of the Father, the Son, and the Holy Spirit."

Everyone begins to cross themselves as I nervously chew on my lip. I'm completely out of place and uncomfortable as Travis prays to *our father,* and everyone says it along with him like drones.

"Amen," he ends it and sits back in his seat. I stare at him intently, trying to figure out if this Father, Son, and Holy Spirit has entered him or not when he looks at me. "You aren't Catholic, huh?" he whispers as he leans toward me.

"I'm baptized, but that was it. My mother—" I choke a little. It's still so hard to talk about her. I clear my throat and continue, "My mother wasn't a practicing Catholic. She baptized me, so I had the option when I was older. Church just never appealed to us."

"I see—" He's cut off by the teacher clearing her throat and looking directly at me.

"Looks like we have a new student. Would you mind coming up and introducing yourself? My name is Mrs. Giovanni, but everyone just calls me Mrs. G," she explains in her soothing voice as I begin to sweat a little. What if she asks me to pray? All I know is 'Rub a dub dub, thanks for the grub' and something tells me that just wouldn't fly here. She seems to sense my hesitancy and smiles at me. "Or just sit in your seat and tell everyone your name and where you came from?" she suggests.

"My name is Emberlise Craven, but most people call me Ember. I'm from the Bronx in New York and now I'm living with my aunt and uncle here in Whitsborough." I turn in my seat to face everyone behind me. My eyes land on Vin's friend with the umber skin and twinkling eyes. He winks at me.

"Welcome, Ember. It's so nice to have you. Maybe one day you can tell us more about the Bronx," Mrs. G says as she claps her hands.

"Just like *Jenny from the Block*," a deep voice says from the back.

"Now, now, Daniel, *don't be fooled by the rocks that I got*. You make another comment, and we'll have a singing contest after school for an hour together," Mrs. G chastises with a *tsk*.

I chuckle softly with surprise because the religion teacher knows her pop music. If she's offering the Kool-Aid, then I'm taking it. She's won me over. I'll pray to whoever's father while I drink it too.

"That's Danny. He's one of Vincent's buddies," Travis whispers to me from behind his hands. Maybe Danny's close to Marlana too. If he thinks he can pick on me because his friend's girlfriend is targeting me, he'll learn the hard way. With my fist through his teeth.

The rest of homeroom goes by quickly, and I've learned just how much Jesus loves me. We're given passages from the Bible to read, and I got my very own to bring home. I can't wait to make Uncle Scott read some of it out loud.

The bell rings, signaling the end of class, and I stand to get my books and bag together.

"It was nice meeting you, Ember," Travis says from beside me as he pushes his books into his bag.

"You too," I reply, looking into his green eyes. He may give me Tommy vibes, but he's so much prettier.

"You can eat lunch with me. I'll wait for you at the

cafeteria doors. I understand how hard first-day lunches can be," he offers with a shrug of his shoulders.

"Or you can sit with me, and after many years of friendship, I wouldn't ditch you like a bad habit," Adrianna interjects, her words shot like venom at Travis. It's obvious something must've happened between them because of the initial tension, but suddenly I'm thrown into a lake of lava as the tension becomes hostility.

"Um…" I begin as I look back and forth between them.

"It's okay. Sit with Adri. I can guarantee she's less boring," Travis mumbles a little glumly before grabbing his bag and leaving the class.

"I like you, Adrianna," I tell her while pointing at her face, because I do. I like honesty and even though I'm protective of Travis, I won't come between what was obviously a prior relationship. It was clear from the moment we sat beside her and he was looking at her like a kicked puppy and she wouldn't give him the time of day.

She lets loose a genuine laugh. "I like you too. Call me Adri. What's your next class?" She stands from her desk and swings her bag over her shoulder.

"Biology in J Hall," I read off the timetable in front of me and huff out a breath. Where the fuck is J Hall?

"That's me too. Then we can have lunch together after. I'll introduce you to a few people." I exhale in relief as the nerves slowly dissipate. It's hard enough being stared at while I walk the halls, but to do it as I search for a classroom? I would want to curl up in a closet until the final bell rang.

We step into the hall and I immediately drop my eyes to the floor, not looking forward to being treated like a freak show exhibit. "Where are you going?" The familiar rasp sends a shiver down my spine. The missing chemistry I was talking about with Travis is certainly there with this one, and it's even worse because we haven't even touched.

"Hi, Vince. I'm off to biology with Adri." I look up with

a flutter of my lashes to find him leaning against the wall outside the classroom door, his mouth sporting a lazy grin.

"Hey, Adri, long time," he says as he looks her up and down. Of course, this is what I'm attracted to. A guy who has a girlfriend, follows another girl, and then flirts with everyone else. I know how to pick the winners.

"Not long enough, little dick, and I mean that both ways," she deadpans with a pointed look at his dick, then she raises a brow at me before turning and walking slowly down the hall.

Vincent just laughs her off, the sound sarcastic and forced. I laugh along too because this girl has completely won my heart, and I declare her my new bestie, whether she likes it or not.

"Your girlfriend, Pink Head, isn't in this class. You can run along to your next period," I inform him with a pat to his cheek. His skin is so soft, and the little electric currents racing up my arm are alarming.

"I don't have a girlfriend," he states, grabbing my hand and removing it from his face. "I'll see you at lunch." Then he abruptly turns around to walk in the other direction, his swagger once again catching my eye. He's stalking me and I like it.

I catch up with Adri, and we walk toward our next class, the silence ringing a little uncomfortably between us. I want to ask about Travis, but I don't want to push her away either.

"So, you've met the Greene brothers." She slips her thumbs under the straps of her backpack and gives me a look from the side of her eye. "Our town's very own walking scandal."

"The Greene brothers?" I question. I haven't met any brothers yet.

"Travis and Vin. They're half brothers. Same father, different mom." The shock has me stopping in the middle of the hallway as students flood around me to their next class. It must show on my face because she laughs and pulls me along into our next classroom.

CHAPTER SIX

Biology is miserably slow, mostly because we're pre-assigned seating with lab partners that can't change all semester and Adri isn't mine. Not that I'm paying the class much attention anyways considering I can't stop thinking about the bomb she dropped on me. Vin and Travis are half brothers, but they're the same age and clearly dislike each other. Now that I think about it, I can see the resemblance. The green eyes, matching dimples, and builds.

Finally, the bell rings, releasing me from the boredom, and I look to my lab partner with an apologetic smile. I barely spoke to her and I don't even care what we did today. I rush to stuff my books in my bag and hurry toward Adri, who is sitting with another cute boy. He has black hair, cut short on the sides, and a curly mess on top. His pale skin illuminates the dark freckles along the bridge of his nose. His eyes are so dark they look nearly black and he's the tall, lanky type, sporting emo vibes.

"Ember, this is Jake. He's really excited to be introduced to you and wouldn't shut up about how beautiful you are," she says in a monotone voice as she reveals everything he was probably saying during class. I laugh at her attitude because it's so similar to mine.

"Hey, Jake, it's nice to meet you." I give him a wide-toothed grin as his face reddens with embarrassment.

"Thanks so much, Adri," he snaps sullenly and gets up to leave the classroom, giving me a nod as he passes.

"I love the stench of embarrassment." She takes a deep breath. "It's what we do, him and I, trying to embarrass each other and see who's the best at it. Looks like I won this week. Doubt he could top that. I haven't seen him blush like that since fourth grade when he pulled his pants off to escape a bee." I'm laughing so hard I have tears in my eyes. She laughs along with me and gathers her belongings. "I just need to go by my locker to drop these textbooks off before lunch, cool?" she asks.

"Yeah, I should do that too. Where's your locker?" Adjusting the backpack on my shoulder, I wince as the strap digs into my skin.

"M Hall, number 346," she answers as she leads us out of the classroom, her braids swinging with her steps.

"Really? I'm number 296. Our lockers are so close." She smiles at me over her shoulder, and this time, when I look around at the students in the hall, not nearly as many are staring. This day just keeps getting better.

"Sweet, let's go." She leads me down the hall past our homeroom classroom. It's a labyrinth, but I'll get used to it. We make it to our lockers, and I head toward mine, only to find Pepto bitch is at her locker too. Maybe if I don't look at her, she'll disappear.

No such luck. "Hey, skank. You smell like a Tim Hortons slut, giving blowjobs out the back." She cackles at her own joke and slaps the locker on the other side of hers, once again making me a spectacle.

"I bet you know exactly what that smells like since you and your mom made it your family business," I snap back, unable to hold it in if I tried.

"You're a whore and I want you to stay away from Vin,"

she sneers at me, her eyes narrowing with warning.

"And you're a delusional side piece who needs to be reminded of her place," Adri retorts from behind me, her voice like a balm over the rage threatening to put me in jail.

Hubba Bubba twirls around to face Adri with an evil expression on her face. "Looks like the new loser has bonded with the old loser. So exciting, such a fitting friendship." She laughs out loud, the sound like nails on a chalkboard. Then she whirls back to me, her eyes burning with intensity. "Stay away from my Vin." She points to my face before stomping off in her six-inch stilettos. No wonder she looked so tall this morning. Her face is model material, but that attitude belongs in the trash.

"Don't mind her. Vin fucks her every other weekend when he can't find anything else, and she has it in her mind that she's important," Adri huffs with a face of mock pity.

"Ah… I see. Well, she can keep him. I'm not interested." I shrug as I open my locker and dump my books inside.

"That's smart because the Greene brothers are nothing but drama." Closing my locker, I tip my head to look at her. This is the perfect opening to ask her about Travis.

"What was that about in homeroom? Were you and Travis friends before?"

"Travis and I were best friends from junior kindergarten until grade nine. He dropped me as soon as his body grew into his fat head." Her mouth purses as her brows drop close to her eyes. "He started playing baseball and joined the school varsity team. He's good and has been scouted since last year. Naturally, dirty skanks started dropping their panties, and he left me behind. My panties firmly kept in place, of course." She gives me a wicked smile, but the lingering hurt in her eyes is clear.

"Of course." I laugh as she leads us back down the hallway. Once my chuckling stops, I give her a sympathetic look. "That's really sad. I'm sorry that happened."

"It is what it is." She shrugs, trying to sound unbothered, but I've already witnessed the pain in her eyes. "I'll tell you more about the Greene drama while you drive me home after school. Saves me from taking the bus and I get to sit in the sweet Mustang." She grins wide at me, hauling another chuckle from my mouth.

"How'd you know that's my car?" I raise a brow at her.

"Are you kidding? We not only stare at the new students like circus freaks, but we also check out their cars." She waggles her eyebrows.

"Okay then, you got yourself a deal." I laugh. Adri is quickly filling the void that's been growing in my chest since my aunt and uncle drove me out of the only home I've known and thrusted me into a foreign place. I haven't laughed this much in a really long time.

We push through a set of double doors and the sound of chatter is magnified as I take in the entire room. Off to the right is the lineup where everyone is buying their food and to the left are tables and a few vending machines.

Glancing around the room, I find the typical high school cliques everywhere. The jock table is in the center, and of course, sitting dead smack in the middle is Travis. He gives me a little wave and a smile, and I wave back. Then you have the smart kids with their chessboards out and it looks like they're having a tournament. I love chess. I could totally be down to play a round. Next is the table of what I assume are the resident mean, popular girls, eyeing all the guys within a ten-foot radius. Any guesses who's sitting at that table? Ding, ding! Big ole Eraser Head herself. I wave at her too, because why not? She scowls at me and her bitchy minions do the same. Among them is another familiar face sitting at that table and it takes me a few seconds to place her. It's the desk girl from the gym.

Scanning over the rest of the room, my eye catches on long locs. Vin is sitting at a table with that dick, Danny, and a few other guys. Danny sees me looking and nudges Vin, nodding in my direction. I won't avert my gaze because his friends have already noticed me. Besides, I'm no coward. He looks over his shoulder and gives me a once-over before slowly rising to his feet.

"That one is trouble," Adri warns from beside me as she sucks on a tooth. "He loves to hit 'em and quit 'em, and trust me, he's hit quite a few."

"How do you know I'm not the same?" I give her a pointed look.

"Okay, girl, do you. I'm getting lunch." She laughs and walks toward the lunch line, leaving me to face the guy who is becoming a danger to my well-being.

"Did you dump the loser already?" I begin to melt the moment I hear his familiar rasp. "I don't want his ass bringing you into drama later."

So, he somehow searched up my timetable. He either has the ability to hack the system or maybe he worked his magic on Anna Gushy Underpants. I should be put off by the warning flags surrounding him, but red is my favorite color. "Why? Are you jealous?"

"No." His answer is quick and without much thought, knocking my ego around a bit. "You don't have a tray. Aren't you hungry?" I look into his pretty eyes and preen a little. His attitude shouts big man, but I have experience with that type and figure I can play this game better than him. So I close the gap between us and press my body against his. We're touching from chest to groin and the heat of his body is seeping past my uniform to alight my skin in fire. We have an audience with Cotton Candy Brain and her minions, so I wrap my arms around his neck, making sure she knows I won't be warned away from anything. His eyebrows shoot up in surprise, but he recovers quickly and wraps an arm around my waist.

"What I'm hungry for, I'm not sure you can handle. *Not long enough*," I tease, throwing Adri's line back at him as I stare up into those light green eyes.

"Adri is full of shit. She's never seen my dick," he groans and rolls his eyes. "Her allegiance has always been to Travis. Even though they hate each other now, she still avoids me."

I run my hand along his chest and lean up to place my lips near his ear, awakening butterflies in the pit of my stomach. "How's my acting? Good enough for drama class or no?"

His other hand moves and skims slowly over my ass, pulling me even closer. Then he turns his face to bring his lips just a fraction from mine. The near contact makes my body shiver with a want so strong, it surprises me.

"Not near good enough if you're trembling at my touch." He leans in farther and his warm breath fans my mouth. "Now, go grab your lunch, and if you want, you can sit with me." He finishes with a light squeeze to my ass then steps back to release me.

The cafeteria is quiet as I look around, finding everyone's eyes on Vin and me. Some are looking curiously at us, but mostly they're watching him with shock. So much for not being the center of people's attention. I think I've met my match. I'm speechless and completely turned on as I gravitate toward the food line, giving him one last look over my shoulder. I find Adri already at the end of the line, paying for her food, and she looks over and waves her hand. I quickly order a grilled chicken salad and make my way to the end to pay, my body still buzzing in all the places Vin's touched.

"That was fun to watch." Adri snorts as I pay for my food and my heart picks up as I give her a flustered look.

"I need a cold shower and a stiff… drink." I grin at her as she laughs. "He smells divine, by the way."

"I bet," she adds, smirking and shaking her head. "He's never been one to show girls too much attention in public."

"That explains the looks we were getting from everyone." I turn around to move toward Vin's table when I find Cotton Candy Brain already there and sitting in his lap. He's engrossed in a conversation with Danny, but she's looking right at me with a smug grin. I refuse to be added to his merry-go-round of girls and I won't give her the satisfaction of seeing how disappointed I am, so I smile widely and blow her a kiss. She gives me a confused look before it turns into a glare and then she presses herself closer to Vin, who seems oblivious to her advances.

"She doesn't know what to think of you. She was hoping you'd cause a scene." Adri points in my face as she says, "I like you."

"I like you too." I laugh.

"Let's go. I'll introduce you to my people." I follow Adri toward a corner table and we pass by Vin's on the way. He sees me, then as if he's just noticing Marlana on his lap, he pushes her off to the chair beside him and glares at me. I look at him over my shoulder and blow him a kiss too before facing forward again.

"Hey, hey, animals!" Adri calls out to a table of three people as we set our trays down. "This hot ass here is Ember. She's so sassy, you'll all love her."

"Hey, guys." I wave at each of them.

"You've met Jake. Then there's Jordan and Cara," she finishes her introductions and sits across from Jordan.

I smile and sit down with them as they return to eating and talking. Jordan is your typical funny guy. He's cracking jokes and making everyone laugh. His brown hair is long on top, pulled into a man bun, and shaved on the sides, and he has piercings in his eyebrow and lip. Cara is shy-looking and for the most part hasn't said much. She's tiny with light blonde hair touching her shoulders and has big blue eyes.

"Where are you from, Ember?" Jordan leans on the table, pushing his empty tray aside.

"The Bronx. I came here to live with my aunt and uncle." I push down the groan threatening to bubble up. I don't want to have to tell this story over and over again.

"Why? Do the schools in New York suck or something?" Jake asks, leading me further into the trauma I've somewhat packed away.

"No, not much different from here, to be honest. Although, I've never been to a Catholic school before. A few weeks ago, my mother passed away." I take a deep breath, swallowing down the lump in my throat. I'm not usually this forthcoming with my life, but I'm trying to change, become someone people want to be friends with. "My aunt and uncle are the only family I have left." I play with the salad on my tray, avoiding looking up at them.

A murmur of condolences circles the table as I slowly lift my eyes from my tray. Everyone looks slightly uncomfortable, and as much as I do too, I don't want them to treat me based on what they've just learned.

"Thank you, guys." I smile at them, then rub my hands together. "So… give me the scoop on this school. Who do I watch out for?"

They flow back into simple conversation for the next half hour, telling me silly rumors about some students and faculty. I haven't laughed this hard since before I arrived in Canada, and even though the guilt is still present, it's not as prominent as before.

"What's your next class?" Adri cuts in as Jordan talks about his new skateboard.

I reach into my breast pocket and pull out my schedule. "English Lit. H Hall again," I read out loud.

"You'll be with Travis in that class. He's a bookworm," she says nonchalantly. I don't say anything about her knowing his schedule by heart even though it's a little surprising. How did she get Anna to comply? Or is Adri a hacker?

"So am I. That's why I was so excited to have it as an elective. That and drama. I took part in a few plays at my old school." I shrug as I tuck the schedule back into my pocket.

"The drama department consists of everyone sitting at Vin's table, save for Marlana and her posse. They can barely read, let alone memorize lines," Cara deadpans, finally contributing to the conversation. It's her first full sentence and I can't help myself, I burst out laughing which causes everyone to join in.

"That's Cara. She's quiet, but when she speaks, it's all truth." Jordan is looking at her with an admiring smile.

The warning bell rings, and I stand up. It's a good thing I was in H Hall already this morning, so I remember where I'm going… I think.

I dump my tray and say bye to everyone before walking toward the doors. "Adri, meet me by my car after school!"

"You bet, girlie!" she calls back.

I'm heading down the corridor and turning into H Hall when a deep voice sounds behind me. "Going my way?"

I turn to look into a set of green eyes, these darker than the ones I was swooning over not too long ago. "English Lit?" I ask Travis.

"That's the one. You're into the classics?" He begins to fall in step with me as I keep an eye out for the room number.

"Most of them, yes." I look at him from the side of my eye and smile. "They were free at the local library and provided a great escape from real life most days."

He nods and walks quietly beside me, his silence telling me maybe he understands exactly what I meant by escape. He's different from the guy Adri described. He's sad and withdrawn, and it's vibrating from him in thick waves. He's not some panty-dropping douche. We arrive at our room, and it's completely different from the other classes. There aren't any desks, just tables with chairs scattered around them.

"We sit wherever we want each day. Mr. Adams likes us to mix it up to experience different perspectives," Travis explains when he catches my confusion.

"That's different," I state as we walk inside. Then I follow Travis as he leads us to one of the front tables.

"You want to be at the front, right?"

"Yeah, but it's okay if you want to sit in the back. You don't need to take care of me," I reassure him.

"I enjoy spending time with you, Ember. Unless you would rather me sit at a different table?" He seems so unsure, nothing like the playboy he's accused of being. Interest is blooming in his eyes and a part of me is curious if something would blossom between us. I could change my usual trajectory when it comes to relationships and go for the good guy for once.

"I'd love to sit with you." The way his face lights up has my stomach flipping with unease, because I'm also worried about hurting him when he seems so vulnerable already.

He continues to grin and pulls out a chair for me, making me swoon a little. Every girl wants to be treated like a lady, and Travis seems the perfect gentleman. Which has me conflicted because of what Adri has said. I'm not going to judge him though until I learn his side of the story because there's always two sides to a coin.

"I'm not going to lie to you. I've heard some things about you that aren't so nice," I murmur quietly to him as other students begin to file into the room.

"Okay… Well, I guess my first question would be from whom? Vincent or Adrianna?" His hand curls around his chin as he looks at me with a questioning tilt of his brow.

"I haven't spoken to Vin about you, just Adri," I reply. I won't lie to him, but I also won't tell him what was said. She's my friend too.

"That situation is complicated. I'm hoping one day we can clear it up. I have nothing bad to say about her. She's amazing, but the things she thinks I've done are severely misconstrued." He shrugs as if it's no big deal, but his tone says differently. He misses her.

"Here's the thing. I will help you, but only if I think it's worth it. She's been great with me today, and I don't want to step where I don't belong. It's easy to tell you both are feeling the same way." He shrugs again and turns to look out the window, effectively ending our conversation before class starts.

During class, we talk about *Pride and Prejudice* and since it's one of my favorite books, I answer almost all the questions. Travis is watching me with a look I recognize all too well. Admiration mixed with lust. Each time my hand goes up, he grins in my direction. Then all too soon, class is done and I'm packing up and getting ready for my last class of the day. My first day turned out better than I expected, and it seems I'm walking out of here with two new friendships.

"Where to next for you?" Travis leans over a little too close to be just friendly as other students rush out of the room. We stand from the small table we're seated at as I put away the school copy of *Pride and Prejudice*. Mr. Adams tells us he'll see us tomorrow as he's the last one to leave the class and when I look up from my bag, Travis is standing a little closer to me. I roll with it and let him crowd in close. It's the first thing I've let myself feel since the death of my mother, and if it becomes a good thing, then I would've lost nothing.

"Drama in the cathedral. I was going to ask you where that is because I've been wondering all day. I have a map, but there's no cathedral in the school." Looking up, I find him staring at me intently as I wait for the butterflies to scatter in my stomach.

"Drama? Vin is in that class. Be careful of those drama guys." He bites his lower lip, and even though it's sexy as hell, my heart doesn't speed up and those butterflies remain sleeping. Not that it's much of a surprise. "The cathedral is another building not attached to the school, that's why."

"I can handle myself. Which way is the cathedral?" His eyes dip down to my mouth as I speak and I find myself biting my bottom lip to gauge his reaction.

"I'll take you. It's the same direction as the gym. I have baseball last period." His voice is husky and full of heat, and for once today, he doesn't sound sad or dejected.

"Thank you." I let out a squeak when he leans in close

and wraps a piece of my hair around his finger.

"You're stunning, Ember," he says softly. No one has ever called me stunning before.

"Thank you, Travis," I whisper back as my heartbeat finally begins to pick up. After being up close and personal with both brothers, I can see their eyes are a little different. Where Vin has a dark green outer circle and light moss-green inside, Travis' are all green with flecks of gold. Both sets are breathtaking. He leans in closer as his eyes grow heavy with want, my hands moving to grip his waist. Is he going to kiss me?

Maybe it's the part of me that wants to soothe the sad boy or maybe I'm trying to open my heart and somehow fill the void, but I find myself leaning in as well. It's too soon and I've only known this guy for a few hours, but something inside of me is tugging on my heartstrings. He's going to become someone important; I just don't know in what aspect yet.

"Can I…?" he breathes as his thumb and forefinger grip my chin. I nod, unable to form a word. He closes the gap and presses his lips gently to mine. There's some heat, but it quickly fizzles out, much to my disappointment. He pulls back, and I guess the dismay is written all over my face because his mouth curves downward instantly. He looks back and forth between my eyes with question as I stay where I am, looking back at him with a bit of a challenge. He can do better than that. "Fuck it," he growls, and then he crushes his mouth to mine. Now this is what I'm talking about. My fingers dig into the waistband of his pants as I lick my tongue along his bottom lip, and he opens for me. Our tongues dance, our teeth clash, and still, I feel like I'm not close enough.

Those butterflies finally take off and I moan into his mouth as he answers with a groan of his own. The ringing bell pulls us out of our stupor and we part, our breaths mingling in the short space between us as I sharply inhale. Maybe this is his panty-dropping persona because that was so damn hot.

"That was the warning bell," he says quietly, his lips still brushing mine. "We should get you to the cathedral." I give him a nod and his eyes darken when I lick my lips. "Don't do that." His voice is husky and deep as he steps into me again.

"What?" I give him a fake confused look as he tucks my hair behind my ear.

He mumbles something unintelligible before pressing his lips to mine again, biting my lower lip lightly. Then he pulls away and waggles his eyebrows, a small smile dancing on his lips.

"Let's go." He turns quickly, starting for the door as if to put space between us. Laughing, I follow him out of class, the butterflies once again falling into a slumber. As hot as he kisses, I think that's about the only bit of chemistry we have.

We leave the main building and walk across a large running track, something my school back in New York didn't have. Travis points out the gym, the baseball field, and the courts. Then he points to a building with stained glass windows, the top decorated with spires.

"That's the cathedral. We have Mass in there once a month," he points out as his head tips back along with mine to look up at the looming structure.

"It looks older than the school," I remark as an ominous feeling comes over me.

"Yeah, this was one of the first buildings built by the founders of Whitsborough," Travis explains, contempt filling his voice.

"Founders, huh? Sounds prestigious." I turn to find him watching me.

"Prestigious? No. Authoritarian? Elitist? Absolutely." The hard glint in his eyes and the firm set of his jaw tells me there's a history here in this small, sleepy town.

"Mass?" I change the subject, hoping to erase the irritated look in his eyes. "Like a church service on Sunday?"

"Yeah, exactly." He nods, his eyes softening. "We also

hold drama class here on the top floor. It's large, with a stage and lots of windows."

"I've never been to Mass," I mutter, more to myself.

"Never?" he asks, and I shake my head no. "I'll take you to one. This Sunday?" He's looking a little bashful now. "I know your uncle. He and my dad go golfing together. So I can pick you up, if you'd like?"

"I'll let you know." I wouldn't mind checking out a service, even though my sins may set the place ablaze once I step inside.

He shrugs as we continue toward the building and stop in front of a pair of ornate doors. "Straight inside, there's a set of stairs to the left. Go up two floors and you will come to the rotunda."

"Thanks again for helping me out today." I grab the door handle in my hand, the cold metal a shock to my heated palm.

He smiles and leans in to kiss my cheek—not even a single flutter—then turns and walks back in the gym's direction. I'm about five minutes late by the time I reach the rotunda, and the classroom is already full. Looks like I'm the last to enter. The teacher is sitting behind a large desk; she's middle-aged and eccentric-looking with big bottle-cap glasses and frizzy hair.

"Emberlise Craven, I presume?" she asks in a nasally voice.

"Yes, ma'am. Sorry I'm late. They kept me behind in my last class to catch up a bit." Not a complete lie.

"That's just fine, Emberlise." She waves me off with a kind smile. "Take a seat."

I look around the large open room and find everyone lounging on cushions on the floor or sitting on couches. I spot Vin and Danny on a couch in the corner and Vin crooks his finger, beckoning me to him. Putting a seductive smile on my face, I start toward him as his tongue darts out to lick his full bottom lip, a gleam of metal catching the light. Vin has a fucking tongue ring. The butterflies erupt in my stomach as my pussy clenches in anticipation. She has no regard for red flags.

Danny smirks at seeing me approach and nudges Vin with his elbow, a smug look on both of their faces. I'm still not over what happened at lunch, no matter the happy dance my vagina is doing right now. If Vin really wanted me to sit with him, he wouldn't have entertained Pepto. To say I'm irritated and slightly jealous would be an understatement, and it's an emotion I'm not familiar with. Vin's grin widens the closer I get to him as I sway my hips a little more, running my finger along the top of my cleavage. Then I plop my ass down on an oversized cushion and direct my attention to the teacher, who is babbling to a student about the upcoming play.

"What the hell…?" Vin whispers loudly as I drop my face to look at my kilt and hide my smirk. He's going to have to learn he needs to work for me because I won't be some playboy's toy for a week. Despite that, Travis is occupying my thoughts. Am I into him? I guess if I really must ask, it's a no. The attraction is there, and my body ignored my brain when his mouth and hands were on me, but I think that's the extent of it. Unfortunately, his brother causes the same reaction with just a glare. It looks like just friends for Travis and me. I will have to tell him before our church date this Sunday.

"Miss Craven, did you perform at your last school?" the nasally voice interrupts my thoughts and I look up to find her watching me expectantly.

"Yes, I did. Juliet from *Romeo and Juliet* as well as Fantine from *Les Misérables* were a couple of the leads I had. I have prepared a list of the plays I took part in and the dates for you." I pull out the sheets from my bag as a few students turn to look at me curiously. The moment I chose to put acting ahead of fighting, I knew I would have to make it a priority. "Also, I marked the ones that were recorded and uploaded to YouTube if you are interested in seeing more."

I bring the sheets to the front of the class, and she smiles warmly at me. "It's nice to have a student take this so seriously."

"I do. Acting has been one outlet for me. I'm sorry, I didn't catch your name?" I've always made it a point to personally speak to each of my teachers, letting them know I take my education seriously, and just because my living conditions have changed, doesn't mean my ambitions have too.

"You can call me Lisa. All my students do." She takes the papers and places them on her desk.

"Then please call me Ember," I reply. I return to my seat as she looks over the sheets I handed to her. I've listed quite a few roles on it. Besides school plays, I did an actor's workshop twice a week and every weekend, and a summer camp as well.

"This is truly impressive, Ember, and I look forward to your audition for the play we are preparing for. Lance here is our very talented screenplay writer, and he has provided us with an original play for the end of the year." Lance turns on his cushion to face me. He has long, dirty-blond hair pulled back into a ponytail and thick glasses perched on his large, hawk-like nose. He waves at me with a genuine smile, so I wave back with one of my own.

"As we are coming to the end of April, we need to start auditions this week. I am going to hand out the play and I want each of you to read it over and decide who you want to audition for or if you want to be a stagehand." She stands from her desk and moves around the room to hand out booklets. "Afterward, I want you to pair up and read lines together."

I receive a booklet and read the title page. *The Shortest Summer* by Lance Hawkins. I scan through it quickly and realize it's good. It's very good. The play is about two high school students who hang out in different groups and come from different walks of life. They fall in love during the summer months, only to go back to school and break up. It's sad and lovely at the same time. I'm so engrossed in my reading that I don't hear him approach, but my body senses him as goose bumps erupt along my arms, making my hairs stand on end. I look up into green eyes that look clouded with irritation.

"Hey," I say slowly when he doesn't speak.

"Hey… I was hoping…" He shuffles from foot to foot, looking perturbed.

"Vin, sit. You're making me nervous with your stuttering and shuffling." I motion to the cushion beside me.

"I didn't stutter," he retorts as he drops to the spot I pointed out.

"Yeah, you did. I was embarrassed for you." I chuckle as I look back down at the booklet.

"Why didn't you sit with me at lunch?" So, he's a straight shooter. I like that, but that's why I'm about to be just as up-front and avoid playing around the bush.

"I won't be a plaything, Vin. I've heard about you, and I can see you and how you are with your group. You're a player and that's great. I won't tell you not to be or anything. It's just not my vibe." The way I feel let down is a bit concerning because if Vin had even an ounce of Travis' chivalry, I would be hooked.

"Plaything? That's a little presumptuous, don't you think?" He leans in closer, his breath fanning my neck. My pussy clenches and I nearly moan into the play in my hands. Fuck, I'm screwed. "I haven't even figured out if I like you yet."

"Don't play with me, Vin, and we can be friends," I implore as he scoffs.

"I don't need more friends." His words are cocky as he leans back on his hands.

"Then why exactly are you sitting next to me?" I huff. "Did you think I would become another weekend booty call like Marlana?"

"My mother texted me at lunch and told me to play nice with you." A light bulb goes off. This is Sharla's son. I don't answer him and go back to reading the script, hoping the lack of conversation makes him leave. I won't be a pity project; I can take care of myself. "I'm auditioning for Michael." He breaks the silence. I guess he's not leaving. *Pity.* "I want you to be Clara."

Clara and Michael are the leading roles of *The Shortest Summer*. Clara, being the uptight, straight-A student, does nothing she shouldn't, and is top of her grade in school. Michael is the bad boy who runs with a gang and is failing school. They both end up working at the same cinema during the summer and fall for each other. When I don't reply to him, he leans in once more, his breath fanning my ear. "I won't play Michael otherwise."

"Is that an ultimatum? Why would I care if you aren't the lead?" I ask incredulously, my head snapping to gape at him.

"It's not about you, it's Lance. He approached me and said he wrote this play with me in mind as Michael. He would be so disappointed to learn I won't do it." This guy has nerve, I will give him that, but it's clear he's never dealt with a girl who doesn't melt at his feet.

"I won't be strong-armed into a role. I need to feel it. So, you can take your idle threats elsewhere. If I want the role, I will audition for it." I stare him down, a part of me hoping for a fight, just a little spat to alleviate the pressure that's been collecting since I moved here.

"You're not like most teenagers." I roll my eyes at the same fucking line I've heard many times before. Sorry, I don't bend to the will of men. Disappointment rolls through me when he remains cool, not giving me the confrontation I'm wanting.

"Like I said, Greene, I had you pegged from the moment I first saw you." I look him right in the eyes again. "Word of advice? Maybe you should just stick to those other teenagers you chill with."

To be honest, the role of Clara stood out to me and I'll audition for it, but it won't be because he forced me into it. He can wait until auditions to see what I choose. The last bell of the day rings and I realize I'm tired but also excited to talk to Adri.

"I'll walk you to your locker." Statement, not a question.

"Sure." I shrug. It's a free world and if he wants to escort me around, I won't complain about the view.

Danny walks up to us with a shit-eating grin on his face.

"Hey, loser," he says to Vin, his eyes flicking between us as he slips his hands into his pockets. "Are you coming to my house after school or going on a date?" I struggle to hold in my eye roll as Vin chuckles beside me.

Then Danny winks at me, and the tiny motion sets me off. "Do you have an infection? Apparently, a symptom of eye gonorrhea is incessant twitching." I nod sympathetically as I stand, wanting to be on even ground with the jerk. "You should really have that checked out." Danny's mouth falls open as he shakes his head and walks off, muttering to himself.

Vin's face lights up with the biggest grin as he stands beside me. Fuck, he's pretty. "You have a sharp tongue, Em."

"My fists are pretty sharp too, *Vince*," I reply with a sweet smile.

"I'm really starting to believe that." He grabs his bag and we leave the classroom, descending the stairs together in silence. There's something brewing between us, but I can't tell how it'll turn out. Though, right now, I want to punch him in the mouth more than I want to kiss him.

We walk through the field, and I stop when I find Travis batting at the baseball diamond. He's shirtless, his body sculpted to perfection. He hits a home run and lazily trots around the plates, a smug look on his face as his teammates cheer.

"I can't help but hate him. We have the same blood running in our veins, but I can never accept him," Vin says, his voice making me turn to look at him as he watches Travis as closely as I was. His eyes are filled with malice as his hands clench at his sides.

"Hate is a strong word. We should use it only in situations most deserving. Has he done something to you personally to cause such hatred?" I press, my head tipping to the side.

"Yeah, he was born." He turns and walks away, leaving me on the field alone.

Slowly, I make my way back inside the school and

luckily find the hall with my locker on the first try. I drop off my stuff and grab what I need for my homework tonight. Irritation hovers over me as I slam my locker shut. We barely had time to speak before his mood changed.

As I approach my car, I find Adri leaning against the passenger side, smiling as I unlock the doors. We get in and she breaks the silence. "This ride is so fucking sweet," she purrs, running her fingers along the dashboard.

"I kissed Travis today, and yes, it was hot, but I quickly figured out that I don't have any genuine feelings for him beyond physical attraction. So, I am going to tell him we can't be more than friends," I rush out in one breath as I rest my hands on the wheel, not bothering to move out of the parking spot until we've hashed this out. I need to be honest with her, especially if what I suspect she feels is true. I don't want to ruin a great friendship before it's had a chance to flourish.

"Oh, wow," she breathes out as I turn my head from the windshield and find her looking at me with wide eyes. "Why did you tell me that?"

"Because I think you have actual feelings for him and I just needed you to hear it from me. I don't want to ruin our friendship over a boy." My hands grip the steering wheel as she averts her gaze to her hands in her lap.

"Thank you for telling me, even though it hurts to hear it," she finally whispers, confirming what I suspected is true.

"Are we okay?" I reach out and rest my hand on her shoulder.

"Yes, very much okay. I'm really glad you were honest with me. That isn't easy," she says, her eyes watering as she looks up at me.

"It's my policy." I start up the car and give her a smile. I'm glad she trusts me enough to give me another chance, and I vow not to fuck it up.

"I think we need some ice cream floats, and I believe I owe you a juicy story about two brothers who hate each other."

She smirks at me, her teary eyes filling with mischief.

"Tell me where to go, missy."

Chapter Seven

Adri directs me to a little mom-and-pop diner about fifteen minutes from the school. It has retro fifties decor and booths designed like the interior of a car with racing memorabilia all over the walls. The music is old-school fifties bops, and they even have their servers on rollerblades taking orders. I immediately fall in love with the place.

As we sit in front of our ice cream floats and funnel cakes, I patiently wait for Adri to tell me about the Greene brothers. "I don't even know where to begin. I guess I'll start with my friendship with Travis," she starts as she swirls her straw in her cup. "He and I were in the same preschool, but we didn't get along at all. There was hair pulling, toy stealing, and pantsing." I laugh along with her as I take a sip of my float.

"For JK, his parents started him at some prestigious school for the rich and it separated us. Travis really kicked up a stink every day for an entire month. The teachers were tired of his sulking and his parents finally caved and sent him to the school I was in. We were inseparable ever since." She sighs, taking a sip of her float, her eyes becoming misty as the story continues. "Vin also went to that school, and that was when

Travis learned this other boy had his last name."

"What?" I say as shock tears through me. "They didn't know about each other?"

"No, they didn't." She stiffens and then grits through her teeth. "Their father is a grade-A jerk. He got Sharla pregnant during senior year of high school, and just four months later, he got his now wife pregnant in college."

"Oh my gosh!" I nearly choke on my float and begin to slap my chest to clear it. She wasn't joking when she called the brothers the town's scandal.

"Yep. So he leaves Sharla—well, Robert says he broke up with Sharla before knowing about the pregnancy—and goes off to college. Sharla insists she told him, and Robert told her he was off to college so he would be able to provide for their new family. Then he meets Catherine and just doesn't come home for a few years." She shrugs. "Sharla says he called her and tried to convince her to have an abortion, but she was already six months along. Sick, I know."

"I have no words." My stomach churns as I think about Vin's mother and the hardships she had to face raising her son alone.

"During elementary school, Vin and Travis got along. They hung out at recess, and they played T-ball together all the time. Mind you, the mothers just ignored the situation completely and acted like it didn't exist." She takes a drink of her float and fiddles with the straw. "I was a part of the group. They were my best friends too. Travis and I were closer because we lived closer to each other, but Vin was our school best friend for sure."

The server comes to our table and plants his hands on the wooden top. "Hey, girls. I have a guy at the counter that insists on paying for your bill. I came by to tell you." Then he smiles and skates away.

Who is paying our bill? As Adri looks at the counter from her seat, I stand up from mine. I don't see anyone until I look at the door and find long, light brown locs swinging by the exit.

"Who was it?" Adri asks as I smile and sit down.

"They must've left. I couldn't see anyone." I shrug. I don't like lying to her, but if Vin wanted us to know he paid, he would tell us himself. I decide to keep his little secret. "Anyway, continue." I wave her on as I pop the straw back in my mouth.

"Right." She bites her bottom lip. "Um… Where was I?"

"You were all best friends at school," I answer her, eager to hear the rest.

"Yes! Anyway, we began first grade and that's the year you can start enrolling for the Whitsborough science fair. The fair was a big thing for us and we wanted to do an erupting volcano." She gets a far-off look in her eyes, like she's back in first grade. "Vin was easily the smartest of us. He figured out the formula for the lava while Travis and I papier-mâchéd the volcano. We got the invite to the fair and we were so excited, but we had to bring home forms for our parents to sign for permission to travel to Toronto, ya know? On those permission forms, it had all our group members' names. It's a mystery how Vin's mom reacted, but we all knew how Robert reacted. He read Vincent Greene and nearly blew their roof off. Travis said he was the maddest he had ever seen him."

"What happened then?" I lean in, my words rushed with trepidation.

"Robert is not a good person, clearly. Instead of sitting Travis down and telling him who Vin was, he forbade him to go to the science fair. To top it off, he also told Travis that Vin and his mother were so poor they were practically homeless. He told him to stay away from Vin for good." Her hand tightens into a fist on the table as her eyes burn with anger. I don't blame her, this is heartbreaking.

"Are you fucking kidding me?" I practically scream, my rage bubbling close to the surface. "What the fuck is wrong with that man?"

"It gets better." She shakes her head and looks out the

window. "Robert took a trip to Sharla's house that night and I'm guessing he paid her off. They pulled Vin from our elementary school the next day and moved to Toronto." She looks sad as her chin trembles with the memory. "I missed Vin after that, and our group was never the same. Anyway, we didn't see him again until eighth grade."

"They moved back? But what did Robert do about it?" My heart begins to pound as I picture a scared Sharla coming back to her hometown, despite a man who was dead set on keeping her out.

"I'm not sure about the specifics, but Sharla ended up buying the restaurant and coming back. Vin was completely different. He was mean and a bully, but mind you, he knew Travis was his half brother, and he thought that was the reason they were shipped off. He grew to resent Travis during the time he was away, and as soon as he was back, the hatred was evident."

"I get it, but why take it out on Travis?" I press my hand to my chest as sadness fills it and I suck in a breath.

"Because I'm guessing Travis had the life Vin thought he should've had? It's no secret that Sharla struggled to raise Vin with how little they had. Robert never acknowledged him, and I guess Sharla never took him to court over it. I wouldn't want that man in my child's life either, to be honest," she spits out, her mouth turned down in an angry scowl.

"Things are making more sense. I still don't get why he took it out on Travis, or still is for that matter. He should take it up with his deadbeat dad," I snarl as I envision Travis' sad eyes. Vin's anger reminds me so much of my own, and even though I should be wary of him, I just keep seeing myself instead.

"When Vin and Sharla came back to town, Travis still didn't know that Vin was his half brother. None of us knew. I'm sure the adults all heard the gossip, but we were oblivious to it. It was Vin who told us in eighth grade, after he beat Travis to a pulp for the first time." She leans in to sip her drink as tears pool in the corner of her eyes.

"Oh no!" I cover my mouth with my hand as I envision the two brothers fighting. A mix of rage and horror consumes me and I can't help but feel sorry for them both.

"Travis obviously didn't believe him and told Vin he was delusional, that Vin just wanted Travis' life. It was a terrible day." She sighs. "When Travis went home that night and his mother saw his face, she freaked out and asked him what happened. After Travis finished, he said his mother remained so quiet he just knew everything Vin said was true. He was broken after that. What's even sadder? Travis grew up as an only child too and would always ask his parents for a brother."

"I feel for them both. That's a hard situation. Their father is scum," I growl and slap a hand to the table.

"Complete scum." Adri nods in agreement.

"So obviously, that hatred is still going strong to this day," I say, then lean in with a smirk. "But what happened with you and Travis?"

"I've loved Travis Greene since we were in seventh grade, but I kept it to myself because I didn't want to ruin our friendship." I nod because I had guessed as much. "Then in ninth grade, just before Christmas break, I thought we were going somewhere finally. We went to a party, and it was boring as fuck, so we got drunk. Without getting into too much detail, we ended up making out, then not even an hour later, he goes into a room upstairs with an eleventh-grade slut. I haven't spoken to him since." Her jaw is clenched so tight that the muscle bunches beneath the skin.

"Wait, you didn't even tell him he was being a douche? Or that you saw what he did?" My eyebrows raise with shock. "Why didn't you confront him?"

"He knew. That's why he has never even tried to explain himself." Her eyes water again as she bites her lip to stop the trembling. "I thought I was worth fighting for, ya know? But he just let me go."

"And he's been a whore ever since?" I try to imagine the

guy I met today as a playboy, but something is just not adding up. He didn't kiss like it was something he did often.

"Pretty much. I stay away from him, but I hear shit. Today was the first day he's spoken to me in two years." That explains her reaction in class.

"Because of me, I'm sorry," I reply as I reach across the table and cover her hand with mine.

"You didn't know. Don't worry about it. You need to be careful about Vin, though. He's got a chip on his shoulder and he has anger issues," she implores as she flips her hand around to link her fingers with mine.

"We have chemistry between us, I won't deny that. To be honest with you, I don't think I can stay away. There's just something about him that draws me in." I pull my hand back to my float and shrug like it's no big deal, but it is. He's a walking red flag and I'm already infatuated.

"Just promise me you'll be careful and smart about the whole thing." She tips her head forward and looks at me through her lashes.

"You got it, doll." I stick my fist out, waiting for a bump. She raises an eyebrow and looks at me skeptically. I shrug again and then drop the fist. "Or not. Look, I'll be smart, I always am." She nods and turns back to her float.

We finish the rest of our drinks and leave the diner, our minds buzzing with everything we spoke about. Then we sit in the car at the end of Adri's driveway as I stifle a yawn. It's been a long day, and I just want to go home to process all I've learned about Whitsborough and its residents. I also want to have a conversation with my aunt about the Greenes, she's Sharla's best friend after all. I promise Adri to pick her up in the morning before we exchange cell numbers, and she leaves the car with a grin and a squeal.

Pulling into the driveway of my new life of wealth and privilege, I find a cute red car parked near the garage. Don't ask me to tell you what kind of car it is because I don't have a clue.

I grab my bag out of the backseat and head inside the house. As soon as I'm dropping my bag in the foyer, Aunt Debbie's laughter filters out from the kitchen, and the husky chuckle in response sounds very familiar. I enter the kitchen and both my Aunt Deb and Sharla are sitting at the table as they turn toward me with a smile.

"Hey, honey! How was the first day?" Aunt Deb asks as she motions for me to come closer.

"It was good." I step up to the table and give Sharla a wave. "Most people are very kind here."

"Did you meet Vincent?" Sharla inquires as she tips a wine glass up to her mouth.

"Yes, I did." I nod. "I also met Travis." I don't care at this point if I have no tact for mentioning that. Both boys were screwed out of a relationship because all parents involved had their heads up their asses. Sharla is the least to blame, but she still kept information from her son, even if her intentions were good.

"Travis is a good boy." Sharla sets her glass back on the table, her mouth set in a grim line.

"They both are," my aunt agrees as she sips from her glass, her eyes on Sharla over the rim.

"I also met a girl named Adrianna. We'll be riding to school together." Sharla refills her glass as Aunt Deb reaches out and squeezes my arm.

"Adrianna is a sweet girl. I'm glad for you, hun." Her eyes become glassy with emotion as I imagine she's thinking of my mother. I swallow down the lump forming in my throat and back up toward the foyer, planning my escape.

"Well, I'm going to go start on homework. It was nice to see you again, Sharla, and thanks for the coffee this morning." I point toward my aunt. "Make sure you collect your payment."

Sharla laughs and gives me the gun salute, and I head toward the staircase when my aunt says, "What payment? Am I being pimped or something?"

Chuckling, I head to the foyer and grab my bag, then run up the stairs to my room and throw myself on my bed, trying to digest the amount of information I ingested today. Poor Travis and Vin. They're family but don't have the option to act that way. I don't know them well, but I want to help Travis and Vin reconnect. I want to help them heal and maybe become friends. Expecting them to be brothers overnight is foolish. Am I trying to be a savior and fix the damaged? Maybe. Am I doing it because I can't fix my own damage? Probably.

I push aside the Greene drama and pull out my textbooks to lose myself in the heart and its functions until dinnertime.

"Ember! Dinner!" Uncle Scott yells from the bottom of the stairs.

He's home? What time is it?

Looking at the alarm clock on my side table, I see it's been a few hours since I cracked these books open. I change out of my uniform quickly and run downstairs, looking out the window by the front door as I pass it. Sharla's car is gone. Good, because I need to do some digging. I enter the kitchen to the scents of garlic toast and spaghetti, and it makes me nostalgic for my mom's meals. I put a wall up at the sudden rush of grief and sit at the table, clearing the lump in my throat. "Dinner smells great, thank you."

My uncle looks over his shoulder from his position at the stove, his shirtsleeves rolled up, and he's elbow-deep, stirring the pasta. "Are you ever going to be a regular teenager? You know, acting disrespectful and moody?" he teases with a wink and grin.

"Most definitely when the honeymoon period is over." I nod with a grin of my own as I sit beside Aunt Debra at the table.

"That's good. I thought we were going to have to open you up to check if you were actually real," he reveals with a laugh. My aunt and I join in.

"Seriously though, you're amazing, Ember, and your mom clearly did a great job raising you," Aunt Debbie adds before clearing her throat. She's also going through her grieving process, and it's filled with guilt and regret. I reach my hand over to cover hers, hoping it eases some of it.

"Thank you," I whisper as she offers me a watery smile. Then Uncle Scott comes to the table with a tray of garlic toast and my mouth waters as I exclaim, "That smells so good!"

"Dig in." He rubs his hands together as he sits across from Aunt Deb and me.

After we have all stuffed our faces and rubbed our full bellies, I break the silence. "I found out about some drama today." Straight to the point, Ember style.

"Tons of that around here," Aunt Deb hums as her eyes skip to my uncle.

"About Travis and Vincent," I clarify, leaning on the table to look him in the eyes.

"Mm-hmm." He nods and folds his hands behind his head, his expression turning serious.

"Two sons with a father who didn't know how to keep it in his pants, and two mothers who would rather pretend none of it existed." I place a finger to my chin and tap it.

My uncle bursts out laughing and falls forward, slapping his hand on the table. "Nailed it."

"Why did he do that?" I ask seriously as I look from him to my aunt.

"Who? Robert?" my uncle inquires as he straightens.

"Yeah. Why not acknowledge Vin? He's his son too." Familiar feelings of being unworthy flood me at the thought of deadbeat fathers. Maybe this hits a little closer to home because I have a father whom I've never met.

"I can't answer for him, but I would say he isn't the most dependable guy around. The Robert you face and the one behind your back are very different." He's trying to keep his answer unbiased, but disdain is coated through his words. "Anyone dealing with him understands to never turn their back on him. I tolerate Robert because he makes me a lot of money, but anything beyond a few games of golf and one meeting a month, I try to steer clear."

"It must be difficult since Aunt Deb and Sharla are best friends," I dig a little deeper, wondering how far I can push for information.

"Not really. I don't bring Robert around the house. It's just unnecessary, and it's no secret Sharla and Debra are close, they've been that way since middle school. So it doesn't come up." He shrugs and leans back in his chair. "Besides, Robert is just business, and Sharla is family."

"Those brothers hate each other because their parents really took an unpleasant situation and made it worse," I think out loud as I look down to my hands folded on the table.

"I agree," my aunt chimes in and places her hand over mine as I look up at her. "I tried so hard to convince Sharla to accept Travis for Vincent's sake, but in the beginning, she was so blinded by betrayal she couldn't move past it to the bigger picture. Now, as much as she tries to encourage them to communicate, the damage has already been done."

"I see," I murmur, and Aunt Debbie squeezes my hand. Does Sharla deserve a break because she's now trying to patch the destruction she had a hand in from the beginning? In my opinion, no.

"Are you familiar with the quote 'The sins of the father are to be laid upon the children'?" Uncle Scott asks me as he folds his arms on the table and leans forward.

"Yes, *Merchant of Venice*, Shakespeare." Literature has always been my strong point.

"Beauty and brains." He snaps his fingers.

"And brawn too, apparently," my aunt adds, giving me a side eye.

"That too." I nod in agreement. I won't sugarcoat my

past, and fighting was a part of it. MMA training is a part of who I am.

"Robert is a stubborn, emotional, and vindictive man. He makes rash decisions based on his emotions, and unfortunately, I believe his boys—both of them—have inherited one or more of those traits. That's what's making it impossible for them to move past their anger." He looks me in the eye as he speaks, his serious expression one I've rarely seen. "But I also believe, one day, something or *someone* will change that." The way he's looking at me makes me think he might mean me. If that's the case, he would be terribly wrong. Today I made out with one brother while pining for the other. Speaking of, I should call Travis and explain about today and how I'm feeling. I don't want to lead him on any further.

Rising from the table, I start collecting dishes as my aunt and uncle move into the den. The rule of my mother's house was if you didn't cook, you washed. After I wash the dishes, I find my aunt and uncle cuddling up on the couch. They look so in love and it's obvious he adores her. It's really unfortunate they couldn't have children of their own.

"Hey, guys. I'm going upstairs to finish my homework, then call it a night." I thumb over my shoulder. "Thank you for dinner."

"Okay, honey. I'll check in on you later." Aunt Deb lifts her head from Uncle Scott's chest to look at me.

"Night, kid." My uncle grins over his shoulder.

Chapter Eight

I'm lying on my bed, typing a text to Adri, asking for Travis' number to tell him that I hope we can remain friends. Something tells me these people and being here in Whitsborough is fate. That them being in my life was always meant to be, no matter how terrible the path was getting here.

Me: Hey!

Me: I need Travis' #.

Adri: Hiiii. I only have his house number.

Adri: He's changed cells since the last time I spoke to him.

Me: Ok cool, I'll take it.

Me: Thanks, bitch.

Adri: You got it, skank.

Chuckling to myself, I press on the contact card she

provides and fall back on the bed as the phone rings. I drum my fingers on my bedspread as my heart spears up into my throat. I need to do this with the most transparency but also while being mindful of his feelings, which is something I've never been too good at.

After the sixth ring, Travis picks up. "Yo."

"Seriously? You answer your phone with *yo*?" I chuckle.

"Yep." He exhales an irritated sigh. "Who is this?"

"Ember."

"Oh… Oh! H–hey, what's up?" he sputters. The shock coating his tone has me stifling a laugh into my fist.

"I just wanted to call to talk about what happened in class today." Suddenly, my heart begins to pound in my chest, the sound reverberating through my ears. What if he hates me? I want a fresh start here in Whitsborough, to be a different Ember, but that won't happen if people begin to avoid me like they did in New York. Being a girl who likes to pound her fists into people's faces isn't a likable trait, apparently.

"Like homework?" he asks, sounding slightly confused.

"If you have to ask that, then I am totally right about how I'm feeling." I adjust myself on the bed and sit up straighter.

"You mean the kiss," he states, his voice sounding a little disappointed.

"Yeah…"

"You're not into it, or me," he mumbles with a sigh.

"I won't deny that the kiss between us was great, but it's missing the fire, the irresistible need to be in each other's orbit. I'm trying to be honest with you, and right now, I think we both have too much baggage." It all pours out of me as the words meld.

"Okay…" he hesitates, the word dragged out as he waits for me to continue.

"I want to be friends and I don't want to fuck that up by forcing an attraction," I persist.

"Yeah. I mean, I agree. I was into it too at the time, but I'm living a curse of trying to forget someone in other people. The truth is, I'm still not over that person. I'm sorry."

I bet he means Adri.

"Anyone I know?" I tease as I try to lighten the mood. His answering chuckle has my whole body relaxing with relief. We're going to be okay.

"You don't know many people yet, fool," he retorts.

I laugh as I say, "It just better not be Marlana."

"I would never," he vows.

"I'm here if you ever want to talk, and I still want to hang out." I mean it. Travis has a pure soul, it's there beneath the heavy blanket of sadness. Is it wrong that I want to curl up under it with him, just so he's not alone?

"Yeah, let's do that." I can hear how lonely he is, and right here and now, I make a vow to show him he matters, even if no one else will. Maybe he can heal me too.

"I'll see you tomorrow?" I ask, my voice sounding small and unsure.

"Yeah, you will. Good night, Ember."

"Night, Travis." I stay on the line until the dial tone hits my ear. Then I drop my phone to the bed beside me and stare at the ceiling. Uncle Scott's words from dinner come back to echo through my mind. Maybe I am the bridge that helps the two brothers overcome their anger. I sit up and grab my phone when it pings with a message.

Adri: Did you let him down easy?

Me: Didn't need to. Travis is into someone else anyway.

Adri: Better not be any of the skank squad.

I laugh out loud as my thumbs move quickly over the screen.

Me: LOL! He said he would never!

Adri: Seems I'm popular tonight for handing out #s.

Me: What do you mean?

Adri: Vin asked for your #. I hope it's okay I gave it to him?

My heart picks up into a quick staccato again as I stare at the screen. Vin asked for my number?

Me: That's cool.

Adri: You're a dork. But in case he chickens out, here's his #. I'm off to shower. See you tomorrow.

Me: Night!

I stare at the contact card she sent me. What would I even say to him? He ditched me twice today with no explanation. I can't blame him for his attitude, not after everything he's been through and the fact that he faces it daily whenever he lays eyes on Travis.

Ten minutes go by without a message or a call, and I figure if I want to be that bridge, I have to start building it.

Me: Leaving me on that field to walk all the way to the school alone was cruel.

I wait. He takes a few minutes, but he finally replies, sending my heart into overdrive with apprehension.

Vince: You're a big girl. I'm sure you were good.

That's irritating. My spine straightens with surprise at his nonchalant tone and I'm typing my reply when another text comes through.

Vince: Sorry, though.

Me: Sorry isn't enough. You'll have to make it up to me.

Making it up to me will entail his complete attention and a better attitude toward his brother, he just doesn't know it yet. Yeah, I'm still irritated with his initial response, but I have to let it go. It's clear Vin and I are similar in the way that we react to anger with more anger.

Vince: Whatever you want, Em.

Typical guy, not much of a texter. Even with so little said, I'm smiling widely. Yeah, I'm crazy about this one already, and that can only mean heartbreak in the near future.

Those three dots appear again and I stare at it with excitement.

Vince: Ma and I are coming to Aunt Deb's on Friday for dinner.

My eyes widen on the screen as I swallow past the dryness in my mouth.

Me: Is this a usual thing?

Vince: Yeah.

Vince: Can't hide from me.

I giggle and throw myself on my bed, my phone chiming with a new message.

Vince: I'll see you tomorrow.

Vince: No more ditching. I wouldn't want to be on your bad side.

Me: Good night, Vince.

I send him a kissy face emoji and he replies almost instantly.

Vince: I'll only accept the real thing.

Setting my alarm for school, I lie in bed, running everything over in my head. Maybe he'll make it up to me with a hot kiss tomorrow, since he only accepts the real thing. I roll over, cuddling into my pillow as I close my eyes and try to dream of dark sepia skin and bright green eyes.

I've got it bad.

I'm on my way to pick up Adri when my eyes flick to the time on the dashboard. I ended up sleeping in and didn't allow enough time to pick up a coffee from Sharla, which means I'm going to be a mean bitch today. I'll have to wake up earlier so I have time to acquire my caffeine fuel.

Popping my sunglasses on, I pull up to the bottom of her driveway and tap my fingers impatiently on the wheel before hitting the horn. I can't drive up to the house because the huge golden gates, monogrammed with Hilton along the front, are closed. It seems like a legit thing to do, putting your name everywhere in case you forget it. Must be a rich people thing. I've seen it a lot in my neighborhood. Although, we don't have it on our gates.

Adri comes jogging down the driveway at the sound of my horn, her maroon hair flowing around her face in loose curls as she waves at me. How can she be so happy in the morning?

"Hey, bitch!" she yells and opens the door, her voice like nails on a chalkboard.

"Are you always this chipper?" I ask, looking at her above my glasses as she bounces on the seat.

"Oh, you're a morning bitchy bitch." She snaps her fingers before putting on her seat belt. "Noted."

I chuckle and say, "Just need coffee. Didn't plan my morning right."

"Did I fuck it up?" she asks while fluttering her eyelashes at me. "Not that I'm suggesting you don't pick me up anymore, 'cause this ride is now my morning orgasm." I laugh out loud while pushing my sunglasses up on my head and then pull out of her driveway. "So, tell me what happened with Travis," Adri begins as she tries to look unbothered.

"I basically said I wasn't that into him and he agreed." I shrug. "He said he was into someone else. Any idea who it is?"

"I haven't really paid any attention to him. So no goddamned idea." I stop at a red light and look over at her with my brow raised.

"Sure," I drawl out.

"Fine!" She throws her hands up. "I've made it a point to make it look like I haven't been paying attention to him." Then she slouches in her seat. "He's never really dating. I just hear the rumors."

"Like?" The light turns green, forcing my eyes back to the road.

"Like who he's sleeping with and it's usually never the same girl twice," she answers with a huff.

"Interesting." I tap my fingers along the steering wheel.

"Not really." Her eyes flick to me as her mouth curls up into a sly grin. "Vin is the same."

"Well, Travis is into someone, regardless of who he's sleeping with. I have an idea who." I look at her and ignore the Vin dig. I won't be the next to fall victim to rumors. I'm good at digging for the truth anyway.

"Me?!" she squeaks, straightening in her seat as her hands press to her chest. "Are you nuts?"

"Just an inkling." I smile as we stop at another red light.

"What happened with Vin?" she asks, changing the subject as she links her fingers together in her lap.

"I texted him and said I didn't appreciate him ditching me yesterday."

"You texted him first?" She gasps. "And?"

"And... he said he was sorry and wouldn't do it again." I shrug as I move through the green light and turn onto the stupid gravel road toward the school. "He asked for a kiss."

"He did?" She puts her finger to her mouth and taps her bottom lip. "That's weird."

"Why's that weird?" I ask as I keep my eyes on the huge potholes.

"Vin doesn't do PDA. Like, at all. Nothing."

"He's never had girlfriends?" Shelby bounces over bumps as we slowly make our way along the road.

"He has. He just doesn't pay them much attention in public. Like I told you yesterday, that's why people were staring, because he's shown more affection with you than his actual girlfriends."

That's a little weird, but then I think back to yesterday when Marlana was on his lap and he pushed her off. He didn't want her attention at all, and from what I understand, they fuck all the time. "Weird," I echo her previous statement.

We pull up to the school and I park in the same spot I had yesterday, slipping my sunglasses firmly over my eyes and keeping them there until I can get to the cafeteria to grab a coffee. If anyone looks me directly in the eyes before then, God help them. *Look at me, a good Catholic already.*

"You realize you parked beside Travis, right?" Adri snickers while pointing out her window.

"How the fuck would I know that? I barely know what kind of car I drive."

I *tsk* as she laughs and points to a cobalt-blue car. Pretty color. "It's the newest model Honda Civic. Fully Loaded." She sounds like she's reading the owner's manual but in French.

"Speak English. My tank"—I tap my temple—"is on empty, remember?"

She continues laughing and gets out of the car. "We were meant to be, Ember."

"How romantic." Smirking, I lower my glasses to the bridge of my nose. "Will I receive routine head with that declaration?"

"Now this is a conversation I can get behind." His raspy voice sends a shiver down my spine as my eyes widen on Adri.

"Dirtbags." Adri snickers at us with a shake of her head, but I don't miss the wink she sends me before she walks away.

I finally turn to face him as my heart tries to jump out of my chest. He's so fucking gorgeous standing in the sunshine. He has his trademark scowl on his face—the one I want to sit on—and is holding a cup toward me. "My mom sent me with this since you didn't come in this morning," he growls as his eyebrows furrow together.

My mouth falls open. "Is that coffee?"

"Yeah, I think so?" He looks confused as his mouth dips into a frown. "She said it's the same as what you got yesterday."

I don't think, I just launch myself out of the car, throwing my arms around him and burying my face in his neck. He smells like soap and sunshine.

"Whoa," he murmurs, his one free arm coming around my back. "It's just coffee."

"You don't understand," I tell him, my voice muffled by his shirt. "I'm going to marry your mother." Pulling away from his neck, I look up at him, my hand cupping his cheek as I stare into his beautiful eyes. "I'm your new stepmommy, honey."

His hand is rubbing slow circles on my back as he pulls me in closer. He's chuckling, the sound vibrating from his chest to mine. Then he bends his face down to mine before whispering in my ear, "I'll have you before she does."

A shiver runs from my toes all the way to the top of my head. His green eyes, cushioned by his thick black lashes, grow heavy as I tip my face back. I've never wanted to kiss someone so badly. He looks from my eyes to my mouth as he slowly leans in.

"Get a fucking room!" Vin pulls back and looks across

the parking lot with annoyance. Standing with her hands on her hips is Cotton Candy Head. Her face distorts with jealousy and rage as she snaps, "Seriously, Vin?"

"What, Marlana? Can I help you with something?" he asks, sounding tired of her shit. Stepping away from him, I place the coffee on the roof of Shelby as he turns to face the bitch whose jealousy is written all over her face.

"Yeah, actually, how about you move away from the skank and walk me to class?" She bares her teeth as she talks, her cheeks reddening with anger.

Oh, hell no. I warned this bitch multiple times yesterday. "That's it. I told you yesterday not to push me."

"Hey!" Vin yells as I dash toward her. I make it three steps before he grabs the back of my shirt to hold me in place. My body stiffens as I fight against him, my anger clouding any other feeling.

"I warned you too!" she shrieks. The fear in her eyes fade when she notices Vin has a firm hold on me, and she comes up to me, her long nail pointed toward my face. "What made you think he would want a poor, orphaned bitch over me?" she spits out. "We've been together since the eighth grade!"

"Mar! Stop! We haven't been together for months!" Vin exclaims from behind me, his admission making me snort.

"You stupid bitch! He's mine! Take that smile off your face!" Then she does something that shocks me. She bitch-slaps me hard across the face, making my head snap to the side. Blood floods my mouth and it sends a familiar red haze over my vision.

"Holy shit," Vin hisses and moves to grab her.

He lets me go, and I don't waste the opportunity to fly toward her and grab her head in a guillotine choke hold. Her hands fly up and grab my arms as she screams, only making me tighten my hold.

"From this day forward, Pepto, you will never touch me again. You understand?" I barely recognize the sound of my own voice as I sink farther into the red haze. She's losing her breath and still grabbing my arms, trying to pull me off.

"Ember, let her go," Vin says calmly beside me, but I refuse to step down now, not without her tapping out.

"Do you understand?" I can't do much to her beyond cutting off her air supply unless I truly want her dead. She's just having a hard time breathing. I could go tighter and make her pass out, and she realizes it when I flex my arm. She finally nods, and I let her go with a shove.

She coughs and grabs at her throat. "You're a psycho!" she screams hoarsely, her eyes wide as they scan the parking lot around us.

"Yes, I am. Better to keep that in mind the next time you want to throw hands." My adrenaline ebbs when I notice a crowd has formed around us, and Danny appears, looking shocked. I must've blown his little brain. Who would've thought a female could fight?

Idiot.

Marlana's goon squad is here too, as well as Travis and Adri, the latter laughing while bent over at the waist. Marlana walks away, still gripping her throat, and Travis is not too far behind, his shoulders shaking with restrained laughter.

"Ember!" Danny yells, coming closer. "What are you doing Friday night? I love being choked during sex."

"You know what, Danny? I would actually consider fucking you if it meant I'd be able to choke you to death," I reply, rolling my eyes. The crowd disperses, but I catch a few looking at me with caution. Good.

"Great! Friday night it is!" Danny exclaims, his face exuberant, before walking back toward the school.

"He's not that bright, huh?" I ask Vin. When he doesn't reply, I turn to look at him and find him staring at me with his brows tugged together. "What?" I rear back, giving him a glare.

"Nothing." He points to the coffee on top of my car. "Don't forget that." Then—shocker—he walks off toward school. *Without me.*

"You are so badass!!" Adri squeals and launches herself at me. "Can you teach me?!"

"Sure." I carefully detach her arms from around my neck and shrug. "I may have a class starting up at the gym. Sign up."

She touches my face where the bitch slapped me, the sting flaring throughout my cheek. "You're going to be wearing her handprint for a bit." Her brows crinkle with concern as I gently push her hand away from my face.

"Meh, I've had worse." Adri lifts an eyebrow but doesn't say anything. I'll have questions to answer later for sure.

The warning bell rings, so I grab my coffee and backpack and head off to start my day. Adri and I hurry to homeroom, and we sit in the same seats as yesterday. Travis isn't up front today though, because he took his regular seat in the back. I give him a little wave and he smiles in return. We're going to be okay, I'll make sure of it.

Mrs. G rushes into class wearing a full black dress with long sleeves, and the skirt to her ankles. The collar of the dress is white and very nun-like. "Good morning, children of God!" she sings out. I plant the biggest fake smile on my face and keep it there for the rest of the period.

I make it to lunch unscathed. A few people asked where I learned to fight and it gets boring reciting the same story, so I just tell them to sign up for classes at the gym and maybe I'll divulge.

"I have so many questions," Adri begins as we walk toward the cafeteria.

"I figured." I click my tongue as I side eye her before grinning at her curiosity.

She leans in to whisper, "Is it private? Should we sit outside?"

"Private?" I look at her with confusion. "I trained as an MMA fighter. What were you thinking?"

"Oh, that's cool. I wasn't thinking anything," she says hurriedly, her eyes flickering to the side.

"I'm from New York, so I must be a gangbanger, right?" I grin.

"Maybe? Or like a drug runner? Or! You would collect the flesh of people who owed your mafia boss money!" she exclaims, her voice growing louder as she continues.

"Are you sure *you're* not on drugs?" I tease as she giggles. "You're sort of close. I wasn't just training, I did some other stuff. Nothing I want to talk about at school, though, understand?"

"Call me tonight?" she asks me, her eyes bright with curiosity.

"Yeah, sure."

We step into the cafeteria and people turn to look at us, some leaning together to whisper about the new girl being a savage, I bet.

"Ember! Hey!" Looking around, I spot Danny waving his arms from his seat at the table. "Come sit with us. You too, Adri."

Adri is shaking her head and walking toward her usual table, intent on ignoring him as I grab her shirt to stop her. "I want to sit with Vin. Please, please come with me."

"Fucking shit, you owe me big time," she grumbles while stomping off toward their table.

I walk behind her and when we reach the table, I place my tray beside Danny's, right across from Vin. He doesn't even spare me a look as he's completely engrossed in a conversation with a busty blonde from our drama class, but I bet he can see me in his periphery. She's saying she's trying out for the part of Clara and she's so excited to work beside him, her tits bouncing with her enthusiasm. He's agreeing and smiling widely, blatantly ignoring me.

Fuck this. "Come on, Adri, I think Jake is looking for us." I grab my tray.

"Thank fuck," she breathes out, getting up quickly from her chair beside mine.

"Wait, what?" Danny says, looking at me like I just stole his puppy.

"There, there." I pat his shoulder. "I changed my mind, but I'll be seeing you later in drama."

Vin's attention suddenly snaps to me and he has that same look on his face he had this morning when I grabbed Marlana, wary and cautious, like I'm a rabid animal. I can't deny that it hurts, especially because I thought he was different.

"You'll sit with me?" Danny stares at me with puppy dog eyes as I fight to keep my eyes from rolling.

"Sure thing, pumpkin." I walk away, putting an extra swing in my step and feeling the heat of Vin's eyes searing through my back.

Lunch goes by quickly with Jake and Jordan cracking jokes and Adri razzing Jake as much as possible. I'm proud of myself because I didn't look at Vin once, although, Adri told me periodically that he was staring a hole into my back.

Good.

Gathering up my things, I prepare for English Lit as Adri calls out from the double doors, "Bitch, I'll see you later at my orgasm machine."

"Do I want to know?" Jordan tips his head to the side, his brows furrowed.

"My car. It's replaced her multispeed bedroom companion," I reply with a wink.

"Ew." Jordan rears back, his face full of distaste.

My phone pings with a message from Tommy as I step through the double doors. He sent me the new emoji of his animated face and I giggle as I leave the cafeteria. It's been a few days since we've texted.

"Anything interesting?" I'm proud of myself when that familiar sexy rasp doesn't make me pause.

"Not really," I mutter without stopping and then continue down the hall toward English Lit as I tuck my phone back into my breast pocket.

"Hey!" he yells, running to catch up to me. "Ember, wait." Vin grabs my arm, forcing me to stop, and I don't think as my instinct kicks in because all I feel is his hand grabbing me. My heart rate picks up and red explodes in my vision.

"Get your hand off me, pretty boy, unless you want to be choked out like your friend was this morning." My words are low and deadly, filled to the brim with threat as I step in closer to him.

"She's not my friend, and don't threaten me. You should know I'd take that threat with pleasure." He looks around at the gathering crowd, trying to keep his face impassive, but I can see the growing agitation in his eyes.

"It didn't look pleasurable for you this morning. You talk big game but really you're just another man who can't handle a strong woman." With that, I shrug off his hand and walk off while he struggles to speak, his mouth opening and shutting like a fucking goldfish.

"You told him." I try to calm down as Travis comes up beside me, his presence like a soothing balm over my rage.

"He's all talk," I snarl as my heart rate levels out.

"Look, he and I don't see eye to eye, but he's not all talk. My face will tell you he's not all talk." I look up to find him nodding, his eyes wide, and then I laugh as the last of my anger filters out through the sound. "He's not used to seeing a girl fight like that. Around here, we have nail scratching and hair pulling. Obviously, some slapping."

"You didn't look at me like I was a disgusting monster after, though. That's the difference." I hoist my bag up higher on my shoulder as I huff.

"I don't think he thought that. Fuck, I don't know why I'm sticking up for him," he mumbles the last part as we approach our classroom.

"He's your brother." I turn to him with a smile.

"You're wrong. We share a father, but we were never brothers. Maybe he was thrown off guard, but not disgusted," he explains as my heart breaks for the guy.

"Well, he has a ball sack. It's about time he acted like it." I grin as I cross my arms over my chest.

"That is so fucking sexist." He snickers, shaking his head. "Ball sacks are sensitive, you know?"

"I'm saying he should man up." I stop and look at him, putting my hands on my waist. "I trained for years in MMA and because of that, no one will lay their hands on me."

"I agree they shouldn't." He holds his hands out to placate me. "Maybe he should woman up instead."

"Huh?" I raise a brow.

"Those things can take a beating," he says, pointing between my legs and walking into the classroom with a wink.

Fuck, if he isn't right.

I sit through English Lit, a class I absolutely love, but don't absorb a single thing. Nothing is retained because I can't seem to shake the images of Vin looking at me like I belong in a cage. I snap out of my thoughts when the bell rings at the end of the period and now I'm off to drama. Probably toward actual drama as well.

"Take it easy on him, Ember. He's different around you," Travis admits as he puts his books away.

"I like him. I barely know him, but I like him." I shake

my head because this whole thing is so silly. I've never had a reaction to someone like this before. "He disappointed me this morning."

"I think all guys are programmed to be a constant disappointment to girls," he mutters as he slings his bag over his shoulder.

"You're probably right," I agree with a heavy exhale.

"Anyway, give me your cell." He holds out his hand.

"Why?" I ask, giving it to him anyway.

"Nobody calls our house phone anymore except for scammers and telemarketers." I laugh as he texts himself with my phone. "Text me later if you want to talk." With that, he gives me a quick hug and leaves the classroom.

I arrive at the rotunda on time with Vin and Danny already there, sitting on the same couch as yesterday. As I enter the room, their eyes land on me as I head to the same pillow I sat on yesterday, pulling the script out of my bag. I read over it again last night and decided to audition for Clara.

"Okay, I'm here. Please kick my ass any way you please," Danny interrupts my reading as he plops down on the pillow beside mine.

"I'll take a rain check, but I might cash that in sooner than later," I mutter as I keep my eyes on the script, hoping he'll go away.

"Fuck, I hope so. That was so hot this morning," he says, dropping his voice to a whisper as he leans in. "Marlana needs someone to knock her down a few pegs."

"Yeah, well, that's not going to be my prerogative." I shake my head and look up at him. "I just want her to stay out of my way."

"Won't happen." He leans back on the pillow and looks over at Vin, who's shooting daggers at the both of us. "My boy wants you, and she has always wanted him."

"She can have him." I glare back at Vin.

"Nah, she can't." He snickers. "Not anymore. The moment your sweet-ass climbed those stairs and fed Marlana attitude, he was done."

"Whatever." I look back down at the script in my hands, hoping the jerk will go back to his asshole friend and leave me alone.

"Want to make out?" he deadpans instead.

"Not particularly." I slowly lift my head to stare at him. His face is alight with mischief as his eyes flick from Vin then back to me.

"It'll make him jealous, and we'll keep it totally PG." He crosses an X over his heart.

I lean in close, our breaths mingling. "Not particularly," I repeat slower, in case he's hard of hearing.

He groans loudly just before a large hand wraps around his collar to drag him off the pillow. I stand up quickly in a defensive stance, readying myself for a fight. "What the fuck is wrong with you?" Vin asks through his teeth, his face in Danny's.

"She's hot!" Danny shoves him off, his face darkening with irritation. "No one else is making a play."

"Are you both for real?" I demand with my hands on my hips. "I'm not interested in either of you. Move along out of my way." Turning my back, I sit down on the pillow once more, ignoring the children behind me.

"Fuck this!" Vin snaps, then the classroom door slams shut soon after.

Looking around, I find Danny sitting on the couch with his elbows resting on his knees as he perks an eyebrow at me and grins. "You got him so twisted, baby girl."

Lisa arrives soon after and I force myself to concentrate on the class, refusing to think about the boy with green eyes and a hot temper.

Walking to my locker after class, I mull over Vin's actions earlier. He's so hard to read. He's clearly attracted to me, but after this morning, I'm pretty sure I've turned him off. I shouldn't be stressing over a guy who's intimidated by a female, but seriously, there's just something about him I can't let go of.

As I near my locker, laughing and snickering pulls me out of my thoughts. I look around to find groups of people watching me and whispering to each other. *What the fuck?* It's like I'm thrusted back into my old high school in New York and everyone is talking shit about me. It makes my stomach flip as I grip the straps of my bag tighter. I don't have Tommy here to back me up. Not a single friend to take my side.

Approaching my locker, I notice a piece of paper taped to it. It's a picture of two mangy-looking dogs fucking on the side of the street as people look on with the words *project whore* scribbled on top. My pulse sings with violence the longer I look at it, but I don't rip it down because that'll give people the reaction they're looking for. I've seen and been through a lot worse than this weak-ass attempt at bullying. I open the door and a strip of condoms falls to the floor as everyone laughs louder. I know who the culprit of this little scheme is, and noticeably, her pink head is nowhere to be seen.

What a ball sack. I'll have to thank Travis for that. It makes so much more sense.

I pick up the condoms—which have project whore written on them too—and stand in front of Marlana's locker. I open the first condom and fling it on the metal, the lubrication really helping it to stick. A few collective gasps sound around me as I fling the other three to stick on her locker as well.

"She's lucky this project whore is short on time, otherwise, I would've used them beforehand," I declare loud enough to every nosy person watching. Some laugh and others rush away. "Bunch of ball sacks," I mutter to myself.

I grab my homework for the night and remove the photo from the outside to pin it up on the inside of my locker. I look at the few still standing around as I say, "I'll save that as reference for my next client." I wink at them. "Looks like a good time." Then I slam the locker shut and walk outside.

That pink-headed bitch better not push me too far. I need to prove to my aunt and uncle that I'm well-behaved. I don't want them to give me up, but if a bitch needs to be reminded of where her lane is, I'll do it.

Adri is chilling against my car, and standing across from it, leaning against a gunmetal Hummer, is Vin. His arms are crossed, and he looks pissed. Yeah, well, he can kiss my ass. How dare he look pissed?!

"Looks like he's been waiting a while." Adri snickers as she leans farther over the trunk of my car.

"Probably. He stormed out of last period before it even started." I pull my keys out of my bag.

"Ember, he's never been like this for anyone." She looks over at him. "Maybe you should talk to him?"

"Fuck that, I don't chase, baby. Let's get the fuck out of here." We both slip into the car, my eyes moving to the rearview every few seconds to see he hasn't moved an inch. As I peel out of the parking lot, I chance a final look in my rearview mirror and find him still watching with that scowl on his face.

Chapter Nine

After dropping off Adri, I decide to drive around a bit. My mind is a jumble of different thoughts, and I can't concentrate on one from the other. In the end, it kept running back to my mother and the many times she would grab my chin and tell me I am who I am and to never change for anyone. No matter where I come from, I am my own person. I will always hold that close, and for that reason, I just can't bend to Vin. I will never change for him or anyone else.

After circling the block a few times, I notice a matte black, blacked-out sedan following a few cars lengths back. I turn down a few random streets, noticing they still aren't far behind, and from my rearview mirror, at least two shadows appear through the windshield. *Fuck that.* I pull over to the side and turn my hazards on. Whoever the fuck this is, I'm going to force them to come face-to-face with me. I step out of the car and wait for them to pull up, but to my surprise, they just drive by, and unfortunately, their windows are tinted so dark that I can't see inside. With my stomach twisting with unease, I make a mental note to talk to Tommy. Maybe the gang has a tail on me. It wouldn't be the first time they've followed me, although Whitsborough is a little far to come to keep an eye on me.

I make my way back home in a worse mood than when

I left school, and when I pull into the driveway, I spot Vin's gunmetal Hummer idling. "What the fuck?" Pulling up beside him, I park my car and wait. We have a stare off for a minute, neither of us moving until he realizes I won't give in. He gets out of his SUV and crosses to my passenger side before folding himself into the car.

"Hey," he rasps as he shifts his big body to find a comfortable position in the small seat.

"*Hey*?" I look at him incredulously as his head snaps up to look at me. "That's it?"

"I just got in here?" He raises a brow and looks around with a confused look on his face.

"What do you want?" I turn off the ignition and undo my seat belt.

"To apologize," he mumbles as he scratches the growth on his cheek. It's clear apologizing is not something Vin is used to doing. "I fucked up. I was just surprised and maybe a little freaked out this morning. I thought you were going to kill her."

"Kill her?" I scoff with a sarcastic laugh. "What do I look like? You know what really pisses me off, Vincent?" He narrows his eyes at the mention of his full name. "You didn't bat an eye when she slapped me hard enough to draw blood, but I grab her, and oh no! She's going to die?" I chuckle. "Why don't you go check on her if you're so fucking worried?"

"It all happened so fast! I didn't have time to react to her slapping you! Then suddenly you have her in some death hold!" He throws his hands up as his voice raises.

"Say it again," I grit out through my teeth and lean across the center console, putting our faces inches apart. "Accuse me of trying to kill her one more time and I will never breathe in your direction again. Understood?"

My breathing is erratic as blood surges to my face. I close my eyes and rely on the techniques I learned to control my emotions. I really don't want to fly off the handle right now and do something I will regret, like a quick jab to his throat.

Vin is also quiet, giving me the time to de-escalate. His fingers on my cheek jars me as he drags them down to my lips. "I'm not good for you," he whispers.

"Whatever." My eyes remain closed, but I don't push him away as his finger outlines my lips slowly.

"Doesn't mean I'm staying away from you." He groans when I run my tongue along my lips and swipe it over his finger. "When I looked into your eyes after the whole Marlana thing, I saw a darkness inside of you that calls to my own." His thumb presses against my bottom lip before he opens the car door and leaves. When I finally open my eyes, he's already at the end of the driveway.

Exhaustion hits me once I enter the house and close the front door to kick off my shoes. I spot my aunt and uncle curled up on the couch, watching some housewife's bullshit. Uncle Scott does that for her, and it melts my frozen heart.

"Hi, baby girl," my aunt says, spotting me in the doorway. "I saw a certain Hummer sitting in our driveway."

"Yeah," I answer noncommittally with a shrug.

"Everything okay?" Uncle Scott asks, his eyebrows coming together.

"Oh, yeah… Yeah, nothing to worry about." They both have concern in their eyes and it makes my chest swell. I love them. "I love you guys." My voice shakes as I let out what's been trapped inside my heart.

My aunt smothers a sob with her hand and stands up before coming over to me and wrapping her arms around my back, her shoulders shaking. "We love you too, baby girl."

"You're ours now, Emberlise," Uncle Scott says with a nod.

I hug my aunt back quickly and then start upstairs to my room. I'm so emotionally tired and just want to sleep.

The rest of the week goes by without issues. Marlana still mutters bullshit and her little mob of skanks snicker when I pass, but she mostly keeps her head down and avoids my path. Travis and I have gotten into a comfortable cycle of hallway chats and evening texting. As for Vin, I haven't seen him in the last few days and haven't received so much as a text. He's either away or he's having lunch off the school grounds and skipping drama. So much for my darkness calling to his.

It's Friday and it's audition day. I've picked apart Lance's brain the past few days about Clara and what he envisioned her to be when he wrote the script. He's been my pillow partner in every drama class and the excitement gathering in his eyes more and more each day is addictive. He really believes I'm his Clara.

Danny has been his annoying self, following me everywhere and constantly hanging around. He peppers me with questions, most I don't even absorb, but the good ole smile-and-nod has been working wonders. I have wanted to ask him where Vin was these last few days but held it in. Desperation has never looked good on me.

"Earth to Ember!" Adri screeches me out of my thoughts of Vin. "Answer my question, bitch!"

I smile at her, showcasing all my teeth. I love this girl. "Don't know what you asked, hoe."

"Oh my god, I asked if we were hitting up the party tonight!" She slaps her hands on the lunch table, jarring my tray.

"What party?" I quirk my brow.

"You haven't heard? Do you live under a rock or something?" She throws her hands in the air. "Danny's party!"

"Nah, I'm good." He probably did tell me about his

party this week, and I probably smiled and nodded at it. Jake and Jordan laugh while Adri shoots daggers at me.

"Vin will probably be there." She waggles her eyebrows, thinking this is enticing, and fuck her, it is. I can't let it show how badly I'm pining for the asshole.

"I'm super good," I drawl and drop my attention back to the salad in front of me.

"Cool, I'll bring my stuff to your place to get ready. Be super good for nine." She grabs her tray and leaves the table, dropping it to the dirty stack before exiting the cafeteria.

"And she says I live under a rock." I shake my head and stab at some lettuce.

"You both need to fuck those brothers and get it out of your systems," Cara deadpans. I choke and sputter on my chocolate milk as Jake and Jordan laugh out loud, catching the attention of everyone in the cafeteria.

"Cara with the zingers!" Jake yells. I wipe my mouth of dribbling milk and smile at Cara.

"I'll borrow some condoms from Pepto. She seems to have enough to go around."

"Thank God, otherwise, a few dudes in this school would have penis rot, including Vin," she retorts.

We all go into another round of laughter as the bell rings. I stand up and dump my tray, then make my way to English Lit. This time, I sit beside Travis and convince him to come to the party. He grunts and groans until I mention Adri is going, then he perks up and says he 'may make an appearance.' He also says he had a weird couple of days, and that he'll tell me about it later. I'm a little intrigued but decide not to push him for more if he's not comfortable talking about it here.

Drama again is a no-show for Vin. I guess he's not going to be auditioning after school either, which everyone is surprised about since he'd been in every school play for the last three years.

The rotunda is packed with students when I arrive and I'm excited to finally see the theater. Our classroom has been on the opposite side of the hall and I haven't ventured through the double doors to check it out. Sitting down on the couch nearest to the classroom door, I try to listen in on a few conversations, catching the tail end of one that really interests me.

"Last year, when we did Snow White together, and he was the huntsman, I could just feel the sexual tension, couldn't you?"

A few murmurs reply as I look around and my eyes settle on the busty blonde who was talking to Vin in the cafeteria the week before. Instantly, my blood boils. They probably did have chemistry. I saw it for myself with how he smiled at her, something he rarely bestows on people.

Lisa finally graces us with her presence with Lance on her arm. "Thank you, everyone, for coming to try out. It's really amazing how you all want to be a part of something different. As you all know, we are doing an original piece this year and Lance is the scriptwriter. I am sticking to his vision of everything and therefore having him on the judging panel with me." A few gasps and groans rings throughout the room.

This is perfect because all week Lance has been telling me I'm his Clara. A slow smile works over my face as confidence settles inside me. I've never been nervous before an audition because I always enter a place of calm. The stage is my second home and a place where my mother lived to see me act, so I will channel her love today.

"Let's file out and move into the theater. Take a seat in the first two rows in front and we will call you up." She smiles and continues, "Good luck, and remember, everyone is called up randomly."

She leaves the room and we all follow in a single file. When I walk through those double doors, the sight of the theater takes my breath away. It's beautiful. The area is sunken in with the stage bottom center, six aisles of stairs, and five sections of seating. The seats themselves are dark red and cushioned velvet, and the stage consists of a dark wood and rounds at the front. Its depth is large, looking to go in about fifty feet. The front curtain is made from the same rich red velvet as the seats.

Making my way down to the first row, I sit next to Danny as he slouches in his seat. He's not auditioning for a part because he loves doing stage effects and lighting more so than acting.

"Nervous?" he asks me with a nudge to my shoulder.

"Nope." I shake my head as excitement bubbles in my stomach. "I just want to get up there already." He nods and shoots me a smile.

For this audition, we were told we could use any part of the script. I decided on the scene when Michael breaks up with Clara at the end of summer. He doesn't want his friends knowing he was ever dating her because she was nerdy and picked on. She's completely heartbroken and becomes a little unhinged. I can't wait to portray the amount of anguish needed for this scene. I have enough of it buried inside I can set free.

"Britney Barnes, you're up first!" Lisa calls out. The blonde makes her way to the stage, her face a mask of arrogance. So, her name is Britney… still skank to me. As she starts her monologue—she picks the part where Clara decides she's giving Michael her virginity—I see why she had most leads for school plays. She's actually good. Although, I would never admit that out loud. We go through I don't know how many auditions because I have completely zoned out, immersing myself in Clara.

"Ember Craven, you're up!" Lisa breaks through the haze as I blow out a breath and stand.

"Hey, break a leg, boo," Danny enthuses.

A wave of tranquility comes over me as I climb the stairs to the stage. This is home for me. I walk to the center and look out at everyone. "I will be auditing for Clara. I've chosen the bedroom scene after Michael has broken up with her and she is alone."

Lance and I had discussed this particular scene this

whole week. He picked this one because it's Clara's mental breakdown and her only solo scene. With no other actor on stage, it would be up to me to capture the audience's attention. The only other scene that is just as emotionally testing is the final one, but that involves having a Michael character to truly capture the agony. I do my scene, which entails a lot of screaming, ugly crying, and hair ripping.

When the four-and-a-half minutes of gut-wrenching pain is over, I calmly stand up, thank everyone, and make my way off the stage and back to my seat. Everyone is quiet, and as I sit down, Danny gives me a quick one-armed hug.

"Fucking amazing, Ember," he whispers.

"Ahem," Lisa clears her throat. "Well, okay then. We have one last audition today." Good, I'm ready to get out of here and shake off Clara's lingering sorrow. It mirrors my own and threatens to open the gates of grief I've sealed so meticulously. "Vincent! You're up!" Lisa bellows.

Wait… what? He's here? A few excited murmurs and gasps sound collectively through the front rows. People turn in their seats, looking behind them for the beautiful man who's held my mind captive all week. I turn as well and find him making his way down the stairs. He must've been sitting in the back row. He keeps his eyes downcast and doesn't spare me a look as he makes his way onto the stage.

"I went through this script multiple times, looking for the best solo Michael scene I could find," he rasps out. I've missed the rough sound and hearing it now makes me shiver in my seat. "Yeah, he has many," he continues, "but there was one scene I just kept coming back to. The last scene, but to do it justice, I would need a Clara character."

Murmurs rise in the theater and we all look at Lisa, who shrugs. "Well, it's never been done, and you take the risk of people's attention being drawn to the other character, but I'll allow it."

Britney starts to make her way toward the stage stairs. It makes sense that they've planned this because they've acted with each other before.

"Ember, would you help me out and play Clara?" he asks. I look at him with confusion and then look at Britney, who's halfway up the stairs. "Please?" He turns and looks at me imploringly.

I stand up slowly as Britney opens and closes her mouth. "I thought… since we've acted together before…" she stumbles over her words as she watches me approach, making people snicker.

"Thank you, Britney. You're a great actor, but I already had someone else in mind." He grimaces toward her.

I make my way to the stage as Britney shoulders by me. "Bitch," she mutters under her breath. *Great, another one who hates me.* I walk up the stairs and come to stand directly in front of him.

"You know this scene?" he asks quietly, his scent washing over me. I didn't realize how much I missed it and him. Not trusting my voice, I simply nod, just once, and look at him to start. This scene is wonderful. Possibly my favorite. As we begin our scene, I become immersed with Vin in his element. This ending scene is heartbreaking. Clara finds Michael at one of his gang's hangouts to tell him she's pregnant.

At the end of the scene, we both stay standing where we are, panting. The scene is hard, but I can't deny the chemistry we have because it has clearly shone through on this stage. Finally, the room erupts with clapping and hooting. We look out to the audience and almost everyone is standing and applauding. Even Lisa wipes a tear from the corner of her eye. Vin grabs my hand to bow together and I gasp as a current snaps between our clasped palms.

I quickly release his hand and walk off the stage to retake my seat next to Danny. He chuckles and playfully punches my arm. "You're a force, Ember."

"Thanks, Danny." I grin.

"Ladies and gentlemen!" Lisa calls out. "That was truly

some great acting. I will post all roles on Monday in the rotunda. Have a great weekend."

Vin makes his way off the stage, and again, he walks by me without a glance and exits through the double doors. Well then, I guess that's that. I'm not going to lie, my heart feels like it has dropped into my stomach.

Soon after I leave the rotunda, my chest heavy and my mind racing all the way to my locker, I grab my things. I'm relieved it's the weekend and not really paying attention to my surroundings as I'm pulling out the textbooks I need for homework.

"Thanks for helping me out." His warmth rolls against my back as my heart kicks into full gear, and I squeeze my legs together as need tears through me.

"Mm-hmm." I freeze, dropping my textbook back onto the shelf, and swallow as my mind scrambles to form words. He grabs my arm and turns me around to face him as he slowly backs me into my locker, putting his hand up beside my head and effectively caging me in. His face comes down so we can look each other in the eyes. Those beautiful green eyes.

"Sorry I've been absent. I've had some shit to deal with," he whispers, his breath washing over my face. My eyes are on his plush mouth as his pierced tongue darts out to lick along his bottom lip. *Panties officially soaked.* "So, I'll see you tonight?" He leans back and drops his hand from the locker, putting some space between us.

"Um, I don't think I'm going to Danny's party." I find my voice, even though it sounds a little huskier than normal, thanks to my roller coaster vagina.

"I meant dinner at your house, remember? My mom and your aunt have those biweekly gossip fests." He quirks a brow.

"Right!" *Totally forgot.* "Sure. Yeah, I'll see you then." I swallow thickly as he backs away and walks down the hall.

Chapter Ten

I have half my closet thrown all over my room looking for something to wear, and trust me, when you have an overzealous aunt who loves to shop, half your closet is a lot. I've always been in a school uniform when I see Vin, so tonight, I want to wear something that showcases my personality and the body I work hard on.

I finally settle on black skinny jeans, ripped at the knees, and a dark gray AC/DC band shirt with the sleeves ripped. I tie it to the side to show off my toned midriff, hoping for sexy, but not too obvious. The doorbell rings and I rush into my bathroom to check my makeup and hair. I left my hair straight and hanging to my waist, and my makeup from school is still intact. I apply a light coat of gloss and I'm done.

"Ember! Our guests are here!" Uncle Scott yells from the first floor.

"Okay!" I'm so fucking nervous and it pisses me off. I never get like this, not even when I'm fighting dudes twice my size in the ring. I run a hand over my stomach and will it to chill. Finally, I pull it together… slightly, and make my way downstairs. My aunt and Sharla are chatting and laughing in the kitchen, and the TV is on in the family room. Sports are my uncle's favorite, and I assume Vin is inside with him. So I head into the kitchen first because I don't want to face those green eyes just yet.

Sharla and my aunt are sitting at the table with a bottle of wine already opened and half-filled glasses in front of them. "Oh, my!" Sharla exclaims when she sees me. "It really is like looking at your mother. You even dress like she did. Mind you, she was as pale as a ghost with white-blonde hair, but the features and your eye color are the same."

"I envied Rebecca for those eyes. Our father had the same and his mother before him, apparently," Aunt Debbie adds. I soak in the information about my family because my mother never told me a single thing. I sit down with them at the table, hoping they'll continue.

Sharla grabs me a wine glass and fills it with a wink. My aunt just shakes her head with a smile and cheers me with a clink of our glasses. I take a sip and settle in my chair, waiting for more information.

"Your mother, aunt, and I were inseparable in middle school and high school, causing havoc and breaking hearts." Sharla laughs. "Debbie has loved your Uncle Scott since fifth grade."

"I did. He punched Kirk Oakwood in the face for yanking on my pigtail." She nods with a faraway look in her eyes.

Sharla snickers, her eyes sparkling with the memories of her past. "Your mother and me, though? We ran wild. From twelve years old, we knew exactly what to say to get boys and men alike to do our bidding." She drums her fingers along the tabletop. "Remember how we had Doug Adams at the gas station sneaking us a pack of smokes every day?" she asks Aunt Debbie.

"Yeah, you two were something else." My aunt snorts with obvious affection. "But I loved every second of the time we spent together."

"So, you were best friends with my mother?" I ask

Sharla. "Did you know she was planning to run away?"

"No, I didn't." Her face becomes a little dark as she takes a sip of her drink, her eyes avoiding mine. "She ran with a different crowd during our tenth grade."

"Let's not get into all this," my aunt groans. "Let's set dinner on the table." They both stand up and start pulling the lasagna out of the oven and tossing the salad. I can't help but let the disappointment sink into my bones as I get up from the table and start toward the family room.

Tenth grade would make her fifteen and my mother had me at seventeen. Maybe my father belonged to this crowd she ran around with. There are reasons why bringing this up is difficult. For one, Aunt Debbie has already left the conversation, and two, anything to do with my mother after she ran away is a sore spot.

"You're going to have to tell her at some point, Deb. She deserves to know," Sharla says quietly when they think I'm out of earshot, but my aunt doesn't reply. Know what exactly? I worry my lip between my teeth as I get closer to the family room. How bad was it? Why did she leave Debbie and Sharla behind without a second thought? What happened to her?

"There she is." My Uncle Scott's voice filters through my thoughts as I step into the den.

"Hey, Em," Vin says as he slowly scans me from head to toe.

"It's Ember," I retort as I sit on the couch beside Uncle Scott and he wraps his arm around my shoulders.

"True."

Bastard.

"That's true too, actually," he deadpans.

Did I say that out loud?

Uncle Scott chuckles as he turns down the TV. "How's my girl?"

"I was listening to Sharla and Aunt Debbie talking about their childhoods. You were included too." I nudge him in the ribs. "The moment you two fell in love."

"Ahh… Kirk?" he asks with a raised brow.

"Yup." I pop the P with a smirk.

"I rigged that." He exhales with a smug look on his face.

"Huh?" I tip my head in question.

"Yup." He pops his P too. "Total set up. Cost me twenty bucks too."

"You paid him to pull Aunt Debbie's hair?" I ask, aghast as I push his arm off me.

"Shh!" He covers my mouth with his hand. "Are you crazy? If she finds out, that's at least a week of sleeping on the couch."

Vin is chuckling into his fist and I'm struggling to keep the smile off my face as I push Uncle Scott's hand away. "You're a fraud!" I whisper harshly.

"Worth the whole twenty bucks, though. Would've paid double if twenty didn't work." He shrugs.

"That's inspiration right there." Vin nods. "OG shit."

"That's right, I'm OG." My Uncle Scott puffs out his chest.

"Yeah, you're pretty outstanding," I reply honestly. Did I mention how much I love my aunt and uncle?

"I'm going to grab a beer. Try not to kill each other, yeah?" Uncle Scott gives me a wink and heads to the kitchen.

Vin slides over and sits next to me, his thigh touching mine. I can't help the shiver that runs through me, then it fades as a knowing grin spreads along his mouth. "You're an amazing actor, Em."

"You are too, Vince." He winces at the name and I do an

imaginary fist pump.

"Are you nervous about the results on Monday?" He leans in and I bite my lip as his scent wafts under my nose. I want to breathe in deeply and soak it all in.

"Nah, what's done is done," I answer as I squirm, trying to put some space between us. "I never let myself worry too much."

"Come with me to Danny's party." His voice is low as he leans in and brushes my hair back from my face. I turn away, not wanting his touch to crumble the fragile walls I've built to keep him out.

"No way." I swallow as my voice trembles from his touch.

"Why? You don't want to be seen with me?" He chuckles as if that would be absurd and the arrogant tone has me turning to face him, our noses inches apart.

"Not like that," I snap back.

"What does that mean?" He narrows his eyes at me as he rears his head back.

"I don't want anyone to mistake we're dating." His eyes widen with shock, and his mouth opens and shuts. Bet he's never been told that before. Again, I give another imaginary fist pump.

"Come on, kids, grub's up!" Uncle Scott yells. I stand without a second glance at Vin and walk toward the kitchen.

Dinner is awkward, Vin and I barely speak unless we're asked questions and his eyes never leave me, the heated stare like lasers. The adults are oblivious to the discomfort and continue to chatter around us.

"What's the plan tonight, kids?" my uncle asks as he leans back and throws his arm over the back of Aunt Debbie's chair.

"Nada," I mumble as I push my empty plate away from me.

"A small gathering," Vin says at the same time.

"You look after Ember." Sharla points at him. "She's family too."

"She better not be," Vin retorts. "I'll check into the mental hospital if that's the next revelation." Sharla tips her head back and roars out a laugh and my aunt and uncle join in. I look at them like they're all insane. How can they just nonchalantly joke about that? Sharla catches my expression and her face softens.

"Ember, Vincent and I are very open with each other. Trust me, that situation is not a sore spot for us. We've talked it out a million times over." I want to disagree with her and tell her it is a sore spot for Vin. She doesn't see how he is with his half brother.

"Truth." Vin nods. I shrug and begin to clear the table because this is none of my business.

The doorbell rings and I give a questioning look to my aunt. "I have no idea who that could be," she says with a shake of her head.

"I'll get it." I walk to the front door and throw it open. There, standing on my front porch, is Adri. She has her backpack stuffed to capacity over her shoulder and her hair is a tangle of maroon curls all around her face.

"I'm here!" She smiles wide, throwing out her arms. "Let's get ready to party!"

"Sounds good to me." His rasp hits my back and I roll my eyes.

Adri's eyes widen as Vin wraps his arms around my waist and buries his face in my neck, his mouth pressing against my skin. It takes all my concentration not to react to him, but every single inch of my body sings with his touch.

"Vin's here?" she whispers the obvious.

"Yeah," I reply, shrugging him off. "Unfortunately."

"Oh stop," he says with a grin. "Let's go party."

"He's here with his mommy for their biweekly dinner with my auntie and uncle," I sneer in a mocking voice as I step aside to let Adri in.

"I love my mommy." Vin shrugs. "And your auntie and uncle too."

"Whatever," I huff out, motioning for Adri to follow me up the stairs.

"Don't take too long, girls. I got to be at Danny's by ten to help set it up." We ignore him as we head to my room, closing the door on his voice.

"Wow, I know you're probably going to want to kick me in the cunt, but you and Vin really look amazing together." She flutters her eyelashes at me. "You are both so gorgeous, and your kids would be—"

"Adri," I cut her off with a warning. "It's getting to be more than a cunt kick at this point."

"Okay, okay!" She laughs as she throws her hands up in surrender. "Let's do some braids in your hair."

I let her take full rein over my hair and makeup as I scroll through IG on my phone.

"I told my dad I was crashing here when he dropped me off. Is that cool?" she asks when she's done, and I look up to find two Dutch braids and a full face of makeup.

"Yeah, yeah." I turn my head from side to side, admiring the finished product.

"I won't be intruding on you and Vin, right?" She squeaks with fear when I form a fist and grin at her.

Adri has given me a smoky look, making my turquoise eyes pop. She uses some magical mascara because my eyelashes nearly touch my eyebrows. Then she applied some shimmering powder that highlights my high cheekbones and pouty lips. My lips, she left natural with just a touch of gloss.

"Holy shit," I gasp. "I don't even look like myself." I look at her makeup and notice she went the opposite to my dark. Her eyes shimmer with gold and she painted her lips a deep red to match the color of her hair.

"What are you going to wear?" I eye her as she pours her bag out all over my bed and a few scraps of clothing falls out to mingle with my pile from earlier. "Are these outfits?" I ask, lifting a tube top.

"That's my favorite skirt." She snatches it out of my hands. *Skirt?*

"My uncle will flip if he sees you leaving wearing that." I laugh.

"That's why I have this." She holds out a long, black leather trench jacket.

"Ooh, I like!" I touch the smooth material.

"Let's figure out what you're going to wear." She moves toward my closet as she hums.

"Not a dress or skirt," I tell her, then hold up her *skirt.* "My ass would never fit in this."

"Girl, not all of us are blessed like you!" She laughs as the sound of scraping hangers filters out from the closet.

Then she comes back holding out my floor-length, gray maxi dress that has a slit to the thigh. All trimming and the bust are leather, including the straps which are pulled into a halter in the back.

"I don't know..." I trail off as she smiles wide. She also pulls out my cropped leather jacket and black leather boots.

"I won't take no as an answer. Everyone now knows you're a badass, so fucking look it." To be honest, I'm glad she pulled out the dress, I wouldn't mind driving Vin a little crazy. I grab the clothes and walk into the washroom.

After we're dressed and Adri is completely covered in the trench coat, we go downstairs. The sports channel is still blaring and Vin's loud voice talking to my uncle hits my ears. I walk to the family room while Adri waits by the door. The less interaction with her attire, the better. As I approach, Vin looks up and I preen when his jaw drops. His eyes do a slow perusal from my head to my feet as I lift my eyebrow, making him grin when our eyes meet.

"You look like you could deck a bitch while having a fun night on the town." That's my uncle, he just gets me. Vin is nodding in agreement.

"Let's get going. I'm already on the verge of changing my mind," I groan as I shift from foot to foot.

"Vincent, have my girl home safe and sound." Uncle Scott points at him with a stern look. "I know these parties and you'll be lame if you leave too early." He turns back to look at me. "If you're going to drink, don't drive. Don't let anyone drinking drive you, and if you're stuck and need a ride, always call me. Don't do hard drugs. Smoking a joint is cool, but I'd watch out about mixing it with alcohol if you're not used to it." He taps his chin, thinking of anything else. "Don't have sex, I don't want to be a… grandpa uncle? Would I be Uncle Grandpa? Shit, that's weird. Just don't have sex!"

"Gotcha," I reply, watching his eyes grow frantic as I try to hold in my laughter. "There's no one I'd bone anyway." He visibly relaxes.

"Bone?" Aunt Debbie calls from the kitchen doorway.

Sharla is grinning behind her. "You look gorgeous, Ember!"

"Hey, Deb?" Uncle Scott shouts. "If Ember has a baby, would I be Uncle Grandpa?"

"Sounds about right." She nods enthusiastically. "Uncy gramps."

"You guys are weird." I turn away from them and walk toward Adri at the front door. "Am I driving?" I look at Vin over my shoulder as he follows me.

"Ma?" He looks at Sharla. "You okay to get home?"

"You kids go. I'll drop her home when they're done with all the clucking," Uncle Scott interjects. "Remember my one rule, Ember!" he yells out as we leave the house.

"What's the one rule?" Adri asks me as we're climbing into Vin's backseat together.

"No boning."

"That's a good one rule." She nods in agreement.

We pull up to Danny's house and the music is thumping down the street, sounding like he's getting a head start with the night. He lives in another enormous house, which seems to be the theme with most students at Precious Blood. It's a red brick, Tudor style, surrounded by immaculate lawns.

"Ready?" Vin asks, holding his arm out. I ignore his offer and hop out of the Hummer. There's no way I will be on his arm. The boy has not earned it yet. "That's how it's going to be?" Adri is already inside as Vin shoulders past me into the house, his anger vibrating off him.

Stepping into the foyer, my breath is stolen right out of my chest. Danny has a beautiful home. Large Greek columns line his grand staircase and accents of gold are scattered everywhere. There are actual oil portrait paintings of his family. Everything is so prestigious here in the little town of Whitsborough and so is every person. Some are just better at hiding their money than others, like my family. Although we have an oversized garage filled with classic cars. Mine being one of them.

"Ember! Our very own star in the making!" Danny booms as he's walking toward me, arms outstretched. *He's not wanting a hug, is he?* His arms wrap around me and he lifts me in the air. *Yes. Yes, he is.*

"Okay, friendly giant." I tap his shoulder. "You may release me."

"Fuck! You are fucking hot!" he groans and lets me down to bite his fist. *Charming.* "Head to the theater room. We're just setting up the booze and snacks before everyone gets here. Adri is already there, flicking through Netflix."

"Cool." I walk toward the double doors he's pointing to.

Theater room, huh? I amble inside and again, my breath rushes from my lungs. There's a large projection screen at the front and about fifty leather recliners lined up. Adri has indeed started up Netflix and is currently watching *Dirty Dancing*, one of my favorites.

"Bitch, look what I found in the hidden panel." She's holding up what looks to be a very expensive bottle of amber liquid.

"Couldn't have been too hidden if you found it." I walk toward her as she shakes the bottle.

"Right? Dumb rich snobs." She twists off the top.

"You're rich too," I state as I sit in the recliner beside her.

"Not this rich. You know? Like *stupid* rich. Endless pools of money, rich," she hiccups.

"Have you had some already?" I eye the bottle.

"On my second crystal glass full." She holds it up, and I'm astonished with how fast she downed the first. "Can't sully the bottle with my not-as-rich lips. Yours either, unfortunately," she sneers while filling up a second glass for me.

"Cheers." I tip my glass and down half the contents.

"Your tits look so big in that dress," she says, poking my cleavage.

We polish off two-thirds of the bottle and we're halfway through the movie when the theater doors open. The music rushes into the soundproofed room, startling us. "Girls, party is in full swing. Get the fuck out here!" Danny screams.

"Oh yeah!" Adri snaps her fingers. "This is a fucking party."

I snort and try to stand up, just to fall back down. "I'm hammed." I snort again.

"Let's go dance!" Adri squeals as she staggers toward the doors.

I follow her out on wobbling legs and see that the place is completely packed. People are grinding on each other everywhere. I look around for Vin, because I'm weak and can't help myself, and find him in the kitchen, leaning against the counter with Bitchney hanging off his side.

Hauling out a stool at the counter, I take a seat to enjoy the show. His mossy eyes flick up, barely scan me, then slide back to Britney's face. *Well then.* She grins up at him as he wraps his arm around her waist. I get it. I pissed him off by not letting him claim me or whatever, but I know I'm right and he has to earn it. I already told him I won't ever be one of his playthings.

"Oh, look, girls! The drama sluts are all here!" a whiny voice penetrates the music. Marlana comes and stands to my right and looks down at me, her mouth curling into a sneer. I swear, if she touches me right now, I'll jab her eye out. "You meant nothing. She doesn't either. He'll always come back to me," she says, close enough that only I can hear.

"Back off, slut. Are you possessed or something?" Adri yells at her from my left. Shit, maybe she is. I watched that show and I know exactly what I should do. Sam and Dean taught me well.

I reach over the counter and grab the salt shaker, shaking it at her. "Spirit be gone!" I scream. "If this doesn't work, grab me some iron," I tell Adri. Everyone begins laughing as Marlana screeches.

"I fucking love that show!" Adri hollers, her voice filled with amusement.

Marlana and her cronies finally leave the kitchen with her trying to dust the salt out of her hair while I decide if I want to pocket the shaker for its magical effects.

"My bitch! Let's go dance!" Adri grabs the salt shaker, placing it back on the counter, and hauls me off the stool. We make our way over to the crowd as an old-school Biggie Smalls song plays and I move to the beat.

I grab Adri's hips with both hands and bring her in close. Wrapping my arms around her waist, I slowly gyrate my hips into hers. Her eyes widen at first, but then she moves with me, her arms wrapping around my neck. We garner an audience as Marlana and her crew look at us with disgust. Vin is leaning against the far wall next to Danny, watching us with hooded eyes. Then *Bitchney* steps in front of him, pressing her ass in tight. She dances on him, smirking at me like she knows just how affected I am. He doesn't move to touch her, but he doesn't move her away either.

I bring my left hand up to Adri's chin and tilt it back, her eyes darkening as she whimpers. My eyes find Vin as I drag my tongue up the column of her throat and he bites down on his lip while one hand grabs Britney, bringing her in closer. Adri lets out a moan and cups my face with her hands, bringing me in closer. I kiss down her neck and my right hand grabs her ass cheek, grinding her onto my knee.

"Fuck me, Ember. I totally want you." She's looking at me with lust in her eyes.

"Maybe one day." I wink at her and flick her lips with my tongue. She moans loudly as her body shudders.

"Travis is here behind you, laughing at Tracy Bertrand," she says into my ear as her arms drop from my neck.

"Who is that?" I look over my shoulder as she steps away from me.

"She's in your Lit class. She's wanted Travis for a while. He hasn't even looked at me." She kisses my cheek and turns, walking toward Danny with her head held high. Looking around the room, I notice both Britney and Vin are gone and I can only imagine what they are up to as I dance alone for a bit. Heat hits my back as I close my eyes, disappointment flaring through me. It's not Vin. I know his scent. I look over my shoulder and find another set of similar green eyes full of mirth.

"Quite the show you put on there." Travis crosses his arms over his chest.

"So, you watched." I spin to face him with a smirk on my face.

"I see everything, especially when it involves people I care about." His smile drops as he looks toward Adri and Danny. I follow his line of sight until I see she has positioned herself in front of Danny and they are sensually making out, grinding into each other.

"That's my fault. I think I riled her up," I try to explain as I turn back to find his face hard as stone. "Vin left with Britney," I sulk as he wraps his arm around my shoulders and kisses my temple.

"Need a ride home, kid?"

I nod and point to Adri. "She's with me too."

"Okay, go get her. I'll wait outside." He brushes by me without sparing another look at Adri and Danny, striding for the door.

I finally convince Adri that having sex with Danny would be a bad idea—much to his dismay—then dress her in her trench coat and force her into Travis' backseat. "Oh! Hi, Travis. It was great seeing you tonight, and you know… talking." Her sarcastic tone fills the car.

"You were a little busy. I didn't have time to say hi," he retorts as he pulls out of Danny's driveway, white-knuckling the steering wheel.

I sit in the passenger seat and look out the window, listening to them go back-and-forth. They want each other, it's so obvious. Finally, my house comes into view and I exhale in relief until I see the tail end of a black sedan driving down my street. I straighten in my seat until the taillights disappear.

Fuck, I really need to talk to Tommy.

Once Travis is parked, Adri rushes out like her ass is on fire and marches up to my porch.

"You guys are crazy. You know that, right?" I say to Travis as I open the door.

"Whatever." He leans in and kisses my cheek. "Sleep it off and don't dwell on the asshole. He's not worth it." I nod and get out, waving goodbye.

Adri is huffing on my porch, giving me major side eye when I approach. "What is it?" I ask.

"So, you and Travis?" She crosses her arms over her chest and sways, her drunken mind filled with jealousy.

I shake my head. "Travis holds a piece of my soul, just like you, but nothing romantic." She visibly relaxes and pulls me in for a hug, and I accept her apology with a chuckle.

It's a bit of a struggle getting Adri upstairs and into her pajamas, but luckily, my aunt and uncle are on the main floor and can't hear how many times she falls to her ass. I pull out my phone as we get ready for bed, hoping for something from Vin, but find nothing. No messages or phone calls. That fucking jerk. I pull up his name and hover over the text icon. I know I shouldn't because I'm not thinking rationally. So, I toss it on my night table instead and decide to forget about him and get some sleep.

Chapter Eleven

A constant pinging seeps into my sleep-addled brain as I slowly come to consciousness, the pounding of my head and the sandpaper consistency of my mouth invading my senses. The ping sounds again and I groan out loud. With my eyes still shut, I reach out and pat around for my phone on the side table. My hand closes around it as the ping goes off once more.

Who the fuck is messaging me this much?!

I crack open one eye to find Adri is still very much in my bed and still very much snoring. Bringing the phone up to my one squinting eye, I see it's eight in the morning. Someone is going to die. It's Saturday, I have a brutal hangover, and someone has lost their fucking mind. I unlock the phone and check my messages.

Dickfacebitchfuckerasshole: Ember, call me.

Dickfacebitchfuckerasshole: I know ur pissed. Can you just call me when u wake up?

Dickfacebitchfuckerasshole: Fuck! I was supposed to take u home. I couldn't find u!

Dickfacebitchfuckerasshole: Just tell me u got home.

Dickfacebitchfuckerasshole: Ember!

Dickfacebitchfuckerasshole: I will call ur house.

Dickfacebitchfuckerasshole: Fuck!

Tommy Boy: Hey, Blur.

Tommy Boy: Sorry, I've been MIA just had so much shit to deal with.

Tommy Boy: I got some info to tell u. Will FaceTime tonight.

I snort out loud because I must've changed Vin's name last night. Fuck, that's pretty spot on. Then it all floods back, him and Britney, both of them disappearing, and me having to grab a ride home from Travis.

He tried to find me, my ass.

My spirits rise a bit at seeing Tommy's messages. At least I have his face to look forward to later, despite the ominous message. It'll be good to tell him about that car I've been seeing. I lock my phone without responding to either of them and turn over to fall back asleep. I'm just getting comfortable when a strange ringing reverberates off my bedroom walls, then Adri's groans sound around my head.

"What time is it?" she snaps. "Where's my fucking phone?"

"Eight-thirty," I respond, keeping my eyes shut. "Sounds like it's at the bottom of the bed."

"It's probably my dad. Just ignore it." The ringing stops and we both sigh with relief, only for it to ring again. "What the fuck!!!" she screeches, the noise assaulting my throbbing head. I turn and open my eyes as she crawls down the bed and grabs her phone, looking at the screen. "Why the fuck is Vin calling my phone?!" She narrows her eyes at the phone before answering it with a scowl on her face. "What the fuck do you want?" I snort and bury deeper under the blankets. He totally deserves her scary mood right now.

"Obviously, we are home, you idiot! No thanks to your dumbass! Travis, the more considerate brother, made sure we were safe. I hope Britney gave you herpes!" She hangs up, then throws her phone back on the floor.

"You're perfect," I mumble from under the covers.

"And you deserve better," she soothes as she snuggles into my back.

Sunlight is streaming through my window and becoming harder to ignore as I stretch out, my hand connecting with Adri's face. "Shit, my bad." I pat the top of her head in apology.

"I barely felt it through the pounding in my skull." She slowly rolls out of bed, her eyes barely open. "I'm totally using your shower."

"Cool," I respond before picking up my phone. I have no more new messages and a small pang of disappointment hits my chest. A part of me wants Vin groveling, but another part of me just wants him to leave me alone. Yes, I've rebuffed his advances many times, but my heart hasn't completely followed my brain to the get-over-him zone. I message Tommy back to let him know I'm excited to talk to him later. He has been so busy lately since Raphael returned from prison.

Adri comes out of my bathroom looking a little more awake and a little less drunk. I'm in desperate need of a shower as well but the thought of moving is so daunting. "Vin has been messaging me," she says while looking at her phone.

"Saying?" I sit up quickly.

"He wants to see you. He's asking me to tell him when we wake up." She looks up at me with her eyebrows raised.

"Did you answer him?" I ask, my teeth gritted as images of him and Britney flip through my mind.

"Nope, I wouldn't do that without speaking to you first." She pockets her phone and begins stuffing her things into her backpack.

"I don't want to see him," I admit, my voice sounding more sad than angry.

"Makes sense. I would think you were nuts if you did." She shakes her head. "I called my dad. He's on his way to pick me up."

"You don't have to leave so fast. I can make us breakfast." I begin to move out of bed when she stops me by raising her hand.

"I have a fucking paper due on Shakespeare for Monday." She's clearly hungover too and probably needs her own bed.

"Gotcha, sister. I'm gonna start on some work too." I slowly make my way out of bed.

After Adri leaves and I finish my shower, I spend the rest of the day studying and trying to nap off my hangover. I finally crawl out of my hole and go in search of my parents. The thought stops me in my tracks. I just referred to my aunt and uncle as my parents. A wave of guilt threatens to drown me as I think of my mother. As much as I miss her and will love her forever, my aunt and uncle really are my new parents.

I find them curled on the couch, my uncle watching sports and my aunt reading a novel. "Hungover?" My uncle snickers.

"Pretty much," I groan as I lean on the wall, my arms crossed over my chest.

"Hey, Vincent called this morning. Something about losing you at the party?" He raises an eyebrow as he runs his fingers through Aunt Debbie's hair.

"He disappeared with a chick. I don't know about the losing me part. Travis brought us home." My uncle chokes at my response as my aunt blinks slowly.

"Well, he's just stupid. There's no one better than my niece," he states. "Speaking of, Andrew called and said he had a phenomenal turnout for your class. Over sixty people. He wants to know if we can stop by today to complete some paperwork and settle on a schedule."

"Really?" I'm amped as I push off the wall, my hangover becoming an afterthought. "Let's go now!"

We finish up the meeting with Andrew and settle on two different classes each Sunday, one in the morning and one in the afternoon. The pay is great too. After telling Uncle Scott to head home, I start in on a bit of a workout. It's been a while, and my body is itching to sweat out the excitement still coursing through me.

I hit up the treadmills and run full speed for fifteen minutes when a hand shoots out, bringing the machine to a jog. "What the fuck?" I turn to find green eyes full of anger staring at me. "Go away, Vincent," I growl at him.

"No." He shuts the machine down completely and leans into me. "We need to talk."

"Fuck you and your talk." Ignoring his huff of irritation, I try to turn the treadmill back on when he grabs the back of my shirt and drags me off the machine, then down a narrow hallway. It would be easy to break away and put the drop on him, but I don't want to. I like him manhandling me a little, and I'm desperate to hear every excuse he has from his pretty mouth. I'm so fucking screwed. He pulls us into a small, dim towel closet and shuts the door before my back meets the slab, the room falling into darkness around us. "Does it need to be dark for you to spew your bullshit?" I snap at him.

He presses his body against mine, bringing us completely flush, as he hardens against my stomach. His face moves into my sweaty neck as he husks, "Why? Are you afraid of me?" Then he licks my neck from my collarbone to my ear. I swallow back my groan to hide my arousal, but he presses his tongue against my pulse, feeling it for himself. "I didn't fuck her," he states, his lips still pressed to my neck. He takes another step into me, pressing my back to the door, his hard cock grinding into my stomach once more.

"I really don't care." I try to say it with grit, but I'm so aroused that it comes out breathy and full of lust.

"I took her *drunk ass* home, because even though I'm a *dick*, I didn't want her to do something crazy like drink and drive after I *rejected her*," he punctuates his emphasis with his cock.

"Sure." I regain some of my senses and twist my face away from him, though it doesn't break the contact from his lips to my skin.

"Ember!" he growls before biting down on my neck hard. "Stop being stubborn." Finally, I put my hands on him and grab his waist, pulling him in tighter. I swear I was about to shove him off until he bit me, making me groan. "Does my girl like a little pain?" He bites me again, harder.

"I'm not your girl," I retort while rubbing myself against his leg.

"Sure," he mocks me with the same tone of disbelief. Then he drops his forehead to my shoulder and starts taking deep breaths, and I do the same to bring myself under control. I can't fuck him in the towel closet where I'm newly employed, as much as I fucking want to. "Let me drive you home. We need to talk."

"How do you know I didn't drive myself?" I push his

chest, making him take a few steps back.

"Because your car is fucking flashy, and it's not here." Facts.

I drop my head back against the door. I should just call my uncle because I really don't need the drama of a guy who's damaged beyond my capabilities, but my heart won't let me. "Okay." I nod.

We're sitting in his Hummer, still parked in the gym lot, when he drops a bomb on me. "My dad dropped by our house a few days ago. Apparently, he has cancer and wanted to right his mistakes. He wants me and Travis to have a relationship and he wants my forgiveness," he says while looking out his window, his jaw clenching.

"Wow," I breathe out. I really have no words.

"My mother is leaving the decision up to me, saying if I want to forgive him, she'll support it, but I don't know if I can." His voice is drenched in anguish as my heart swells inside my chest for him.

"That's understandable. I don't think you have to forgive him if you don't want to, but Travis is a good person, and really, he's not to blame for this mess." I put my hand on his arm as he turns to look at me.

"I know that, but when you've hated someone for so long, it's hard to rewire your brain." He covers my hand with his own, his thumb rubbing circles over my skin.

"True." I nod as I stroke his hand. "I suck at any family advice because I've only ever had my mother and I've never met my father."

"That's the other thing I wanted to tell you." My head snaps up to look at him as my heart pounds inside my chest. "I found a box of my mother's stuff the other day. I was trying to find pictures of when she was with my father, but I also found pictures of your mother with a group of their friends. Then I came across yearbooks with her writing in it."

"Seriously?" I gasp as I cover my mouth with my hands.

"Yeah." He pulls one of my hands down to kiss the back of it, my heart swelling inside my chest as my stomach flutters. I've completely abandoned my promise of resisting him. "You can come by whenever and we'll go through it together. Maybe we'll find answers about your father."

I don't think, I just lean forward and wrap my arms around his neck. He's shocked, but after a beat his arms come around me, making our embrace awkward over the center console. "Thank you," I whisper.

He drops me off at home with the promise of having me over during the week. He would rather we do it while his mother is at the restaurant since I expressed concerns that both she and my aunt were hiding something.

I wave goodbye as he backs out of the driveway, then I enter the house and scream out, "I have a job!"

"Yay!" my aunt hollers back, and I follow her voice to the kitchen.

"Congrats, kid," my uncle says with a smile.

"I'm going to FaceTime Tommy to tell him the news." I bounce on the balls of my feet with excitement. Everything is falling into place.

"Alright." My aunt waves me off. "I'll call you when dinner is done."

After my FaceTime with Tommy, I'm left with more questions than answers. He says Raphael has become crueler since his time in prison and doesn't trust anyone. Tommy thinks it's a good possibility he put a tail on me to make sure I'm not spilling gang secrets. Not that I knew much, as I wasn't a part of the inner circle. The reason for the call was so he could tell me he's heard my name come up in passing conversations. This doesn't bode well for me. My only option is to corner this black sedan and get my answers, as dangerous as that will be.

With my phone still in my hand, one person filters

through my mind, knowing he may need someone to talk to right now.

The phone rings and then his quiet voice fills my ear. "Hey, E."

"Hi, Travis." I swallow down the lump in my throat as my vision clouds. I'm familiar with the turmoil he's going through, losing a parent is difficult at our age.

"Everything okay? Do you need something?" He's the kindest person I know. His father is sick, and still, he's ready to help anyone.

"I'm okay. I'm calling to see how you're doing and if you need anything from me." I fall back on my bed as I stare at the ceiling.

He breathes into the phone for a few seconds and then finally says, "He told you?"

"Vin? Yeah, he told me." I exhale a heavy sigh. "I'm so sorry, Trav."

"I still haven't really processed it. I was going to talk to you about it, but I didn't want to make you face what happened to your mom again." His heart must be many times too big for his chest. Having friends like Travis is rare, and I'm privileged to experience his kindness. Besides Tommy, who was never overly kind, I didn't have many friends to begin with.

"You want to hang out for lunch tomorrow? We can talk?" I offer.

"Yeah, I'd like that." Relief filters through the phone as I smile.

"Okay, I'll see you tomorrow."

"Thanks, Ember."

We hang up and I immediately text Adri, hoping she doesn't suspect anything between Travis and me again. I want our friendships to be open books. No secrets.

Me: Hoe, I'm having lunch with Travis tmr. Family issues. I will fill u in after.

Adri: You better, bitch.

Me: For sure.

After having dinner and doing my homework, the rest of my night is filled with restless sleep, trying to figure out how I'm going to corner this sedan and help my friend through a heartbreaking time of his life.

Chapter Twelve

Today my uniform is hiding two switchblades and a set of brass knuckles. It's a good thing the school doesn't have a metal detector. Now that I know the gang may be on my tail, I need to prepare myself and make sure I protect the people around me. Shit is about to turn messy.

After grabbing my free coffee from Sharla—she's spoiling me—I pick up Adri. I have Marilyn Manson bumping and sunglasses stuck firmly on my face when she slips into the car.

"Are we dark today? 'Beautiful People'?" she asks, her eyebrow raised as I turn down the music.

"Baby, I'm dark every day." I look at her from the top of my glasses with a wink.

"That's pretty hot," she hums, making me laugh as I take us to school.

I pull into my usual spot beside Travis' pretty blue car as Adri looks over her shoulder through the rear windshield. "Vin is waiting by his Hummer. You guys okay again?" Adri glares at him.

"I think so?" She turns at my answer with her brow quirked.

"*Okay?*" she mocks my uncertainty. "I'm sure you can handle him. Just cunt kick him when he gets out of line."

I swat at her shoulder as I burst out laughing. "I love you, bitch." She gets out of the car and blows me a kiss, then she walks by Vin, running her finger across her throat. I'm laughing again at her threat and so is he as he walks toward my car, shaking his head.

"Get out here so I can touch you up," he quips into my window. *Panties flooded at eight in the fucking morning.* Deciding not to over-analyze what's happening between us, I emerge from the car and he pulls me in for a hug, his arms wrapping tightly around me and his lips pressing against my forehead. After hearing about him not liking any sort of PDA, his sudden display of affection has left me speechless. "You smell good," he rasps, his voice deeper than usual as he hardens against my body.

"You have a boner," I deadpan, and the full belly laugh he lets loose warms my soul. I want to do that for him every day.

We casually stroll into the school with his arm slung over my shoulder, and by the shocked expressions greeting us, it's a big deal. We make it to my locker and he waits patiently as I drop off my bag and grab the books I need for the first few periods. When I shut the door and turn around, he's slowly closing in, backing me up to the metal. My stomach erupts with butterflies as I melt into the locker. Then he runs his lips along my jaw before pressing them against my ear. "You seriously smell so fucking good."

"Everyone is looking," I chastise as I run my hands down his back.

"Don't care." He presses into me even more, his hard body stealing any coherent thoughts.

The bell rings as I'm about to suggest we find a broom closet and I push him back with a groan. "Keep it in your pants. I gotta get to class."

"I'll walk you." True to his word, he walks me all the way to my homeroom. We're standing in the doorway and the air around us thickens. He's looking at my face and I'm getting the feeling he wants to kiss me, which is apparently foreign territory for him, so I choose to initiate it. I'm leaning in and he instantly grins, his dimple winking at me as his tongue brushes along his bottom lip.

"Hey, morning."

Vin groans and turns his face to glare at his brother as I pull back.

"Morning, Travis." I smile at him and slap Vin's arm.

"I'll see you later. Don't forget roles are being posted after lunch," Vin grunts out to me before shooting Travis another glare and leaving.

"He's pleasant this morning." Travis narrows his eyes at Vin's back.

"No different than usual." I shrug as we walk into class.

The first two periods go agonizingly slow because I'm anticipating the role posting. I doubt I'll be able to eat anything for lunch until I see my name beside Clara's. I may be at home on a stage, but nerves attack me during the wait after an audition.

"Ember?" I turn to find Jake following me to my locker.

"Hey, Jake. What's up?" Reaching for the lock on the door, I begin to spin the dial as he clears his throat.

"I just overheard Marlana talking about fucking up your car." I turn on him as my mouth dries. That car is worth more than I'll ever be. I can't let anything happen to it.

"Seriously?" I ask as my heart pounds through my ears. Then I spin around and dash for the parking lot, not waiting for his confirmation. If she so much as leaves a fingerprint on that car, I will knock her the fuck out. I race outside and find the bitch and a few of her skank posse carrying two paint cans. Stopping suddenly, I take a deep breath, trying to stave off the rage as my vision pounds with a red hue.

Slowly walking up behind them, I grab the two chicks at her back by their uniform shirts and whip them to the ground. A paint bucket drops, alerting Cunt Head to my presence. She quickly turns as her eyes widen, then immediately narrow.

"What the fuck are you doing?" she yells. "Travis, tell this bitch to back off."

I look over my shoulder and see a crowd forming, some recording with their cell phones and Travis sauntering toward us as the two girls on the ground slowly rise back to their feet, their expressions filled with fear.

"What are you doing with paint cans?" My voice is even, effectively hiding the violence I'm begging for. My body shakes with barely restrained rage as I round on Marlana, my blood begging me to let loose.

"None of your business!" she screeches as her cheeks darken.

"According to Jake and a few others, it is Ember's business," Travis answers calmly as he takes the paint can out of Marlana's hand, her fingers releasing it immediately.

Marlana's best friend, Shay, breaks away from the crowd and comes to stand in front of Marlana. "Mar, you can't do that. It's going too far." She picks up the fallen paint can and holds it in her face. "You could be charged. Let this shit go." Marlana tips her head back in defeat and looks toward the sky as Shay continues, "Plus, this one can seriously kick your ass." Shay looks at me with a grin. "I signed up for your class, by the way."

I'm too angry to acknowledge her right now as my fists clench, and it's taking all my willpower not to mess up Marlana's face. I watch with shock and a little disappointment as Shay leads Marlana and the other bitches back to the school, and they walk inside before I turn back around to face my car. It's then I spot two men with black clothing and hoods drawn over their heads, watching me. One of them taps the other and motions for them to go around the side of the school.

With my anger raging and a severe need to sink my fists into flesh, I run toward them. They go around the corner and I slow down. I don't want them to notice me too soon when I draw close.

"Ember!" Travis screams out. "Come back!"

They're walking about fifteen feet ahead of me and I slip on my brass knuckles as I come up behind the first guy who's turning at the sound of Travis' voice. I hit him in the kidney, aiming up and under the rib cage, and he drops with a grunt. The other guy spins around with a shocked expression. He doesn't have time to defend himself though before I'm slamming him in the trachea. His hands come up and grip his throat, leaving his solar plexus open. A hit to that leaves him winded and dropping to his knees. His buddy is getting up behind me, so I quickly punch him on the chin and he's instantly knocked out. Then I turn back to the other, watching as he struggles to move to his feet. He's holding on to his lower back, right against that pounding kidney.

"Why are you following me?" I grit through my teeth, my body tense and ready to continue fighting.

"Orders," he huffs out as he backs away. "Fuck, they warned us about you, but I didn't believe it."

"Orders from who?" I growl. I'm losing my patience and the guy notices as his expression falls with acceptance. His cover's been blown anyway.

"Raphael."

Before I can interrogate them further, Vin and Travis run around the corner screaming my name. Travis must've ran back to get him before approaching us. They stop immediately when they find me squared off with one guy and a second is out cold on the ground. While the guy is distracted by the Greene brothers behind me, I shoot out and punch him in the side of the neck. He dizzily falls to his knees, and I grab his hair, pulling his head back to look him in the eyes.

"Stay away from me and mine. Pass this on to Raphael."

I spit in his face before tossing him to the ground. Then I slip off the brass knuckles, tucking them back into my bra, and walk toward a shocked Vin and Travis.

"What is going on, Ember?" Travis asks, slightly panicked as he looks over my shoulder.

"Bronx business." I shrug, walking past them and back to the school.

"Were those brass knuckles?" Travis presses Vin as they follow behind me.

"I can't process. I'm so fucking turned on," Vin replies. So he's cool with me taking down men twice my size, but not a vile girl hell-bent on winning him back. Noted. Regardless, a smile creeps over my face because they're actually having a conversation.

My stomach growls as we step inside the school, but I'm too amped. A fight always leaves me feeling restless afterward, but coupling that with a confirmation of the Rampage putting a tail on me has my insides boiling. Sitting in the lunchroom to eat won't be an option with this energy coursing through me. I turn to go back outside, needing to run it off and remembering the school has a track. It's not optimal with my kilt, but I have to make do or else I'll be antsy and on edge for the rest of the day.

"Ember, what was that?" Vin grabs my arm, his lust bleeding into concern.

"What did it look like? I'm a fighter, Vin." I shake him off and push open the door to suck in a lungful of fresh air.

"Who were they?" Travis whispers as he stands in the doorway.

"People tailing me from my former life." I run a hand along my forehead, trying to ease the tension pounding through my skull as I walk away from them.

"I'm coming with you," Vin rasps behind me. "I don't care if you're the heavyweight champion of the fucking world. I won't let you fight alone again."

"I'm not going back to fight them. I need to drain my adrenaline or I won't be able to concentrate for the rest of the day," I explain as my stomach flips with his confession.

"Got it. So, what are we doing?" I turn and look into his eyes. He's serious about being with me, so I decide to let him come along.

"I need to run laps."

Leaning against the wall, I study Lisa as she posts the roles on the message board beside the gym. My adrenaline is gone, but my anger is still here and coursing through me. I need to fight, that's my problem. I've never gone this long without one, and it's the only thing that eases the dark energy.

Britney and a few of the other girls are casting looks toward me, and every time I catch her eye, she swallows visibly before dropping her head. It's easy to feel the tension I'm exuding, its dark and thick, coated with pent-up anger. *I need a fight.* Vin is standing with Danny and a few of his other friends, all of them looking excited with anticipation as he keeps his eye on me. After our run, I asked him to back off for a bit. He could read my volatility and did as I asked. The roles are posted, and everyone crowds the board, all except me and my moss-green-eyed bane as he comes to stand next to me.

"Em, let's check it out." He holds out his hand. "Then I'm taking you home. We can grab the stuff I found about your mom too."

My anger subsides a bit, and the darkness recedes a little back into my soul. As people applaud us, I nod and take his hand, knowing we have the lead roles without needing to check the message board. I overhear that Britney is playing the roles of my understudy and my best friend. I'm praying there's no drama with that because I have enough as it is.

"Can we go?" I mumble, my body feeling weighted with exhaustion. As much as I want to celebrate mine and Vin's lead roles, my energy is tapped at zero.

He's so in tuned and hears me over the excited squeals as he nods and squeezes my hand before leading me outside. I don't bother grabbing my bag because I have my cell phone in my bra and it's all I need. I'm Adri's ride, so I do the best friend thing by texting Travis to take her home. Maybe they can work through their bullshit on the way.

Vin is leading me to his Hummer when I stop, the events from earlier flooding my mind. "I can't leave my car here. Marlana tried some shit earlier."

"I'll deal with her later." His eyes flash with annoyance as we go to my car, his hands reaching out for my keys. *Fuck, they're in my locker.* My face tips back and I close my eyes, irritation running through me. With everything going on, I've started to disassociate from my surroundings. Vin wraps his arms around me and brings me into his chest, my forehead falling forward as I exhale with relief. "What's the combo?" His rumble vibrates against my ear, relaxing me further.

"22, 67, 81."

He jogs back inside, and I lean against the car to wait. I have to FaceTime Tommy tonight when I've worked through everything that's happened and tell him about the visitors. He could dig around and get me some information on why I'm being tailed. The answers I've been searching for are within reach and I really should feel something right now. I'm about to learn more about my mother's secret life, but there's nothing except darkness inside of me. She was the only one that could bring me out of it, or fighting. Vin jogs back with my backpack that looks way too overstuffed.

"I grabbed every book. I don't know what you'll need. I also told Anna you were having your time of the month and I had to take you home." I lean forward and pull him to me, burying my face in his neck to kiss the soft skin lightly. "I'm here for you, Em," he murmurs while rubbing my back. I nod and then release him before heading to the passenger side of my car.

The ride to his house is quiet and I try to suppress the rising of my anger as I think about the secrets surrounding me. I always had this terrible temper for as long as I can remember, and with my mother gone, I've been having a hard time feeling grounded. Without her, I could release the pent-up emotions through fighting, but the fights have stopped and training classes just won't cut it. After the little sample I got today, I need more of the rush.

"My mom is at the restaurant until five," Vin says. I snap out of my thoughts and realize we're parked in a driveway. As I look up at the house, I find it modestly prestigious.

"Nice house." My tone is flat and I don't make a move to get out of my car. I'm overloaded with things I have to process and the thought of going in there isn't appealing either.

"How about I go grab the box and we can chill at a nearby park?" Vin must sense my hesitation.

I nod numbly. His suggestion is so much better than being locked inside a house and seeing pictures of a woman I clearly knew nothing about. My anger swells and rises again, and it takes every ounce of restraint I can muster to push it back down.

Vin walks to his front door, his swagger causing ripples of want inside me. Finally, a reaction other than the frustration that's been building inside of me. His locs swing against his back and his black bandana blows slightly in the breeze. Then he disappears inside and comes back out with a medium-sized cardboard box. He places it in my backseat before we pull out of his driveway.

A few moments later, we arrive at a park with some benches, but I don't want to leave the anonymity of the car. If I'm going to be angry or sad, I'd rather it be in private. Turning in my seat, I start pulling photo albums out of the box. They're high school girly stuff, for sure. The album covers are Winnie the Pooh and Disney Princesses, which is surprising because it's nothing like the woman I knew. I open the first of three in my lap and instantly recognize Sharla standing with a much younger version of my mother and aunt. They look like happy freshmen during this time and my aunt looks even younger as they stand inside a mall, arms around each other.

As I flip further through the albums, they become less innocent-looking and sporting more serious facial expressions. They're dressing more risqué and surrounded by bigger groups with what looks to be older guys. My aunt appears in fewer and fewer photos, and my mother's appearance changes drastically. Her makeup becomes darker, her clothing more provocative, and there seems to be one guy she's always pictured with.

"Do you know who this could be?" Vin asks me as he points out the guy my mother has her arms around, her face beaming with elation.

"No," I answer firmly. "He's not someone who lives here?"

"No."

I find myself analyzing the guy's face as my heart begins to pound. He looks older than my mother with dark hair and his skin is like a rich sepia, but what really has me starting to sweat is the mole under his right eye. Could this be my father?

"You look alike," Vin mutters, and I can't help but agree with him.

My skin erupts with tingles and I fear I'm going to have a heart attack. This guy is handsome, with a depraved glint in his eyes, and the smirk on his face is downright sinful.

Sharla is wrapped up in the arms of what looks to be a jock, who has sandy-blond hair and green eyes, almost identical to Travis.

"Your dad?" I run my finger over the couple in the photo.

"Yeah, that's him," he all but growls out.

"Travis is his twin, and you look like your mom." He nods, and I pull the photo out of the sleeve before turning it over. *Me with Bobby and Becca with Ray. Grade 12, 2002.*

Fuck, I'm almost certain this is my dad. The timeline adds up.

"You'll be seventeen, right?" Vin whispers, doing the math as well.

"Yeah."

"Damn, you think—"

"Yes," I cut him off. "My skin tone, the mole—" I choke back a sob.

"We have a name now, Em." He grabs my chin to make me look at him, his eyes filled with determination. "Question your aunt, and hell, I'll question my mom too."

"Thank you." My chin wobbles in his grip as the anger washes away.

"Keep that box." He runs his thumb back and forth on my chin. "Keep all of it."

After packing the albums back into the box, Vin drives us back to the school so he can pick up his vehicle, and pulls into the empty parking lot to park beside his Hummer. "My mom and Debra are going away on an annual spa trip this weekend." I think I remember my aunt saying this in passing. "So, I'm having a party at my house on Saturday. My pool is enclosed so you can swim, and I don't know, maybe you can let this chill and we'll tackle it after the weekend."

"Yeah, okay." I nod as I wring my hands in my lap.

"Em, we'll figure it out. I promise." I look up into his eyes and see the sincerity of his words shining back at me.

"Okay. Can I bring Adri?" I grin as his mouth tips up in answer.

"Of course. Bring whoever you want." He leans in, his

teeth nipping into his bottom lip.

"Travis?"

"Sure," he grits out as he pulls back with a roll of his eyes.

"He won't come if I invite him. You have to do it." That has him falling back into the seat with a groan.

"Em." His voice is full of warning that falls on deaf ears.

"Look, Vin, he's your family and one day he'll be all you have." A tear slips down my cheek as the truth of my words hits me in the chest.

"Okay." He wipes my tear away. "I'll invite him." He leans in and kisses the corner of my mouth, then pulls away. Instead of pushing him further, I give him the benefit of the doubt that he will in fact call his brother.

"Should we bring anything?" I ask, my fingers itching to grab his face and pull him back for a proper kiss, but I don't want to make the first move. "Alcohol or food?"

"Nah, I have snacks and a shit ton of alcohol, and please, for the love of God, don't let Adri cook or bake a single fucking thing." He looks at me with wide eyes, pure fear exuding from them.

"Why?" I draw my head back and narrow my eyes.

"Because she's fucking terrible at it." He winces as he says it, his face pulling a chuckle from me.

"Noted."

"I'll see you tomorrow," he rasps. Then he gets out of my car and I watch him slide into his Hummer before driving off.

My drive home is uneventful and thankfully tailless. Hopefully, my message gets back to Raphael and he backs off. I was never a threat to the gang and my role in their organization was minimal. My time with the gang made me privy to certain information, but that doesn't give them the right to stalk me forever. I leave the box in the car because I don't want my aunt to find out what we've found yet. I plan to show her after the weekend, like Vin suggested.

The house is quiet when I step in, which is normal a few days a week. My aunt must be working still, and my uncle's voice is faint as it floats from his office. I go upstairs and take a long, hot shower. Afterward, with my muscles finally relaxed, I text Adri to see how it went with Travis.

Me: Sorry about leaving without giving u a heads-up.

Adri: That's not what u should be sorry for…

Me: Travis?

Adri: Obv.

Me: Sorry, not sorry.

Me: I trust Travis to get u home.

Adri: We barely spoke, so awk.

Adri: Everything ok with u?

Me: Yeah, all good. C u tmr.

Adri: *Heart Emoji*

Next, I text Travis, to thank him for driving Adri.

Me: Thank u for dropping off Adri.

Trav: At least someone thanked me.

Trav: She just hopped out like her ass was on fire SMH.

Me: So… u think her ass is hot?

Trav: Not answering that.

Trav: U good?

Me: I'll tell u tmr.

Trav: Kk.

I put my phone aside and start on some homework. I'm in the middle of reading lines for the play when my phone pings.

Vince: Wanted 2 kiss U.

My heart almost explodes.

Me: U should've.

Vince: Maybe…

Me: Okay…

He doesn't reply after that and I let it go, then I end up passing out hard in the middle of algebra homework.

The rest of the week passes without incident. We have rehearsal three times a week and I've been pretty swamped with homework. My aunt left on Friday evening with Sharla, and my uncle is at his friend's house for gambling night. I decide to have an early night of self-care with a scented bath, face mask, and personal grooming. This way I look my best for a pool party with the guy I've been blue ovary-ing over all fucking week.

Chapter Thirteen

Adri has been at my house since the crack of dawn. Today is Vin's party and I just want to look good, so I've enlisted her to do my face and hair. My uncle has a meeting that's about three hours' drive from here, so he won't be home tonight. Both Adri and I assured him we'd be sleeping at her place. He wasn't too worried, just kept reminding me about his one rule, but I'm hoping to be breaking that rule tonight.

We spent all day making pot brownies, but I also made some Ex-Lax brownies too. I let Adri help, but I did most of the work as Vin's warning echoed in my head. Marlana is for sure going to show her face with her posse of mean girls, despite not being invited, and I would really love for them to be shitting themselves by the end of the night. It won't be anything painful, just uncontrollable diarrhea. I deserve the vindication of retaliation.

I'm wearing a bloodred, barely-there, string bikini and a leather skirt meeting my mid-thigh, then I'll top it off with my leather jacket and some red bottom heels. Adri is wearing a white crocheted sundress with a white string bikini underneath, the material transparent, and she looks like the goddess she is.

Once we're dressed, she puts my hair in big rollers and

starts on my makeup. We go light on my eyes this time with some silver glitter, and she paints my lips the same red as my bikini.

"I plan to be messed up tonight," I say around the lipstick tube.

"Me too. Is Travis going?" She tries to sound nonchalant, but I can hear the longing in her tone.

"I'm not sure. I told Vin to invite him." Her arm drops from my face in shock.

"What?!" she shrieks.

"You heard me." I nod, a small smile dancing around my mouth. "He has to, otherwise Travis would never come, and I want him there."

"Wow." Her eyes look like they're going to pop out of her skull, the sight making me snort.

An hour later, we walk up to Vin's house—thank God he's only a street over—each carrying a reusable container of brownies. Both have a written glittering message that says, 'For shits and giggles.' I chuckle to myself because I'm not telling anyone what that means. Adri and I had a few of the pot brownies before coming, so we already feel nice.

"Why are you laughing?" she asks, looking at me with a silly smile.

"I can't wait to see who shits themselves." I continue to chuckle as I imagine the chaos we are about to unleash. She stops in her tracks and starts cackling. Not even laughing, it's a full-out cackle straight from the belly. Totally not attractive. She needs to not do that if she wants to get laid by Travis tonight. "Never do that laugh again." I point to her face, then to her crotch. "It doesn't make genitalia tingle."

"Got it." She nods as she straightens, fighting to remain stoic, but snickering as we continue walking up the front walkway.

When we approach the door, it flies open to reveal

Danny with just a pair of low-slung swim shorts on. His rich brown skin is damp, and his chest is wide, pecs defined. His abs are like dinner rolls baked to perfection, dripping butter, with a happy trail sneaking down inside his shorts between a delicious V. His body makes my genitals tingle, but that's it. Not to mention now I'm starving from imagining dinner rolls and butter.

"Hello, ladies," he drawls with a wink. *Always winking.*

"Your gonorrhea is showing," I deadpan as my finger swings back and forth in front of his eyes.

He closes his eyes and throws his head back on a loud exhale. "Damn it, Ember, just move your ass inside," he growls. I give him a two-finger salute and walk through the doorway. "Hey, Adri. Shit, your legs look sweet!" he groans at my best friend like she's a slab of meat.

"I'll pass on the gonorrhea for today. How about a brownie?" She smiles sweetly at him.

"Ember, I swear to God you need to stop saying that shit," he says tersely while biting into a brownie. "What does *Shits and Giggles* mean?"

"They're pot brownies." I shrug, feigning nonchalance.

"Nice!" he exclaims, gobbling down the entire piece as he walks off toward the backyard and noise.

"I hope his sphincter explodes," I hiss. Adri starts a fresh round of cackling and I glare at her over my shoulder.

"Last one. Scout's honor," she replies, still giggling while holding up two fingers.

We walk into the kitchen and place the brownies on the table with the alcohol. A set of glass doors leading outside reveals an enclosure of all glass around a pool, and despite the slight May chill in the air, it looks nice and warm inside. I'm guessing it's warm according to the scantily-clad high schoolers.

I whistle under my breath. "Vin and his mom are doing

well without the sperm donor's help."

"Yeah, her restaurant is really popular," Adri murmurs.

At that moment, the glass door opens, and in walks a wet Adonis. Vin looks so good, and his left nipple is pierced, it makes me groan. Like out loud. I don't care, right now I have no shame. *Dear God, I know Mrs. G just introduced us, but please help me keep my vagina in my panties a bit longer.* There's something about a build up that I love, and when we finally come together, we'll be explosive. His body is not as bulky as Danny's, but it is still molded, sculpted, and bronzy. He has a tattoo of script running up the side of his body. I can't see what it says from where I'm standing, though.

"Hey, Em." His voice is like velvet and my thighs clench together at the sound. He knows the effect he has on me, judging by his grin. "Adrianna." He nods toward her.

Adri looks back and forth between us and giggles as she mixes herself a drink in a red cup before walking to the door leading to the backyard. "I'll be outside if you need me." She grins at me, and I nod as she continues to laugh.

The door shuts behind her as Vin saunters over to me and stops an inch from my body. My hand moves of its own accord and rests against his left pec. His heart is thundering in his chest, telling me he's not as calm as he's acting. I slowly run my fingers over the bar in his nipple and he makes a low noise in the back of his throat as I continue over his chest and down his abs. He sucks in a breath and releases a gasp as my hand continues down and over the front of his wet swim trunks. He's already getting hard against my hand. Build up forgotten.

"Ember," he whispers. I lift my head to look him in the eyes. "You look so good, baby."

"So do you." I finally find my voice as my hand drops back to my side, the feel of his skin still lingering through my fingers.

"Come swim with me," he pleads, but doesn't move away from me as we stand still, looking into each other's eyes. I want him to kiss me. It's all I think about. I want to have his full, lush lips against mine.

He closes the gap between us and bends at the knees, but before I can question him, he lifts me with his hands around my thighs, and my legs wrap around his waist, causing my skirt to slide up my ass. We both groan as our centers line up, and he walks me back toward the counter—setting me gently on top—before watching my mouth closely. He's unmistakably large between my legs, and my mouth waters in anticipation. I'm ready, but first, I need him to kiss me. We've been playing this game for weeks, and I'm tired of it.

I run my hands along the light scruff on his cheeks and over his low ponytail. Then, finally, our lips lightly brush.

"There you are, baby." Like ice-cold water on embers, the high-pitched voice breaks us from our hold.

Vin groans and grinds his teeth before his forehead falls against mine. "Go away, Marlana."

"Want a brownie?" I ask her, grinning over Vin's shoulder as he stiffens in front of me. I give her a quick once-over, skipping over her hot pink bikini to match her hot pink head.

"You brought brownies?" Vin pulls back to look down at my face before relaxing into me.

"Adri made them." I widen my eyes, hoping he remembers what he told me about her baking skills and chooses not to have any, but if he does, well, good luck to his asshole. He makes a disgusted face and I shrug, slightly disappointed that we won't be playing asshole Russian Roulette.

"I'll have one," Marlana says with a smug look on her face. She thinks she's interrupting us. Good, I hope she's stuck on the toilet for days. "Shits and Giggles?" Her brow raises as her top lip curls upward.

"They're actually pot brownies," I clarify as Vin studies her closely, his body filled with tension. I run my fingers along the bunching muscles of his back, trying to force some calming energy into him.

"Adrianna made pot brownies?" She looks at me skeptically.

"I made the butter. She just added it to her recipe. I've had two so far. They're good." I grin wide, knowing I look stoned.

"Nice," she says and takes a large piece. She bites into it and makes a face. "It's weird." I pray that's Ex-Lax she's tasting because the pot ones we made were amazing.

"Adri isn't much of a baker," I explain with an apologetic smile. "Regardless, it does what it's supposed to."

I push at Vin to move back and then hop off the counter. Turning around, I look at the alcohol selection, spotting tequila and grabbing it as Vin moves up behind me and presses in close.

"Tequila?" His mouth moves against my hair.

"Mm-hmm." I nearly choke as he presses a kiss to my neck.

"Come outside, Vin," Himalayan Salt whines as she leans against the counter, her arms crossed over her chest.

I snort to myself. *Himalayan Salt.* I take my shot and pour another into the cup as the liquid swirls inside like melted gold. I'm so stoned. I snort again.

"What's so fucking funny?" Himalayan Salt pesters, and I look over at her just as her eyes narrow.

"Your hair looks like Himalayan Salt." I giggle and take the next shot. My hair brushes my cheek as Vin leans in and laughs.

"What do you have against my hair?" she shrieks. "At least it's not boring like yours."

"It's on your head. That's what I have against it," I deadpan while Vin is shaking with restrained laughter behind me.

"Fuck you," she snarls as she stuffs the rest of her

brownie in her mouth and stomps back outside. "And you too, Vin," she adds with her mouth full.

I pray to the gods of shit and laxatives that she picked an Ex-Lax brownie. Vin is still pressed up against me as I pour and toss back another shot, then I turn to look at him. His eyes are hooded and his breathing has quickened as he drinks me in from head to toe.

"I invited Travis like you asked me to." His eyes flick back to mine as his hands tighten on my waist. "But he still hasn't shown."

"I'll call him and tell him I'm here." His brows fall over his eyes at my words as he takes a step back.

"Do you want him?" His eyes betray his vulnerability, so I reach up and place my hand on his cheek.

"No. He and I click on a different level. He's going to be my best friend." My heart clenches as I think of Tommy. He's also my best friend, and lately, I've been neglecting him. He's always been busy and hates talking on the phone, but I don't live down the street from him anymore. He can't just pop in for daily visits.

"What about me?" he whispers as his mouth turns down into a frown.

"You're going to mix me a drink while I call him." My grin hides the racing of my heart. I don't want to be the first to admit the feelings settling inside my heart.

Vin looks slightly disappointed by my answer but nods and starts pulling different liquors toward him. I look over my shoulder as I leave the kitchen to see him mixing different shit into my cup. Maybe I should've asked not to mix a cocktail of alcohol poisoning? I pull my cell phone out of my jacket pocket and call Travis.

"'Sup, E?" he answers as I snort into the phone. I like *E*.

"Hey, Trav. Where are you?" I look out the front window by the door to make sure he's not sitting in the driveway like a weirdo.

"Home. Did you just snort?"

"Aren't you coming to the party?" I ask him as I hiccup into my hand.

"I don't know. Are you drunk?"

"Almost. Kind of. Adri is here." I wait, and when I don't get an answer, I say, "She came for you."

"What do you mean?"

"She wants you, Travis. Do you want her?" I'm done with the games these two play.

"Yes," he replies softly.

"K, see you in ten." I hang up the phone and slip it back into my pocket. If he doesn't show in fifteen minutes, we can't be best friends because I don't condone cowardice. It's all talk though because Travis has quickly become family to me.

I walk back into the kitchen and Vin is waiting with his arms crossed over his chest. It makes his biceps bunch and my vagina clench.

"Is he coming or not?" he huffs as a pec jumps, stealing my attention.

"Not sure." I shrug as I lick my lips.

"There's your drink. It's a Long Island Iced Tea." He points at my red cup.

"Thank you." I grab the drink and take a sip, the burn of potent liquor nearly choking me as I wave my hand in front of my face. "And thank you for the whole Travis thing."

"Yeah." The music turns up outside, and I see a few people jumping into the pool. I'm ready to head out there.

"Where can I put my clothes?" I take another sip of the drink before leaving the cup half empty on the counter.

"In my room. Follow me." He leads me back through

the hallway and up a very wide, fancy staircase. I look at the top level of the house and whistle. It's a large landing with a few couches and a TV with about four different game consoles and some workout equipment as well. Then there is one door to the left.

"My room is the only one up here. My mom sleeps on the main floor. She let me have the master," he states with obvious adoration for the woman who raised him alone.

"Sharla is in a league of her own." She's also raised a son to be proud of all on her own. I admire the hell out of her for that, the same way I admired my mother for doing the best she could for me.

His room is not anything like I was expecting. Vin has such an aloof personality and he doesn't wear his heart on his sleeve. He has a large king-size bed with black bedding dead center, and as I look around his room, I can see the things he loves. He has different Broadway show posters on his walls, sketches pinned up, and an easel with a painting of what looks like the start of a female's face. He catches me looking at the canvas and quickly moves to cover it with a sheet.

"It's not ready yet." He smiles almost shyly, completely different from the guy he was downstairs. "You can leave your clothes in my bathroom and grab a towel." He points to another door. I nod and open the door to his private bathroom.

It's luxurious. There's a huge jet tub and a large stand-up shower with two showerheads. He has double sinks and a tower to the side holding folded towels. I pull off my jacket and skirt and leave them folded on the counter. Next, I pull my hair out of the ponytail and let it tumble down my back in loose, thick curls. I grab a towel and walk out in just my bikini as my heart thuds against my rib cage.

My body has obvious battle scars, silvery lines that tell a story of the pits I had to claw my way out of and the many times I had to prove my worth. I'm not ashamed of them, but it's probably not the body Marlana and the other girls my age have. Each raised mark on my skin is a note to a symphony of survival.

Vin just stares at me for a long while. "Wow," he finally breathes out. I put a little more swing in my step and walk toward him. He begins to sport a tent in his swim trunks and that alone makes me want to rip off my bottoms and throw myself at him. I reach him and look up into his bright green eyes as his hands cup my face. "You're the most beautiful girl I have ever seen."

"Prove it," I dare him with the help of the liquid courage I had downstairs. Tequila really is a girl's best friend.

His face slowly approaches mine as the anticipation becomes overwhelming. His breath tickles my hair as he places a small kiss on my temple. The feel of his lips on my skin alone causes such a guttural groan to be ripped out of my throat. I feel his mouth turn up into what must be his signature grin, and he moves to kiss the tip of my nose. I lick my lips and tilt my head back farther, so he has unrestricted access to my mouth.

Now it's his turn to groan as he slides his fingers into my hair. He brings his face down and presses a kiss to the right of my mouth, just barely touching my lips. I grunt in frustration as his mouth turns up again.

"I need to take my time and remember everything," he whispers against my mouth. "You're the first girl up here, you know."

"Vin… fucking kiss me." I'm completely out of patience as he looks into my eyes and nods, lowering his mouth again. Just as our lips touch, screaming coming from outside breaks the moment.

We pull apart quickly and rush to his window to investigate the backyard. Himalayan Salt is rushing toward the house, holding her ass, and Danny *also* pops up out of the pool to run behind her. I snort because I know exactly what's happening, and it is so worth the interruption.

"What the fuck?" Vin says while running out of his room as I follow behind him.

"Vin! I need a toilet! Now!" Danny screams. "Mar took

the one on the main level." He's breathing heavily and his face looks a little green as he dances from foot to foot.

"Basement," Vin answers quickly, adding, "Don't puke on the floor."

Just then, the front door opens and Travis walks in. He looks so good in a black beanie covering his sandy hair, black, worn leather jacket, V-neck black shirt, and a dark pair of denim jeans, his tan boots topping it off.

"What is going on here?" He laughs, pointing at Danny running down the basement stairs.

"Laxative brownies," I say with an evil grin as I rub my hands together.

"What?" Both Vin and Travis ask simultaneously, the first spinning around to face me.

"Shits and Giggles brownies. You take the chance, like Russian Roulette for your ass." I giggle as they both stand there in shock. Looking at them both now, I can see the resemblance.

"Oh, fuck." Vin rushes into the kitchen to probably throw them away. At least it hit the two people I was hoping for. Thank you, gods of shits and laxatives.

"Do I want to know?" Travis questions with an amused look on his face. "Are you stoned?" He moves his head to the side as I take in his chiseled jawline.

"It's a very good chance that's wearing off and the liquor is starting to kick in." I start to descend the stairs, my grip firm on the railing.

"So, I should stay away from the brownies?" He looks me up and down, his heated stare reminding me I'm in my bikini and nothing else.

"Vin is probably throwing them out." I pout as I step down from the last stair.

"Hey, Travis. Want a brownie?" Vin comes back with a container, offering it to Travis with a vindictive grin on his face.

I grab it out of his hand and slap his ass before shoving him back to the kitchen. "Don't be a jerk, Vin."

"This is pretty tame for him. We would have been kicking each other's asses by now." Travis looks back toward the front door.

"I'd be kicking your ass, you mean," Vin corrects him as he stands in the kitchen doorway. I give him a warning glare and he raises his hands before walking out to the pool.

Travis whistles under his breath. "Have you tamed the beast? Are you the Vin whisperer?"

"I fucking hope not. I love him wild." I wink and nudge him with my elbow.

He laughs and throws his arm over my shoulders as we move out to the pool. People are beginning to trickle inside, but Marlana is back outside with her little gang and I watch her as she stares at Vin walking along the pool deck. I understand because I find myself doing the same thing as his muscles bunch with each step, and from here I can see what that script finally says, *Tainted Blood*. What does that mean? Is that how he views himself?

"You're lucky those brownies weren't potent enough to make us sick," Danny says when he comes back outside, a smile playing around his mouth, and pulling me from my thoughts. "Shits and giggles, clever."

"I should sue you bitches!" Marlana screams from the other side of the pool. She looks outraged, but her friends, including Shay, look slightly amused.

"Maybe you should question what you put in your mouth more often." I raise my hands with the suggestion as people snicker.

Vin sits in a long lawn chair, his abs flexing as he shifts in the seat, and I move away from Travis to approach him. There's a magnetic pull between us, forcing us to stay in each other's orbit. He drops his legs to each side, and I sit between them, moving back until my back meets his front. His arms come around my waist and his chin rests on my shoulder. "How do you smell so good?" His hot breath hits my ear.

"How is your dick so hard?" I whisper back, making him laugh heartily as he tightens his hold around me.

"Can't blame him, baby," he says between laughs.

Travis sits himself in a chair beside Adri and she smiles at him, but that's the extent of their interaction. I need to liven this up and make Travis a little tipsy. "Hey, Danny!" I call out in a sweet voice. "Could you be a doll and grab Travis a beer from the fridge?" I add a few eyelash flutters.

He shrugs. "Yeah, sure."

Vin stiffens up behind me. I know he doesn't like Travis being here, and it's making him uncomfortable, no matter how much he tries to hide it. I turn a bit in my seat and place a kiss on his neck, smiling when he automatically relaxes.

"You want one too, Ember?" Danny holds up a bottle.

"Yeah, please. Unopened though. I know all about retaliation." I point my finger at him.

"Smart." He laughs. Then Danny passes Travis and me the beers, and we open them together. I air cheers him, and we drink.

"Let's play a game," Clit Head whines from the other side of the pool. I snort into my beer, *Clit Head.*

"How about we play hide and seek?" Adri suggests, leaning forward in her chair with a mean sneer on her face. "You bitches hide and we'll come find you… eventually."

Vin throws his head back and laughs out loud. "Fuck, Adrianna. I really missed that sass. Remember in first grade when you grabbed Jake's balls and threatened to make him a girl? Kid cried for like three hours."

Travis snickers. "I think he pissed himself too. Weren't you in detention for a week after that?" He turns to Adri as she shrugs.

"Worth it. That little asshole told me he was going to kiss me after school to see if that's how girls got pregnant." She still looks pissed about it and the look of her angry face has me cackling.

"Those were the days," Vin says quietly.

Travis hears him and nods, giving him a look over his shoulder. The nostalgia has them quieting and even though I'm the odd one out who hasn't experienced these things with them, I feel the bond still strong between them, it's just buried beneath the surface of anger. I want ten years to go by and be sitting with this group—most of them, anyway—and telling our stories of how we were young and silly together. The thought warms my insides. I haven't felt this need to connect with anyone outside of my immediate family. The thought of not having my mom here anymore to experience these things with me is making it hard to swallow. I suck in a breath to stop the constricting of my lungs as my eyes burn with tears.

"Hey, beautiful," Vin whispers in my ear. "I'm here." His hands splay across my stomach as his face slips into the crook of my neck.

He can't know what I was thinking, right? He couldn't know that at that moment, I needed to hear something like that so desperately. I turn in the chair, kneeling between his legs, and grab his face with both hands to stare into his eyes. His hands land on my hips as he pulls his bottom lip between his teeth, his dimples winking at me from the deep caverns in his cheeks. He's stirring emotions inside me that I have tried to cover up and hide. I lean in and kiss his neck softly, sucking his skin into my mouth and giving it a little bite. His grip on my hips tightens as everyone talks around us, but my heartbeat is the only sound in my ears. I'm falling for him, and fast. Danny's whistle permeates my thoughts, and I turn to glare at him over my shoulder. Dick breath.

"Truth or dare people? Come on, let's liven this up," Clitty snipes. I turn back around as Vin shrugs behind me.

His arms slip back around my waist as he mutters, "Sure,

whatever."

"I'll go first," Danny offers as he lays on a floatie in the pool. "Mar, truth or dare?"

"Truth," she answers as she takes a sip of her drink.

"Is it true you're in love with Vin?" She sputters and coughs on her drink while everyone is looking at her expectantly. I know the answer. She is in love with him. Obsessively so.

"No!" she protests loudly. "His dick is amazing though, especially with the piercing."

Now it's my turn to choke and sputter on my drink. Dick piercing? That will be a first for me. Then I think about how this bitch has probably had Vin's dick in every hole in her body. My body stiffens with restrained anger.

"Let it go," he whispers to me again. "It was before you. Now, all I want is you." He grinds his dick into my ass, and I feel how hard he is. "This has only been happening for you since your ass moved here." I relax and push said ass into him. He chuckles and buries his face into my hair.

"Shithead, truth or dare?" Clit for Brains sneers. I look over at her and grin as I snap my fingers, instantly getting her dig at my hair.

"You can do better than that, Clitoris." I laugh sadistically while everyone snickers along. "Dare."

"Bitch, I dare you to kiss Travis." She slaps her hand to Shay's as everyone falls to a hush around the pool. I see the angle she's pulling. She knows Travis is clearly here for Adri with how he's staring at her, and with Adri being my new closest friend, she could stir trouble between us. Not counting the fact that Vin and Travis have a mountain of issues between them, this could be the last thing to make shit pop off. I turn in my seat and place my mouth to the corner of Vin's.

"Trust me?" I whisper softly. He nods stiffly, but his body is radiating with barely restrained anger.

I get up out of my seat and approach Travis as he visibly swallows and looks at Adri. She narrows her eyes on me, and I send her a wink because I need her to trust me too. She must see the look on my face and schools her features to boredom, as if none of this is worth her time. I lean down to Travis' level, placing each hand on the armrests of his chair, and lightly press my closed mouth to his. Our eyes are open and his are filled with mirth. This is nothing like our actual first kiss in that classroom weeks ago. It's the same kiss you'd give your ninety-year-old grandma. Marlana didn't say it had to be a passionate one.

I stand up and pat Travis' cheek, then close the distance between me and Adri. I grab her face in both of my hands and crush my mouth to hers. She has her eyes wide open, filled with shock and maybe something more? Something close to lust. She gasps and her mouth opens beneath mine. I take the opportunity and invade her mouth with my tongue as she recovers and starts kissing me back with a vengeance. A few muttered curses circle around us, and I know the groan that fills the air belongs to Vin. I comb my fingers through her hair and yank her head back, pulling on the thick strands. She moans, running her hands up my sides and stops on either side of my breasts. I suck her tongue into my mouth and slowly drag my lips along its length.

Then I stand up and turn to face everyone, wiping my mouth with the back of my hand and hiding the filthy grin. Danny has his hand down his pants, clearly stroking himself while floating. Vin's mouth is hanging open and his cock is straining hard against his shorts, and Marlana and her groupies look like they've all swallowed vinegar.

"Sorry. Daring me to kiss Travis was so juvenile. I thought I'd up the ante to what a real dare should look like." I bow a little. "You're welcome." Then I turn to look at Adri over my shoulder. Her eyes are wide as her hands cover her mouth. "Best girl kiss I've had yet."

"I'm questioning if I even like dick right now," she deadpans as she slowly drops her hands from her mouth.

Travis is just staring at her, his cheeks a slight pink color, and his pants are also noticeably tighter as well. I grin to myself while I walk back to Vin. Mission accomplished.

I crawl back between Vin's legs and rub my hands along his thighs, my back once again to his front.

"Are you a lesbian?" Clit Head snarls, and the area once again falls to a hush.

"Sometimes." I blow a kiss to her as she straightens her spine, her mouth turned down in disgust.

"Gross." She gags, then her eyes land on Vin. "Vin can always come back and experience what a woman who clearly loves just dick is like."

"Ask him." I wave her on. "Do it right now. Ask him what he wants."

Her neck flushes red with embarrassment and it spreads throughout her face. She backs down and takes a drink from her cup, unwilling to look me in the eye.

I let it go and notice that most people have left the pool and moved inside. The music has turned up, but I can still hear them laughing.

Danny lets out a loud groan and all our attention snaps to him. "I made a mess in my trunks," he announces. His eyes are closed, his face blissed out with post-orgasm, and he's still lying across the pool floater.

"Don't fucking get that shit in my pool," Vin growls at him from over my shoulder.

"My sperms are beasts. They'd swim around and impregnate your mother." Danny's laughing now, by himself. "I'd be your stepdaddy." Okay, that earned a laugh from me.

"You're dead if you keep talking," Vin warns, his voice cold and deadly.

Danny brings himself to the edge of the pool and hops on the deck. Then he walks into the house, his hand still in his shorts, gripping his junk as he winks at Vin.

"Your turn, Ember. Ask someone," Adri calls out as she tips back her drink. Right, truth or dare. I put my finger to my mouth and look at Adri with what I know is my evil smirk, as she frantically shakes her head.

"Let's play, Trav, and don't be a pussy. I just stuck my tongue down Adri's mouth and played with her uvula." Manipulative, I know, but I need him to pick dare.

"Pussy, huh? Fine, E. Hit me with a dare, but if it's making out with any of them,"—he points at Marlana and crew—"I'm telling you to fuck off."

"Noted. Hmm." I tap my finger to my chin as a sneaky smile slips over my mouth. "I dare you to take Adri into the pool shed and play seven minutes in heaven."

"Seriously?" Adri looks at me, shock lining her features as her body straightens in the chair.

"Yes." I nod and clap my hands as Vin snorts behind me. "Totally fucking serious. Get your asses in there and make up for lost time. I won't even hate if it's ten minutes."

Travis stands up and walks toward the shed while Adri is still stuck in her seat, staring after him. "A dare's a dare, Adrianna, let's go," Travis beckons, his back to her. She gets up slowly and glares at me as I blow her a kiss and toss her a little wave.

"Don't steal my thunder, boy. She doesn't even know if she likes dick anymore," I tease him. Vin's chest rumbles against my back and I look over my shoulder at him. "What?" I ask.

"I always knew they would be together, since fucking kindergarten." His mouth lifts and that dimple deepens as he shakes his head.

"Do you miss having them around?" My hand covers his as it fists against my stomach.

"No, Ember, I don't." His words are heavy with irritation and I can't help but wonder if it's because the opposite is true.

"I really appreciate this, but Travis will always be my friend, and Adri will always be my bestie. You understand that, right?" I want to make it very clear that I will never pick sides and if it comes to that, it won't be the side he hopes for.

"Yeah, I'm tolerating them for you. It's scary because I think I'd do just about anything for you." His words are muffled as he says them into my hair, but I hear every word and inflection of his voice.

Marlana and her crew move inside, leaving Vin and I alone, and I snap my teeth at her when she gives Vin a longing look as she passes by. He chuckles as he draws circles on my stomach and my pussy clenches when I think about where I'd rather those fingers be. As if sensing my thoughts, they slowly move down to the waistband of my bikini bottoms, tracing back and forth. I raise my hips slightly, giving him permission to go inside. He wastes no time and pushes his entire hand in, cupping me as a moan flies from my mouth and my head falls back on his shoulder. My nails dig into his thighs as I grip them through his swim shorts.

"I want to make you feel good," he whispers in my ear before tracing it with his tongue.

"Please," I moan as his finger traces along my folds.

"Fuck, you're so wet." His lips hit my shoulder, the brush of their velvet surface making my clit sing between my legs.

I lift my hips again just to push against him and create some friction against the one spot needing it the most. He pushes his finger against my clit, making lazy circles, all the while he's kissing and sucking on my neck. A slow burn starts in my lower belly, and I know I'm about to come spectacularly. He removes his finger from my clit and slips two deep inside my pussy. I gasp with the intrusion as my hips arc upward. "Vin, I want you inside me."

"Yeah?" he breathes into my ear and presses his cock into my back. I nod and grind against his hand, rubbing my clit on his palm and riding his two fingers simultaneously. My juices are sliding down his fingers onto his hand and an explosion begins as my pussy clenches around his fingers.

"I can't wait until my cock is this drenched," he groans, and that's all it takes as I tumble over the edge, hissing his name as the orgasm washes over me. Then he pulls them out and puts them directly into his mouth, sucking my juices off as I look back and into his face. His eyes are closed, like he's savoring the flavor.

"You made me come but haven't even kissed me yet." My voice is husky as my core clenches for more.

He opens his eyes and gives me that grin I've come to love. "I know."

I snort and lean back into him when I remember Travis and Adri. "What happened to those two? Should I go check?" I sit up as I look curiously toward the shed. It's been a while.

"I haven't heard any screaming yet, so that's both good and bad, I'd say." He pulls me in close to his chest and I soak in the warmth of his skin.

"Why *Tainted Blood*?" I tip my head back to look up at him as his mouth purses in thought. I don't think he's going to tell me when he remains quiet, but then he clears his throat.

"I was angry for a long time." He takes a deep breath. "Why couldn't he accept me like he did Travis? It felt like my blood was different, tainted somehow. I tattooed it so I would never forget the way he made me feel."

The door leading to the house opens and Danny comes back with a bottle of tequila. "Why does it smell like sweet pussy out here?" He looks at me, quirking his pierced brow.

"Probably because your boy had his fingers all in one," I deadpan as Vin chuckles behind me.

"I'm hard again," Danny groans, scrubbing a hand down his face. "Here, let's take shots. I'm going to need it."

We each have four shots passing the bottle around

when the door to the shed opens and Travis comes stalking out, walking straight into the house, without uttering a single word to us. I pat Vin's knee and scoot to the end of the chair. I'm pretty tipsy, but I make my wobbly-ass stand and go find Adri. First, I have to pee… bad. The shed has a sauna in it because there's a sign above the door that says, 'Use sauna at your own risk' made from those cheap letter stickers. Maybe there's an Adri and a potty in there too. Two birds, one stone, you know?

I walk in the door and look around. "Adri, I have to pee, answer me quickly or I'm popping a squat on the shower floor!" I call out as I dance on my tippy-toes.

"Over here." Her voice is muffled by sobs and my heart drops at the sound. I will kill Travis if he's hurt her. She's sitting on one of two toilets when I find her, making me moan with relief as I rush to the other toilet.

"Tell me you're crying because he eats pussy like it's an all-you-can-eat buffet," I say while peeing.

"We didn't even kiss. I tried to bring up the shit that happened with us and we just started arguing." She looks at me with tortured eyes. "I need him to apologize, Ember."

"I get that, Adri, but don't you think maybe tonight wasn't the time for that?" I wipe myself and stand, flushing the toilet, but nearly missing the lever first. "Tonight should have been about the reconnect, then later hashing out apologies."

"I know that now, but it's too late. I fucked up." She runs her arm under her nose and I cringe.

"Bah!" I teeter while trying to pull my bikini bottoms up. "Trust me, it's fixable. He may not have eaten you like a buffet, but that boy has been starving himself."

I go to the sink to wash my hands and I reach for the soap dispenser, totally knocking it on the floor where it breaks open and white liquid hand soap seeps all over the place. "You're so drunk," Adri moans into her hands.

"It's ridiculous, really." I nod my agreement while trying to scoop up some soap to wash with because hygiene is fucking important. "You need to be drunk. ASSP!"

"You mean ASAP."

"That's what I fucking said, bitch." I look at her like she's losing it because she fucking clearly is.

"Get me drunk, Embs." I quickly turn to face her, spraying water from my hands in the process.

"Embs! That's new, I like it." I grin. At least, I think I'm grinning. Adri is cringing, so maybe not. "I'm seriously craving Five Guys."

"Ember!" Adri shrieks, her face one of complete shock as she stands from the toilet.

"What?! You Canadians hate burgers or some shit?" I clap my hands at her.

"Ooh!" She slaps her forehead. "The burger place! Not actually five guys."

"Ooh!" I point at her face—one of the three Adri faces. "Not actual guys! That's a lot of meat."

"Are you trying to point at my face?" she asks, looking behind her while laughing. *Fuck, I missed.* "I need to catch up to you."

We leave the shed a little slower than usual since I'm practically two-stepping everywhere. I turn around to say bye to the shed and my eye catches on the sauna sign. I snicker at the thought formulating in my head. "Wait, Adri. I have to just do this one thing, okay?"

"Okay." She plops down on the grass behind me and waits.

About ten minutes later, I have Adri rolling on the grass laughing so hard she's threatening to pee, which isn't a bad idea because I think I need to go again.

"Vin is going to fucking kill you. No, even better, Sharla is going to kill you," Adri says through her tears.

"Nah, I'll say I saw Danny creeping around out here. They will totally buy it."

I look up at my handiwork while I dust off my hands. I've changed the use sauna at your own risk sign to *Use anals at your own risk*. It was tricky, especially because my fingers weren't cooperating as well as I would've liked, but I had to improvise for the *l*, so I ripped the *u* to make one. It's a beautiful sign and very educational.

Chapter Fourteen

We make it to the table and chairs where Vin, Danny, and I were drinking earlier and it looks like they both went inside but left the tequila on the table. I look at Adri with a smile. "Sit down and start drinking." I point at the chair.

"Did you slur? Or you really want me to *shit down*?" I give her my best dirty look and take a shot from the bottle. "Whoa! I said, 'Let me catch up.'" She takes the bottle from me before giving me a dirty look. "You *shit down* and cheer me up."

"When I called Trav earlier, I asked if he wanted you and he said yes." I cross my legs and my foot slaps against the table, jarring the bottle and glasses on top of it.

"He did?" she asks, her eyes widening with shock as she gulps down tequila.

"I really think it's time you both let go of whatever is holding you back and give a relationship a try. Enough of the holding grudges." I wave my hand back and forth, my fingers jabbing into my eye. "Shit!" I rub it to clear out the pain, but it still hurts. "My hand just attacked my face."

Adri chokes on the tequila as she laughs and sputters while I curl my face into my palm and look through the window into the house. Where did the guys go? I squint into the room and see a few people standing around the center island in the kitchen where the liquor sits.

"Ready." Adri wobbles out of her chair, her eyes nice and glassy.

"Me too." I wobble out of my chair next and steady myself on the table before taking a few steps.

We stumble into the house and the music hits us full blast, the sound making my eardrums pulse. Looking around the kitchen, I find Marlana with her monster squad and Danny sitting at the table in the kitchen doing shots. A few guys I remember from drama are here and are surrounded by a group of overeager girls, but I don't see Travis or Vin. My stomach knots because those two missing at the same time can only mean trouble. Danny gets up from the table and closes the door to the kitchen and the music instantly dies down.

"Adrianna, is everything good?" Danny looks like he's genuinely worried about Adri as he gives her a once-over.

"Of course, they're good. They were probably outside eating each other's pussies," Marlana sneers at us, and all the eyes in the room focus on Adri and I, waiting to see how we'll react. I refuse to back down to homophobic mean girls.

"You videotaped that shit, huh?" I ask with a grin as I fall forward on the counter. "Saving it in your rub bank for later, I got you."

"You're fucking gross," Marlana spits with disgust as she backs away.

"You're fucking hot," Danny corrects as he takes a sip of his beer. Adri snorts and begins to pull different liquor bottles toward her, probably making the same alcoholic poison Vin fed me earlier.

With that single thought of him, the door to the kitchen opens and Vin walks in. He looks like he's had a shower and changed into a pair of dark jeans and a blue polo shirt. My insides instantly warm and the dopiest grin takes over my face.

"Hey, baby." He walks toward me, wearing a dopey smile of his own.

"Your baby was outside eating pussy," Marlana snipes, the jealousy thick in her voice.

"Yeah?" He leans in and sniffs my mouth as he hauls me into his arms. "Adri, you got a tequila pussy?"

Adri laughs. "We had pussy shots." She snorts as she downs the liquid in her cup.

My drunken mind roams as I rest my forehead on Vin's chest, breathing in his clean scent. Marlana reminds me of the middle school bullies I used to deal with, the same ones who liked to mock me by saying my name backwards, making it sound like *Rub me*. Maybe that's why I've been taunting her with cruel nicknames, because she brings me back to the drama I endured when I was twelve. Juan had instilled the importance of not fighting on the schoolyard, so I learned to ignore them. I should start taunting her with her name backwards, just to fuck her up. It takes me a minute because of my inebriated state, but Marlana backwards is fucking epic.

"Hey, have you guys ever tried to flip your names backward? Like I would be Rebme." I totter a bit as I push off Vin, who snickers and rights me before stepping behind me to wrap his arms around my waist.

"That is so fucking stupid. How old are you? Ten?" Vagina Lip squawks as she looks from Vin to me.

"Actually, let's start with you, Vaggie." I point at her, trying my best to hold in the bubbling laughter. "It'll be fun."

She rolls her eyes and looks at Vin again, the longing in their depths making her look desperate. She's devouring him as he presses a kiss to my neck when I blurt out, "Anal ram!"

"Oh, hell yes!" Adri screams before laughing right along with me as Vin steps back, giving me the space to fall over laughing if need be.

"Excuse me?" Miss Anal Ram asks. "Is that your favorite pastime or something?" She acts smug as she crosses her arms over her chest to grin at me.

I'm laughing too hard to answer and so is Adri, the both of us hot fucking messes right now. We're both bent over, losing our breath, cackling with tears running down our faces.

"It's your name backwards, Mar," Vin explains between chuckles, trying his best to hold in the laughter trembling in his tone.

She looks off with a puzzled look on her face as everyone else bursts out into laughter, which launches me and Adri both back into full-out belly laughs. "You both are dirty skanks!" she screams, jumping up from her chair.

"Your parents… must hate… you!" I try to breathe as I speak, my stomach tensing while threatening another round of laughter. "Anal Ram was what they wish they did instead of conceiving you!" I grip the counter to keep my face from planting onto Vin's kitchen floor.

"Fuck you, whores!" she yells and storms out of the kitchen, her pink hair billowing out behind her.

"That was actually genius," Shay says with a chuckle. "Not bad, Ember." She gets up from her seat and saunters by Danny, giving him a flick on the nose. Then she leaves the kitchen, I'm guessing to go find her friend, while leaving the door open and letting the music flood in. The heavy bass hits my chest, making me want to dance.

"Bitch," Danny grumbles while rubbing his nose. I didn't miss the look he gave her, though. That was pure longing.

"That was just perfect." I cover my mouth with my hand and look at Adri while she leans on one of the chairs to catch her breath.

"Amazingly perfect." She smiles wide.

"Why do you keep calling her vagina or clit head?" Danny cuts in, his face filled with curiosity as he takes a sip of his drink.

"Because she really started off on the wrong foot with me. From the beginning, she hated me without bothering to know me. Then she lays hands on me and tries to fuck with my car. So, her pink hair is a prime target." It's suddenly hot in here as everyone grows quiet, listening to why I'm targeting Marlana, as if I started this whole situation.

"Makes sense." He downs his drink and puts the cup on the table. "I'm just saying the cycle needs to end somewhere with someone or this is going to plague the group for the rest of our high school years."

"I only retaliate," I explain. "If she keeps her mouth shut and her hands to herself, I'll gladly act like she doesn't exist." My eye catches on the room beyond the kitchen door, finding a drama classmate behind a DJ set. Travis is leaning against the wall and talking to Jeremy from our Lit class and I smile. I'm glad he stayed, and I think I should go make sure he's okay.

As I'm trying to figure out which foot to lead me in walking, Adri mumbles under her breath, "Oh, fuck no." Snapping my head up, I look and find Anal Ram standing in front of Travis with her hand on his arm, laughing. Mind you, he looks uncomfortable as she sways her hips to the song currently playing.

"Well, that'sss my cue to ssstart sssome ssshit," I slur while pointing toward Travis and the bitch. "Unlessss you'd rather?" I ask Adri. She shakes her head, eyes wide at the threat of a confrontation. I shrug my shoulders and stagger toward the next room. "Done."

"Wait, where are you going?" Vin demands as I straighten my spine. If Anal Ram thinks she can maliciously try to destroy what Adri and Travis are trying to rebuild, she's about to be sorely disappointed.

"To fuck sssome ssshit up!" I scream over my shoulder.

"Should I be worried?" he asks as I leave the kitchen.

"Megatron" by Nicki Minaj starts playing. It's the perfect song because Nicki gets me hyped. I walk directly toward Travis, who spots me almost instantly as his face relaxes with relief. He's going to be shocked because he has no idea what I'm about to do.

The first verse starts and I push my way between Anal Ram and Travis. While facing him, I smile and wink, and he grins back as I turn around. Looking Marlana in the face, I start grinding on Travis, his hands instinctively going to my waist. She narrows her eyes and steps back. Perfect, I need some space anyway. Slowly winding my body to the floor, I twerk my hips in time with the beat. I look up to find Travis, his hand covering his mouth as he takes in my bikini-clad ass.

Growing up in the Bronx really taught me how to work my body. Street parties and basement parties were the hype in my early teens. I bring my body back up, gyrating as I raise my hands above my head. On my way up, I grab the hem of Travis' shirt, dragging it up with me, my other hand skimming along his abs. Holy shit, this man is stacked with muscle. My ass continues twerking with the beat as I close my eyes.

A warm breath fans over my face and I open my eyes, expecting to find Marlana, but instead, I have a furious but aroused-looking Vin in front of me. I peer over my shoulder to Travis, who has both hands in the air, proving to Vin he's not touching me. Schooling my features to nonchalance, I back up into Travis, rubbing my ass into his crotch. I face Vin once more and find his jaw clenched tight and his hands fisted at his sides. Then I reach out and grab his shirt, bringing him in close to me.

He gives Travis a hard glare as his hands grab my waist, yanking me into him and off his brother. A laugh rips from my throat as I throw my head back, my arms going wide. I'm pretty sure Vin is in love with me. From everything I've learned about him, his indifference to the girls he's dated, his lack of PDA, and his refusal to kiss just anyone, he's broken all but one of those rules with me, and that's about to change right fucking now.

I pull away from him, turning around back to Travis. Even with the music blaring, Vin's growl still finds its way to my ears. Putting my mouth to Travis' ear, I yell, "Go find Adri! She was pretty upset seeing you with Clit Head. You can thank me later for—" I'm yanked back into Vin before I can finish my sentence as Travis makes his way back toward the kitchen, shaking his head in amusement.

I'm turned around and forced to face a pissed-off Vin. His eyes are no longer green but a shade so dark they look nearly black, and his jaw is hard as stone. I run my hands along the rigid planes of his face and bring myself up to my tippy-toes, pulling his face down to mine. I press my mouth to his gently and a tingle works its way up from my toes to the top of my head. He doesn't respond and his lips are still tightly pressed together, refusing to participate. I slowly lick his lips and move up along his jaw toward his ear. He tastes so good, his lips, his skin, like he was made to be my own personal ambrosia. Vin was always meant to be mine.

I lightly kiss his ear and whisper, "I love you." He might not hear me over the music and that suits me just fine. I pull back, but before I get any farther, Vin shoves his hand into my hair, cupping the back of my head. His eyes are back to that gorgeous moss green I love, staring at me with an emotion I can't pin.

Before I can drag a full breath of air into my lungs, his mouth crashes into mine. Our teeth clash and our tongues battle for dominance, his tongue ring clinking against my teeth. My knees become liquid putty as I lose balance, my heart pounding a rhythm it's never played before. I'm coming undone with just his kiss alone. His free arm curls around my waist and hoists me up, my legs instinctively wrapping around him. Then he leads us out of the room, his mouth still fused to mine. He is the best ambrosia, and I don't think I will ever have my fill of him.

We climb the stairs as I pull my mouth from his and look around. We are definitely on our way to his bedroom and the thought suddenly has anticipation warming my insides.

"Em, you make me…" His voice is hoarse as he trails

off, his brows crinkling together.

"Mm-hmm." I nod. I know how he's feeling because I'm right there with him. I press my lips back to his. This time, our kiss is not so aggressive, but more seductive and searching. His tongue caresses and the stud rubs a line along mine. We reach his door, and he opens it, the scent belonging solely to Vin wafting beneath my nose. I unwrap my legs and let them slowly lower to the ground with my body still tightly pressed to his.

"I just need to…" I point to the bathroom. My nerves crash through me as I take a step back. It's like my first time all over again, and in some ways, it is. Sex has never meant this much to me before.

"Yeah, sure," Vin husks with a nod. I'm still really inebriated as I try my best to walk steadily to the bathroom. Instead, I'm a stumbling mess.

"You good over there?" Vin asks with a chuckle.

"Yep!" I answer, sticking my thumb in the air.

I reach the bathroom and close the door, relieving myself on his gorgeously elegant toilet. I use the bidet because why not? My lady bits love a good squirt. *Heh… see what I did there?* I snort at myself and totter off the toilet, struggling to pull my bikini bottoms up. *Fuck it.* I let them drop to the floor because I'm not going to be using them anyway. My nipples tighten as I remove my bikini top, then I wash my hands and look at myself in the mirror. My lips are swollen from our kisses, and my eyes are glassy and hooded. I have a red blush appearing across my cheeks from alcohol and anticipation.

Overall, I still look presentable. I smooth down my wavy hair and bring it to the front to cover my breasts. I should teach another class. *Seduction 101.* Giving myself the gun salute in the mirror, I open the bathroom door and stop dead as my breath gets lodged in my throat at the sight in front of me.

Vin is lying on the bed, his arms folded behind his head and his boxers slung low on his hips. He is perfect and all mine. *Forever.* I lick my lips as he does the same, his tongue ring glinting in the dark while perusing my body. That's when a small shot of self-consciousness hits. These white-silver lines scattered all over my body are the downside of cleaning up gang messes, and maybe it's not what he's attracted to.

"Hey, bring me all that sexy over here," he growls, the sound pulling me from my descending thoughts. Instantly, my insecurity fades. He wants me, and the look in his eyes isn't just lust. It's a lot deeper. I'm still unsteady on my feet as I stumble my way to the bed and let my back fall onto it.

Vin chuckles and moves me up beside him. "Baby, you're too drunk," he declares with a sigh.

"Is there such a thing?" I flutter my eyelashes at him as I squirm, needing his hands on me.

"Yes, especially when it comes to me being balls deep inside you." He leans down and presses a sweet kiss between my breasts.

"Give me the balls, all the balls, as deep as you can," I groan as his tongue dips out to run along my skin.

"What?" He laughs and looks up at me, the sound throaty and sexy. "How about I eat you out until you cream all over my face instead?"

My clit pulses with his words as a pout takes over my mouth. "Are you saying no balls deep?"

"I'm saying that is inevitable, Em. I will be balls deep in you, many times, for a long time. You feel me?" His fingers drag along the skin between my breasts, the rough pads eliciting goose bumps to rise in their wake. "You're mine now. Only mine, you understand?"

My back arches off the bed as those slow trailing fingers dip into my belly button. "Okay," I agree in a whisper as he looks up at me, his smile blinding. "You're mine too, Vin."

He lifts himself up to his elbows and moves on top of me before dropping his weight onto my body. My legs open as he falls between them, pressing against me in the most delicious way. When I said Vin was large earlier, I really had no idea. With only silk boxers between us, I feel everything, and he isn't just large, he is fucking huge. He presses in harder, and his mouth lands on my neck as the piercing in his dick prods my clit through the silk. A sudden rush of wetness coats the material of his boxers, the slickness of it creating a sensation as though there's no barrier between us. Vin groans and bites down on my neck as he pushes against me again. This time, he enters me a bit, my wet pussy sucking him in. I gasp and he pulls up to look at me, his eyes like a tumultuous storm.

"I want to fuck you so bad, Em." His voice sounds agonized as his body trembles with restraint.

"Holy shit, just do it." I push myself against him more. He's still slightly inside me and we both groan at the movement.

"Not tonight. I want you completely sober the first time you come on my dick," he grits out as if his own decision pains him. He pulls his cock away from my sopping pussy as I lean up on my elbows, bringing our faces closer.

"What?" I narrow my eyes on him. "I need to…"

"I know, baby." His tongue flicks out against my lip. "I'm still getting down there and I want that cream all over my face." He presses his mouth to mine and I run my tongue along the seam. We both open and he devours me, his hands moving along my ribs to cup both breasts. I fall back to the bed with a moan as my skin tingles with arcs of electricity.

He moves down and sucks my right nipple into his mouth, biting down hard as he tweaks the left one with his fingers. The sensations travel southward, and a sweet vibration begins in my lower belly. He continues kissing down over my chest and dipping his tongue into my belly button, the hard metal ball of his piercing flicking against my skin. Every touch of his tongue causes ripples of pleasure to course throughout my body, and when his tongue licks just above my pussy, I nearly come with the anticipation alone. He's so close. I lift my hips, trying to put his face where I so desperately need it.

He spreads my legs apart, and using both thumbs, he

opens my pussy lips to lick me in one full swipe as his tongue piercing presses onto my clit. I cry out as my back arches off the bed when he latches onto my clit, licking furious circles while holding me down with one hand. The feeling becomes almost unbearable as molten hot lava courses through me, making me come so hard as I cry out his name.

His grin presses against my pussy as he spreads me open again and licks all my juices running down to my ass. His tongue briefly licks into my puckered hole, his tongue ring hitting the rim and then swiftly moving up and over my clit with a final slurp.

The need to taste him is so overwhelming that I sit up and push him onto his back. Then I drag his boxers off and sit on my haunches to stare at the beautiful specimen in front of me. His body is like a work of art as I run my fingers over his pecs and then down between the ridges of his abs. I close my fist around his cock and revel as my fingers don't meet. His velvet skin is hot as I pump him slowly, and his guttural groan spurs me on, so I lean over and lick the bead of pre-cum off the tip.

"Shit!" he hisses as I suck the tip into my mouth.

His salty cum coats my tongue as I take him deeper, then begin a slow rhythm, working my jaw to acclimatize to his size. My saliva pools as I release it to slide down his cock, working it into my hand. His cock jerks and he taps my shoulder to let me know he's about to come. I pull back and quickly jack him off as he lets go, his cock squirting hot ropes of cum onto his stomach.

I pump the last of his seed out as it pools between his abs. My eyes eat up every inch of him until I reach his face, his features completely blissed-out, arms sprawled on either side, and his eyes closed. I run my finger through his cum and drag it across his abs. He's still out of it, so I crawl up his body, careful not to press into his mess, and sit on his thighs to stare down at him. He's so beautiful.

"Simmmbaaaaa," I say in the worst Rafiki impression as I drag my cum finger across his forehead.

He looks shocked as his eyes snap open to look up at me.

"Did you just baptize me on top of Pride Rock?"

I tilt my head to the ceiling and stretch my arms out wide as I sing, "Naaaaants ignoyamaaaa baga ichi baaaa baaaaaa," in a poor rendition of the opening credits of *The Lion King*.

He's laughing and pushing me off him, then he gets up and prods to the bathroom.

"I clearly need a shower. Thanks, Rafiki." His naked ass disappears into the bathroom, my body alighting again with arousal, but instead of following behind him, my eyes begin to grow heavy as I curl into his pillows.

I'm woken up when he crawls in beside me and wraps me up in his arms, his mouth hitting my neck as he drags his blanket over us. "I should check on Adri. I'm supposed to be sleeping at her house tonight." My voice is hoarse and filled with exhaustion.

"I checked already. Her and Travis were doing some questionable shit on my couch. I gave them the guest room," he confesses into my neck as I gasp.

"Like sex?" I hiss with surprise and try to look at him over my shoulder.

"Pretty close. I've seen enough of Travis' dick to know he wasn't as blessed as me." He shrugs as he presses the evidence into my ass.

"Oh, stop." I nudge him with my shoulder. "I felt it earlier. It wasn't bad at all."

"Careful," he warns as we both drift off.

Chapter Fifteen

I wake up less hungover than last time and turn to find Vin snoring softly beside me. This is new to me, waking up naked beside a guy I care about. I desperately need a shower and then I have to find Adri. I'd like to be home before my Uncle Scott to avoid him seeing me in a disheveled state.

I ease out of bed slowly, not wanting to disturb Sleeping Beauty, and head to his bathroom. His shower is pretty similar to mine, and his coconut bodywash is so fucking bomb. After my shower, I tiptoe into his closet and steal a pair of track pants, I have to roll them twice to fit, and then I grab a matching hoodie. Don't all girls take their boyfriend's hoodies? Is that what Vin is? My boyfriend?

I tiptoe back out to find Vin wrapped around the pillow I slept on and I smile as I creep over to the bed. I can't resist putting my lips on him and he groans when I kiss his cheek.

"You're leaving," he rasps. I thought his regular rasp set my blood to boil, but his morning rasp makes me want to strip and ride him until I'm spent.

"I need to get home before my uncle." I kiss his neck, unable to pull myself away.

"You smell like me," he mumbles as he fists the front of his hoodie to pull me in closer.

"I borrowed your shower and some clothes," I confess as his lips meet mine in a sweet kiss.

"Okay, baby. Call me later." I kiss his cheek once more when he releases his hold on me, and I stand up to gaze down at him for another minute. *He's mine.* He suddenly reaches out, grabbing my hand to stop me from leaving, his eyes finally opening. "I'll come by after your classes today. We can confront your aunt together. I'll bring my mother and we'll question them both."

Tears sting my eyes as I say, "Okay." He squeezes my hand before releasing it to turn back into my pillow. Fuck, my heart clenches so hard as I watch him breathe in the scent of me before drifting back off to sleep.

I start my way down to the main floor, looking for Adri. Luckily, I don't have to look far because she and Travis are sitting at the island with cups of coffee. I'm pretty sure I just came from the scent alone.

"Thank you, Mom and Dad." I sigh while grabbing a cup. "Can you adopt me?"

"Sure thing, E," Travis answers as he finishes his and pours another cup.

I study them closer at the tone of his voice. Adri is in her outfit from last night still, obviously. She also looks a little sad, and Travis is sipping his coffee. These two clearly still have some issues they need to work out, but I can't be involved anymore because I love them both.

"I'll drop you girls off at home," Travis says, breaking the silence.

"Sure, thanks." I nod and leave my empty mug in the sink.

The ride to my house is quiet, the air surrounding us thick with tension. I don't know exactly what happened between them last night, but I don't think it was as good as mine and the thought makes me sad. We pull into my driveway, and I rush inside to grab Adri's bags. When I bring them back out, her eyes are swimming in tears and Travis has his jaw clenched tight.

"Everything okay?" I ask, running my fingers through her hair.

"Yeah, I'll call you later." She sniffs and looks down at her hands in her lap.

"Okay. Bye, Travis." I bend to look in at him as he stares straight ahead, his eyes narrowed.

"See ya, E." Then he pulls away quickly as if he can't stand to be in such a confined space with her any longer than necessary.

Uncle Scott walks in the door just as I'm leaving for the gym and my first teaching class. "Knock 'em dead, baby girl." He stops with his hands out and a worried look on his face. "Not like actual dead. You know what I mean, right?" I chuckle and throw up deuces as I walk out, his worried mumbles making me laugh out loud.

When I arrive at the gym, it looks busier than usual, and a lot of familiar faces surround me. Quite a few Precious Blood students signed up for my class and I'm excited to get started. I decided to bring a little bit of my former coach with me to class today and teach everyone the first lesson I learned with Juan. A great fighter understands the anatomy and its limitations before learning to fight. Andrew meets me in the locker room, his giddy excitement a little annoying as he drones on about how this is his biggest turnout. Again, I smile him off and continue to tape my hands. I'm wearing my hot pink grappling gloves today, a parting gift from Juan.

"Ember, I spoke to our sister gym in Toronto and told them about you. They sent their best fighter here to help you teach the class."

"Help? I don't need help, Andrew." I stop taping my hands to look up at him, my eyes narrowing. "Why wasn't this discussed with me?"

"I was thinking it could be more like a demonstration." He holds his hands out to placate me, trying to diffuse the situation.

"He's a fighter?" I ask, my brow tipping upward as I finish taping my hands.

"Yes, and their best." Hmm… that might not be such a bad idea. Maybe he would actually fight me and I could drain this energy that's only been building since I moved here. I let it go, only for the prospect of a good fight.

Entering the gym a few minutes later, I find Danny standing to the side of the full room with a huge smile on his face as he waves at me. I grin and shake my head, moving to the front so I can address everyone.

"Hey! Thanks for giving this class a shot. As most of you know, my name is Ember and I have been training and competing in MMA for almost twelve years. Today is your first class, and to excel in this sport you need to understand your own body. My coach first taught me that a great fighter learns the anatomy and its limitations before learning to fight. Today will not be about any complicated takedowns. You won't be fighting for a while. We will start off with the jab first."

I quickly go over stance and proper body form, then show them the simple jab and have them work on it for fifteen minutes. That's when I notice someone watching at the back of the room. He's average height and not bulky with muscle. He has long hair pulled back into a man bun and his face has black scruff to match his ink-black hair. His taped hands tell me he's a fighter, and the arrogant smirk on his face tells me he thinks he's good. If I had never met Vin, I might think he was attractive.

He strides to the front of the class and stands next to me, his eyes still sweeping over me with curiosity. "My name is Cain. You're Ember, right?" I nod, a brusque dip of my chin. "You're younger than I thought."

"What does my age have to do with anything?" I straighten and turn to face him. Trained fighter or not, they all hit the floor with the same sound. If he wants to continue to belittle me, I'll have to demonstrate exactly what I mean.

"It's hard enough to fight a woman, but you're just a girl," he further explains, his face filled with worry.

"Nice. How old are you?" I sneer as I take in his face.

"Twenty-two." He folds his arms over his chest, making his muscles bunch with the motion, as if to prove he's that much bigger with age.

"You're not that old." I chuckle as I dismiss him and turn back to the class.

When he's figured out he's being truly ignored, he asks, "What are you teaching them next?"

"Roundhouse kick," I tell him begrudgingly as my eyes stay focused on the class. If he didn't want to help me out because I'm a girl, then why is he still here?

He starts back toward where he was standing before as I go through the demonstration of the roundhouse kick. The class begins repeating the move as I make my way around the room, helping them all with proper form and giving praise when deserved. For the final fifteen minutes of class, we use the jab and roundhouse kick in sequence, a first impression of what it would look like in a fight. Class goes by quickly, and when I dismiss them, a feeling of accomplishment comes over me. Juan would be proud of me.

I have a twenty-minute break until my next class, so I pop in my EarPods and chill out to my playlist. I'm lying across the mat with my arms crossed behind my head—deep into "Sicko Mode" by Travis Scott—when a tap hits my elbow. Annoyance hits me until I look up into my favorite pair of green eyes, and my heart automatically gallops through my chest and warmth spreads through my face. My hand curls around the back of his neck as I pull his face to mine. Now that I've finally kissed Vin, there's no way I'll be able to restrain myself in his presence. His lips are soft and warm and the slight scruff on his upper lip and chin deliciously scratches my cheek. I open my mouth beneath his and tentatively run my tongue across his lips. He opens, immediately letting me in, and I run my tongue along his, flicking his tongue ring. His groan reverberates through me as his hand grabs my hip. I forget where we are and I no longer care if we're alone or not. I want him *now*. He pulls back and I let loose a grunt of frustration as his mouth twitches with his gorgeous grin.

He pulls out a pod from my ear and lifts his eyebrow. "We have other people in here." I look over his shoulder to find Adri standing to the side of the doorway and leaning against the wall beside her is Travis.

I pull up to a sitting position and try to shake off the lust claiming every cell in my body. "What are you guys doing here?"

"We're here to learn how to be badass!" Adri exclaims as she steps forward, her hands fisted in front of her as she punches the air. Honestly, not bad form.

Vin laughs at the look of confusion on my face as Shay walks into the room and leans on the wall next to Travis. "We're here for the class, E," Travis explains.

"Oh, really?" I grin, my eyes on Shay. I wonder if she would let me do a demonstration on her today.

"Yeah, I'm mostly here to see if you're actually any good." Shay shrugs, sounding like the snobby bitch she is.

"You didn't see her take out two grown men," Vin says under his breath as he looks down at me with pride.

"What's that?" Shay asks, her head tilted to the side.

"Nothing," I answer quickly, getting to my feet as more people file into the gym. "Let's start with some warm-ups."

I go through the routine like the first class, and just like that one, Cain is leaning against the wall, watching me closely. About five minutes before the class is done, Andrew strolls in with a huge smile on his face.

"Hey, everyone!" he calls out as he claps his hands. "I

have a special treat for you all today. Ember here has agreed to show you a demonstration with a fellow fighter from another gym. Everyone, this is Cain." His hand extends toward Cain, who starts walking toward the front of the class, a look of smug arrogance lining his features.

"Some people stayed from the first class to see this because we've never had MMA fighters here in Whitsborough before," he continues. "I will turn over the center room to them. If you guys could move back against the walls, please."

Andrew walks out into the hallway and back in with mouth guards and headgear. I take a mouth guard but decline the headgear because I can't sense my surroundings properly with one on. Cain does the same and we walk out to the center of the room and onto the thick blue mats.

"We don't have to do this," Cain insists. "There's no pressure."

"I'm fine." I stretch out my arms and drop into a defensive stance.

"Listen, I don't understand why Andrew didn't ask for a girl." He holds out his hands as concern saturates his features, and I straighten up again. "I don't make it a thing to fight girls." Irritation courses through me the more he makes me sound like I'm being forced to be a victim.

"I'm fine," I repeat. "If you want to back out, call it." I grin at him around my mouth guard. He looks around the room and at everyone's attention on him. If he does call it, he could say he doesn't want to fight a girl, and it would be accepted, but I need this fight. "I mean, if you're scared about having your ass handed to you by a girl, I get it." A few snickers rise throughout the room as Cain's jaw begins to tic. No man likes to be called a pussy. He drops down into his stance and my blood sings with the prospect of a real fight as everything around me fades.

We circle each other a bit and right away he reaches in and grabs my neck with one hand. It's the typical grab for the beginning of any fight in the ring. I could do a few maneuvers to make him release me, but since he is stronger than me, I need the element of surprise. So, I go for a variation of the duck under. Instead of using my hand to push the arm holding my neck, I look away from him and use my forearm to slam it into his. The strength of my shoulder forces his head and shoulders down. Then I quickly move to his side and keep his shoulder tight to mine. He's struggling a bit, but I'm quick. I push my palms together, bring my knee behind his, and buckle it. I drop his back easily to the floor and continue to keep my palms tight together. He swings his leg toward my head, so I roll backwards and flip back up to my feet.

We circle each other again, and when he goes in for another neck grab, I quickly shove his hand away, chop my hand into his elbow crease then slam it into his solar plexus. He loses his breath from the force and his eyes widen as I quickly flip into a handstand, swing my legs around his neck, and pull him down. I squeeze my thighs around his throat, cutting off his air supply and forcing him to tap out. Then I flip back up to my side of the mat as the noises filter back in around me. A few claps sound as well as a, "That's my girl."

"Fuck!!" he screams as he gets back up. His eyes shine with anger as he shakes out his hands, his mouth dipping deep into a frown.

We begin to circle again, but this time he plays it dirtier by catching me off guard with a punch to my eyebrow. As soon as I feel the impact, I know it's split open. The piece of shit knew I was keeping it clean, and he chose to up the ante. A commotion sounds from the left side of the room and I know it's Vin struggling to get to me. When Cain tries to punch me again, I drop to my knees and use my momentum to slide between his legs. Then I come up behind him, quickly jab him once in the kidney and again on the back of his knee. As he's falling to his knees, I stand up and roundhouse kick him in the back of the head. He spins and lands on his back with a loud *whoosh* as the air rushes from his lungs. He's out cold.

"And that, ladies and gentlemen, is how important the jabs and roundhouses that you learned today are." The room begins to cloud with red as the blood drips down into my eye and

I reach up to swipe it off my brow.

"Get the fuck off me!" Vin grits out, and I look over to where Travis and a few other guys are straining to hold him back.

"Let him go." I nod to them.

He rushes over, pulling his shirt off and pressing it to my brow. "When that piece of shit wakes up, it's my turn," he grounds out, his voice full of menace.

"Vin, this is normal. Actually, it was a pretty tame fight." I push his shirt off my face and grin up at him. My insides sing with relief as the dark cloud that was gathering inside of me retreats.

Vin leads me back to the locker room and showers area, then gently guides me down to sit on a bench. He goes to the bathroom and comes back with a first aid kit and pulls out some alcohol spray and gauze, then cleans my wound. The way he's fussing over me has me swooning on the bench.

"I've never been so angry in my entire life. Not even my father makes me this murderous," he mumbles as he continues to clean me up.

"Vin, I've had a lot worse. I've fought multiple men at once. I've been jumped and nearly sexually assaulted... more times than I can count." He applies some butterfly bandages while I close my eyes. "I've had a gun to my head, been sliced with knives, and was even chained to a train track, but I've gotten myself out of every single situation nearly unscathed."

"Nearly," he spits out. "That's why you have these." He's touching my knife scars on my stomach below my sports bra.

"Yeah." I look him in the eyes. "And these." I point out more on my arms.

"Why were you in those situations? What were you doing?" He sits beside me on the bench as I begin to pull off the tape on my hands. There's no point in keeping my past from him, not if we want a proper shot at a future.

"I became well-known around the Bronx for being a kid who liked to fight and was good at it. Especially because I was a girl. I was approached and asked to fight in some organized matches, but these weren't legal. The money was good, three times the amount I'd make in a legal fight, but those illegal fights brought me to the attention of a local gang. My best friend, Tommy, was a part of them at the time and he vouched to take care of me. My mother and I were struggling, scraping together pennies to make ends meet, so I took the position with the goal to move us out of the projects. They recruited me to be their muscle, someone to teach certain people a lesson for missed payments or missing goods. The fact that I was a girl? Even better because everyone would underestimate me.

"My mother worked two jobs at the time just to keep up with the rent in our shitty one-room apartment. So I started saving, and one day I handed her twenty grand. She knew I was into shady shit, but she turned a blind eye so we could have a better life. I'd come home busted up with cracked ribs and deep cuts. She would patch me up and pretend everything was okay, because it meant we would be getting out of our situation soon. I think she believed once we were out of the projects, I would also stop what I was doing, but that didn't happen.

"The leader of the gang, Raphael, had been in prison for fifteen years for drug and gun trafficking charges. So I never met him, and according to many people, I wouldn't want to. The night my mother died, I had a fight lined up, and I wasn't home when it happened. That's why I live with so much guilt." I pound my fist to my chest as I suck in a long breath. Vin leans in to wrap an arm around my shoulders, his touch making the memories more bearable. "She was home, probably cooking me dinner when the gas leak happened. Maybe if I was with her, we'd have gone out for dinner instead. She wouldn't have had to light that stove. I don't remember much about those first few moments of seeing our house in flames, but I do remember trying to save her. I ran inside, not caring about the heat, but I passed out from the smoke before I reached the kitchen. I couldn't save her." My words end on a sob as tears begin to fall from my eyes.

The grief I had been so carefully packing away is leaking out, the confines I built threatening to buckle.

"Baby,"—he wipes my tears—"that was not your fault. How were you supposed to know?" He presses a sweet kiss to my forehead, and I wrap my arms around him before burying my face in his neck, his scent soothing my very soul as I pack the grief all away again, strengthening those walls. I can't give in to the tidal wave of sorrow, not yet. There's no time to lose myself in grief.

"Is that who's been following you? This gang?" he asks as he tips his head back to look at me. "Those guys you took out at school?"

I nod and grip him tighter to me, hauling him back in. My stomach tightens as fear suddenly runs through me. I won't let our connection turn him into a target and I will protect him with everything I have.

"Do you want me to take you home? I can pick up my car later." His words brush along the top of my head as his chin rests against my hair. I have never been so content in someone's arms and the thought of having to leave his comfort is daunting.

"Okay." I pull back and grab up the tape I discarded on the floor.

"Do you still want to question your aunt and my mother? They're both at your house. My mom said she was on her way over before I came here." I look down at the floor as more apprehension swirls in my stomach. It's been months since I moved here and I'm still without answers. Each day I have more questions, and even though my aunt has at least some of the answers, I've been too afraid to push her. I don't want to lose the only family I have left.

"I should get it over with." I let out my breath on a quick exhale. I would rather take on a roomful of fighters than to cause my parents any stress.

Vin leads me out to Travis and Adri, and it takes me a few minutes to convince them that I'm okay. Luckily for Cain, he left before Vin set eyes on him, otherwise, there would probably be more bloodshed. We leave the gym and head back to my house as my stomach knots tighter. We enter the house, and the ladies are in the kitchen laughing. I can bet money they've popped a bottle of wine too. Vin grabs my hand and we walk toward the sound, and in my other hand, I have the picture of our parents.

"Ember! What the hell happened?!" My aunt rushes to me, checking my split brow as worry colors her features. "I thought you were teaching a class, not fighting!"

"Andrew set up a fight to entice people to come to the next class." I pull her hands off my face and tip a shoulder.

Sharla stands from her chair and comes closer to take a look at my face, her mouth dropping open in shock.

"I'm going to tell Scott to give him an earful!" Aunt Debbie shrieks as she turns to grab her phone off the counter.

"Aunt Deb, she's okay, trust me," Vin says, placating her as he takes her phone away. "You should see the other guy, knocked out cold."

"Ugh!" she grunts with irritation. "I hate this fighting stuff!" Her eyes well up with tears as my frustration snaps into place.

"Know what I hate?" I ask, my voice calm but the tone deadly. "Secrets."

"Pardon?" she asks, her eyes wide as she steps back.

"Can we please sit down and talk?" I motion to the table, waiting until Sharla and my aunt take their seats, then I sit at the table with Vin sitting to my right. Sharla's eyebrow quirks when her son grabs my hand. "Who's Ray?" I ask his mother as I lean on the table.

"I don't know any—" she begins, only to be cut off by Vin.

"No lying, Mother. You promised me a while ago you

would never lie to me again. So, let's start from the beginning. Who is Ray?" he reiterates, his words brokering no argument.

Aunt Deb drops her face into her hands as her body begins to tremble. It takes everything in me not to rise from my seat and take her in my arms. I just need the answers she's hiding.

"Ray was Rebecca's boyfriend," Sharla admits as she looks at Aunt Debbie, whose face pops up from her hands. Then she looks at me, finding my pleading face as she deflates.

"Our family believed he was who she ran off with," my aunt adds.

Chapter Sixteen

"Ran off with?" I repeat as my brows crash together, and Vin's hand tightens around mine.

"Rebecca was dating Ray when she left home," Aunt Deb clarifies as she scrubs her hand down her face. "At least, I think they were dating."

"Is he my father?"

"We're not sure…" my aunt says at the same time Sharla says, "I think so."

"I think I look like him." I push the picture to the center of the table and keep an eye on both of their reactions.

Both women gasp as Sharla picks it up and turns the photo over, looking at her writing. "Where did you get this?" she asks, her eyes flicking up to Vin.

"I found it in a box in the basement," Vin answers honestly. "I think Ember should find her dad."

"You don't want to be here?" My aunt's voice trembles as her hand covers her mouth.

"That's not it. I love you and Uncle Scott, but I've never known my father. I would like the chance to meet him." I reach across the table to grab her hand. "I'm not leaving."

"I must warn you," Sharla begins, her eyes still on the photo as they fill with tears. "From what I can remember of Ray, he was not a good person. He was a hothead, fighting anyone who looked at your mother, male or female. He just had a dark side to him that, truthfully, scared me." Exactly what I always thought. This darkness inside me comes from my father. At least now I have that answer. "I begged your mother to leave him, but she was smitten. He was older than her by nine years, I believe. He ran with a rough crowd here and I think drugs were involved. When she left, it was to be with him."

"Our parents refused to accept him. He was twenty-six to her seventeen, and they just weren't comfortable with their relationship. They were constantly at odds about her going out with him." Aunt Deb sniffs as her eyes flick to the photo in Sharla's hand. "I believe it drove her to run away."

"If they left and ended up in New York, that would be where I would start looking." Sharla nods and places the photo on the table. "I wish I could tell you more, but when Becca left, she never tried to contact me again." Her chin trembles as sadness fills her eyes. "I missed her so much."

"I should ask my friend, Tommy, if he recognizes him," I mumble as I look at Vin.

"That's a start." Vin runs his knuckles down my cheek. "We could do a weekend in New York as well."

"Your uncle and I will come with you. That man was dangerous," Aunt Debbie says, her tone hard and unyielding.

"What's going on here?" Sharla asks, her finger swinging back and forth between Vin and me.

"Don't worry, I'll make sure you receive the wedding invitation," Vin deadpans as my heart stutters in my chest.

I roll my eyes and look at him. There's no hint of humor, just a straight face. I clear my throat and rise from my seat. "I'm going to go shower."

Once I'm inside my room, I immediately hit the shower. I wonder if my father has any idea I exist. If he does, what's hindering him from finding me? Or why doesn't he want to find me? I remember as a kid, I was always asking my mother where my daddy was because other kids at school had daddies, and I just had her. She never once gave me a proper answer. The last time I asked about him, I was twelve years old, and she flew off the handle, breaking at least six plates as she raged around the house. After that, I let it go out of fear of triggering her. It was finally clear to me she would never tell me anything and my asking was only causing problems between us.

Stepping out of the shower into a steamy bathroom, I check out my newest injury and deem it no big deal. I move to my closet and pull on yoga pants and a sports bra when the click of my bedroom door closing makes me pause. I quickly finish dressing before reentering my bedroom and nearly drop to my knees at what's in front of me.

Vin is lounging on my bed, his pants opened and slowly stroking himself. His eyes meet mine and his lips curve upward as he squeezes the tip of his cock, the ring through the top glinting under the light in my bedroom.

I lean against the wall and cross my arms over my chest as I watch the show. "Need a hand?"

"I need your pussy, actually." The things that come out of this man's mouth. His words instantly make me wet and I clench my thighs to fight the urge to join him.

"I can't fuck you while our parents are downstairs," I husk out as I bite my bottom lip.

"Your uncle warned me about the one rule on my way up here." He continues to stroke his cock as it jerks in his hand, the sight making my mouth water.

"Doesn't mean you can't come in my mouth." I push off the wall and walk toward the bed.

His movements speed up and his breathing becomes

labored as my body moves of its own accord. I crawl up my bed and over his body, running my hands over his jean-clad legs. His face falls slack from pleasure and I have an overwhelming need to taste him. I suck one of his balls into my mouth while teasing the other with my hand, then I move up and suck him straight to the back of my throat. I need to make this quick before our parents wonder what we're doing. I continue bobbing and taking him as deep as I can, gagging each time.

He slips his hands into my hair, directing my movements and pulling slightly on the strands. With one final deep stroke, he groans and comes inside my mouth as his cum coats my tongue. His salty essence slips down my throat and I clean off every drop before I roll over and stand up by the bed.

"Come back, I want to taste you too." He reaches for me as I grab a sweater from my dresser and pull it on over my head.

"Vin, we can't. They're right downstairs. Let's go before they come to find out what we're doing." I snap my fingers for him to hurry and tuck himself away before I do give in to the urge and have us both grounded for life.

"Fine, fine," he groans and pulls up his pants before getting off my bed.

Both my aunt and Sharla are still in the kitchen when we go back downstairs, but they're definitely more subdued than usual. The sports channel sounds from the family room, and relief hits me instantly. Uncle Scott feels like the safer bet right now, so we head in there. He's stretched out on the couch with a beer in hand as he turns to watch us come in. Vin takes a seat on the couch at the other end of Uncle Scott.

"Hey lovebirds, when's the wedding?" His grin is contagious, and I feel my own pulling at my lips in reply.

"After college," Vin answers almost immediately, reversing my grin into a frown at the sudden date, making this conversation feel less joking.

I shake my head and ignore them as I curl myself up on the one-seater chair to zone out for a bit. After years of suppressing the need to find my father, I'm nervous to suddenly be this close to meeting him. What scares me the most is the fact that he may not be a good person, and in all honesty, I think I've always been prepared for that based on who I am at my core.

Sure, I love the stage and acting out a role, to step into another character and experience life through different lenses is amazing, but the feel of flesh crushing beneath my knuckles and the warmth of blood as it runs along my skin? No comparison.

"I heard you're looking for Ray?" Uncle Scott's question pulls me from my thoughts as I straighten in the chair to face him.

"Yeah, I think he's my father," I confess with a wince when his face falls.

"For your sake, I hope he's not." His honesty has always been appreciated, but right now, it's burning my insides.

"He's that bad, huh?" I look down at my hands as they twist in my lap.

"I met him briefly." My eyes land on him once more as he puts his beer bottle aside and leans toward me as he speaks. "I was younger than your mother, so I didn't really hang out with that crowd. Ray had this violent undercurrent, like his eyes always looked as though he was plotting something nefarious." He runs a hand down his face as he exhales a long breath. "Even I can admit though, you look like him. Obviously, not the nefarious gleam in your eyes, but you do have that violent edge and it looks like you had a bit of it today." He points to my brow.

"Yeah, I know," I admit. "I always wondered why I was so different from my mother." All three of us fall into silence until Sharla comes around the corner a few minutes later.

"Ready?" she asks Vin as she squeezes his shoulder.

"Yeah." He nods, then gets up from his seat and saunters over to me, bending and placing his hands on the arms of my chair. "We have rehearsal tomorrow. Bring your script."

"Okay," I breathe out as he kisses me lightly on the

cheek.

"Good night," he rasps into my ear as my core pulses with desire.

"Night," I croak past the lump in my throat.

"Good night," Sharla says as she looks at me, her features saturated with melancholy.

Her expression is a reflection of my insides as I sink back into that pool of contemplation. What if I meet this man and I regret it for the rest of my life? Should I push aside the compulsion to find him when I have the perfect family here in front of me?

The next week of school goes by quickly. It's been so busy between rehearsal and schoolwork that I haven't spoken much to my aunt, nor have I sent Tommy the picture of Ray. The whole search for my father has stalled for the moment and I'm thankful for the time it's giving me to think it all through.

The play, though? It's going to be amazing. Britney as an understudy is not ideal. I certainly wouldn't accept food or drink from her for fear of poisoning, but the comfortable atmosphere in that theater and the comradery of this small group is what I love most.

For Clara's loss of virginity scene—yes, that's what we're calling it—Danny has made an actual bed that rotates on a lazy Susan design. So, for this scene, Vin lies on top of me and the bed rotates around a few turns. We stop at the back of the stage and music plays through the speakers while we act out the deed. It's sensual and tasteful, nothing pornographic.

We have one more week of rehearsals before we do dress rehearsals. Then it's costumes and props and late nights until everything is perfect. I don't open myself to love many things, but when I do, I love them with my entire being. The stage is one of those things. Another one? This green-eyed masterpiece whose heart makes mine whole. The word soulmates used to make me laugh. How can there be just two people meant for each other in this entire world? With Vin, I believe it, and with him in my life, my future looks so much brighter than it ever did before.

"Want to chill tonight?" Vin asks me as he drives toward my house. It's eight on a Friday evening and all I want to do is sleep.

"I want to,"—I run my hand over his locs—"but I'm so tired and we have to be back in that theater at seven tomorrow morning."

"Yeah, I know. This time of year, we don't get much sleep," he admits, his sentence punctuated with a yawn.

"Can we reschedule for tomorrow night?" I yawn in reply and we both laugh as he pulls into my driveway.

"Of course." He leans over and presses a kiss to my temple, the gentle, velvet touch of his lips hauling a soft moan from mine. My heart soars as I turn to kiss him, then quickly pull away to open the door. There's going to come a moment when he and I won't be able to hold back, and I really don't want it to be in the front seat of his Hummer.

"Good night!" I sing out to him as he chuckles, knowing exactly why I'm rushing.

"Night, love," he says quietly. There goes my heart again, speeding up and making breathing difficult. We haven't said it to each other yet, not counting my drunken whisper at his party, but it lives inside me. I know Vin loves me. Adri and Travis are constantly telling me how he's changed since I've shown up here in Whitsborough.

The house is quiet when I enter because my parents are out to dinner. Uncle Scott texted me earlier to say they wouldn't be home until later. A hot bubble bath in my claw-foot is needed as I make my way upstairs, my body heavy with exhaustion.

My bath is filled and I'm down to my bra and yoga pants

when a beeping sounds from downstairs. I pull on my robe and follow the noise to find it's coming from Uncle Scott's office. I open the door and the noise brings me to the monitors behind the bookcase.

I flip open the case and look at the screen that's blinking red with an alarm. It's the view of the backyard and two men, dressed in all black, looking in through one set of patio doors. Good thing they are tinted to see only out and not in. My vision pulses with red as my body thrums with anger. They must know that a house this large has an alarm system, and at that exact moment, one guy looks up at the camera. Half of his face is covered with a balaclava, and his eyes are dark orbs of depravity. He slowly points to his eyes, then back to the camera like he knows he's being watched.

I'm watching you.

The message is for me, and I know it's from Raphael. The men move out of view of the camera and onto the screen for the driveway. They casually saunter away like they weren't just trespassing. My phone begins to ring upstairs and I automatically know my aunt and uncle were alerted.

Running up the stairs, I grab the phone from my sweater pocket. "Hello?" I huff.

"Ember?!" My aunt sounds frantic, her voice pitched to ear-piercing.

"Yeah, hey." I try to sound calm, hoping she brings her anxiety down a few notches.

"The cameras alerted our phones. Looks like a couple of guys were on the property, but they've left. We are on our way home now. Are you okay?" Her words rush together as the acceleration of their car filters through in the background.

"Yeah, I'm fine. I saw them on the screens. Should I call the cops?" I begin to pace my room, needing to exert some of the energy pooling inside of me. The Rampage has found me and they're making it known.

"We're going to call the cops to report it. From now

on, the gates have to remain closed when you get home." Uncle Scott's voice rings through the phone.

"Got it. Gates closed," I repeat.

"Okay, see you soon." Aunt Debbie hangs up.

I need to make a few things clear to the Rampage and getting a message to Raphael will only be possible through Tommy. I can also send him the picture of Ray and find out if he recognizes him as well.

I drain my bath since it's long past cold now and have a quick shower instead. When I step out of the bathroom, the sounds of my parents' voices filter up to my bedroom. If the Rampage are here to confront me or threaten me, then I will have to meet them head-on. If they think they can put their hands on my family, there will be no stopping the darkness and I will become the very thing I've been fighting to avoid.

Maybe Tommy knows something of what's going on, and if not, maybe I can beg him to feel around for some answers. I pull out my phone to call him, but it rings a few times before going to voicemail, so I leave him a quick one, asking him to call me back. In the meantime, I upload the picture of Ray to my phone and send it to him in a text.

Me: Know this guy?

After getting dressed, I slip my phone into my sweater pocket, not wanting to miss a call or text from Tommy, and go downstairs. I find my aunt and uncle in the office, scanning over the footage on the multiple screens.

"There!" Aunt Debbie exclaims. "He's looking right at the camera and warning us. Who are these people, Scott?"

"Looks like a couple of thieves, hoping you two were out and they could run off with one of your theater-sized TVs." They both turn to look at me and I let the grin fall from my face.

They look worried, and even though having goons sneaking around the place I'm living at is not new to me, it's certainly new to them. This is not the life they're accustomed to. "I think they were harmless. If they wanted to come in, they would've."

"As long as you're okay," Uncle Scott breathes out as he leans back in his seat. "They must've noticed the cameras and decided it wasn't worth it."

"Robberies in Whitsborough just don't happen," Aunt Debbie mutters as they rewind the footage and zoom in on the masked guy. "Does he look familiar?"

"No," Uncle Scott says as he leans in. "They could be from Toronto."

My phone pings in my pocket and my heart slams against my rib cage as I head back upstairs. I really hope Tommy recognizes Ray, but also doesn't. Is it wrong to hope the man everyone here knew as trouble has changed? Maybe he has a family of his own somewhere in New York and I have siblings. I close my bedroom door and pull out my phone, instantly peeved and happy all at once. Tommy hasn't even read my message yet, but Vin texted me.

Vin: Hey, baby. Am I picking u up tmr morning?

Me: Sure. Scam ur Momma's coffee.

Vin: Will do

I make it an early night since I have to be up at the crack of dawn for rehearsal, but it's hard to shut my brain off when it's firing on all pistons. I need to figure out how to get the Eastside Rampage off my ass and away from my new family.

The cast is sitting in the theater, all of us looking like something close to death. I've already guzzled my coffee and stole Vin's. After a night of tossing and turning, I need the extra fuel to jump-start my brain.

Our Saturday rehearsals are purely for students only. Vin—being student drama president—has the key to the theater. So today is a skeleton crew of stagehands, including Danny, Lance, and the actors needed for the next few scenes we are perfecting, which is basically me, Vin, and Bitchney.

We are doing the Clara virginity scene today and the aftermath. Two scenes, one of which I am in a bed with a topless Vin. *Hold on, it gets better.* I'm wearing boy-cut shorts and a tube top, so a bunch of skin on skin, meaning a certain type of hell for me. Since the party at Vin's house, I've been a mess of bones and horniness. Speaking of bones, I really want his bone—

"Ember!" Vin yells from the stage, startling me out of my thoughts.

"What?!" I yell back as his eyes narrow on me in frustration. *How dare he interrupt my daydream?*

"Let's start." His eyebrow raises and those delectable dimples make an appearance. I want to sit on those dimples so badly. I take my time to swallow down the rest of his coffee as he stands on stage, wearing a pair of basketball shorts and a scowl.

"Ember… today?" Shit, it's going to be a rough day. I make my way up to the stage so we can begin.

We're on our fifteenth take for this scene, and I am a hot mess. The blanket is a thick, down-filled thing, and Lance has asked Vin to remove his shorts and just be in his boxers. He says it looks better, more believable. *For whom, Lance?! Huh? For whom?!* I don't know how much more I can take of his hard length pressing into me. My shorts are thin, and I can feel everything. Every. Inch.

"Action!" Danny hollers, and the bed starts its slow rotation. This time though, as we round the back of the stage, Vin tugs down my shorts as his locs create a dark curtain around our heads.

"Vin!" I whisper harshly as I reach to grab the fabric, but they're already down to my ankles. My heart quickens with the prospect of being caught and the excitement of doing this in front of an audience.

"Baby, kick them off." His finger runs through my soaked slit. "Trust me." His touch has all my common sense fleeing, and I do as he says. By the time we round back toward the front, I'm completely naked from the waist down with Vin between my legs. We've been here before and I know dealing with blue ovaries again will drive me insane.

"Nice guys!" Lance screams out. *You bet your ass it's nice, Lance.* "Hey, Vin! Can you lower yourself more and place your face next to hers? Or better yet, in her neck."

Vin chuckles and does as he's told while removing his cock from his boxers to stroke himself, pressing the head against my clit each time. The idea of everyone being here and watching but not knowing amps up my arousal as we start our second of three rotations toward the back.

"Ready, baby?" he whispers in my ear. *Ready? Ready for what?*

I don't have time to ask him as he slams into me, his hand covering my mouth in time for my muffled scream. My eyes widen as my hands dig into the mattress I'm lying on. The stretch is teetering on the edge of pain, but the feel of his cock filling me so perfectly has my pussy clenching around him. He grunts as he pulls out a bit, only to push more of himself inside of me.

"Relax for me, baby. Let me in." We're at the back of the stage again, completely out of sight, as I try to relax with a large inhale. My pussy finally takes all of him as he pushes in to the hilt, his piercing dragging along my walls.

"Fuck," we both mutter at the same time.

"You're so tight and so fucking wet," he says as he slides

his hands under my ass and tilts my pelvis up toward him, then he pulls out slowly to slam back in. The sound of my juices gushing around his cock hits my ears as his eyes roll into the back of his head.

The music picks up tempo as we begin our rotation back to the front with Vin pumping shallow thrusts into me, dragging his piercing across my clit each time. My whimpering increases as I'm nearing my orgasm, my pussy pulsing as he reaches between us to press his thumb to my clit. He moves his thumb and pulls up my right leg before slamming into me again, then stays there as we slowly move across the front of the stage.

I pulse and clench around him and he groans, burying his face in my neck and clamping my skin between his teeth. I'm so close to that edge, the pressure of it trying to push me over. I just need him to *move*.

"Nice, guys!" Lance exclaims. "This one is so believable. Hey, Vin, maybe for this rotation you could kiss her."

Of course it's believable. I have his balls resting against my asshole, it can't get any more believable than this. I muffle my groan against Vin's shoulder as he shakes with his weakening restraint, and his smoldering eyes meet mine. Then he leans down for a sweet kiss and uses the movement to press into me farther, his pelvic bone dragging along my clit.

"Perfect! Danny, pull the curtains now! This will be the end of act one!" Lance calls.

We're turning to the back, and as soon as the curtain obstructs their view of us, Vin is pounding into me at a punishing rate. His hand clamps around my mouth at the same moment my pussy clamps around his dick, and I find myself soaring into that oblivion. I'm no longer inside the theater of my high school as my boyfriend fucks me senseless. Instead, I'm drifting through a cloud of bliss as my body quakes with the force. The waves of pleasure heighten each time his piercing hits that sensitive spot, and his groan fills my ear soon after as his warmth shoots inside me.

The bed stops moving as I finally come back down to

Earth and look into Vin's eyes. Our chests are heaving with the aftermath of our bodies' explosion, and he pulls out of me to grab my shorts from the end of the bed.

"Let's go clean up, baby," he whispers before kissing my head. Then he helps me pull my shorts on.

My legs are like putty as I force myself to stand and follow him to the back dressing room. Vin leaves me standing in the center of the room, tired and slightly sore, as he locks the door. Then he gets on his knees in front of me and pulls down my shorts as he grabs a hand towel off the vanity and lifts my leg to rest my foot on his shoulder.

"Watching my cum leak out of you makes me want to fuck you all over again." His mouth is so fucking filthy. I moan and push my pussy closer to his face. He looks up into my eyes, and I can only guess he senses my assent because he gets up and flips me around, bending me over his vanity, the mirror in front of my face. Vin grins as he runs two fingers up my slit, collecting our leaking fluids, then drags it up to my rear opening and smears it around my virgin hole. I clench and draw myself away by instinct, the touch foreign to me.

"Shh," he says, bringing me back toward him. "Anyone been back here before?" I shake my head as he brings more of our combined fluids to the hole, then slips a finger in. I grunt with the pressure, dropping my chin to my chest as pleasure blooms. "One day soon, I will be back here," he promises as he pumps his finger in and out. "Your pretty pussy is crying with my cum. Do you feel it running down your leg?" *Oh, God. I'm ready to explode again.* "Not yet," he demands as my pussy clenches, withdrawing his fingers.

The head of his cock presses against my soaking pussy, then slides inside, filling me up to the brim and more. He grabs my leg and lifts it up to rest on the stool in front of the vanity, opening me up farther for him to push in even more. I thought he was in deep the first time, but I was so fucking wrong. The discomfort of this new position quickly fades as the feeling of having him so deep becomes enjoyable. "Let's see how much more of my cum this pussy can take," he grunts out as he picks up the rhythm.

My moans become loud and fervent as our combined fluids drop to the floor. His filthy mouth and the feel of him stretching me has me teetering over the edge quickly, and when I come, a rush of fluid runs down my legs. Shock courses through me as he meets my eyes in the mirror. That's never happened before.

"Did I just make my baby squirt?" he asks as he bites down on my shoulder. The combined pain and his words stretch my orgasm even longer, my legs threatening to drop me where I am. Vin grips my waist and continues to pound into me, chasing his own orgasm while the sounds of my dripping pussy reverberate off the walls. He finally lets out the sexiest, huskiest groan, and more of his cum is running down my leg as he curls around my back, holding me to him until our breathing evens out. "I love you, Em," he breathes into my neck, and my heart fucking soars.

"I love you too, Vin."

"Yeah?" He looks at me in the mirror, his smile so wide as his eyes glisten.

"Yeah." I nod and wince when he pulls out of me, the sudden ache between my legs has me groaning as I straighten.

"I know. I heard you say it at my party," he confesses as I look at him with shock. He's known how I've been feeling this whole time. It's a relief tangled with annoyance because it would've been nice to know before now. He cleans me up gently and then we dress. I'm so languid I can barely move, and the thought of snuggling in my bed and watching some Netflix sounds so good right now.

The next week rushes by with a mix of rehearsals, school, and constant sex. I'm not exaggerating. In his car, in the dressing rooms, and behind the stage curtains. We are insatiable and it's a blessing my aunt made sure I started birth control. Even Adri is complaining about seeing me only in the mornings and briefly at lunch. Once I explained how Vin and I had taken it to the next level, her face lit up with joy.

"Enjoy that dick, girl." She crashed her fist into mine with pride.

Oh, enjoy it, I did.

Chapter Seventeen

"Em! Hurry! We're going to be late!" Vin yells from the bottom of the stairs. This evening is our last dress rehearsal and then our first showing is tomorrow evening.

"I'm coming!" I'm quickly throwing my hair up into a messy bun when my door opens.

"You're not coming… yet, but if you don't get downstairs now, I will make you come and we'll be even later."

He's a fucking machine, that's the only way I can describe him. His dick must be filled with batteries because he's like the fucking Energizer Bunny.

"My vagina is so angry with you! She's going to fall off," I grit through my teeth as I turn to find his shocked face.

"Seriously?" His eyes widen. "She's hurting?"

"She's sore, yes." I roll my eyes at his concern as he hauls me into his warm body, his arms wrapping around my waist. "Give her a few hours to recoup and maybe an ice pack."

"I'm sorry, baby," Vin breathes into my hair and then pulls back to look down at me. "I suppose we can wait a few hours." He grins as he strokes his hard-on through his sweatpants. *See? A fucking machine!*

"Ugh!" I grab his hand and drag him behind me back out of my room. "Let's go, Energizer."

"Energizer?"

"Yeah, like the fucking bunny," I retort as we go downstairs and outside to Vin's Hummer.

We have a two-hour rehearsal tonight, then Lisa says she's turning her back on the later festivities. Apparently, the drama club has an annual tradition of throwing a modest party in the theater. Vin says the cast and crew shows up, sometimes with a few friends, but it remains intimate. They usually sit around, have a few drinks, and jam out to music. It sounds awesome and I've already invited both Travis and Adri. Tonight, I have plans to make these brothers interact because they're going to need each other more than ever. Doctors have completed testing on their father and he has stage four pancreatic cancer, not a good prognosis. I want Travis to have a brother to rely on when times are rough and Vin would make a great pillar of strength.

My stress level is through the roof, and I need this distraction because I haven't heard anything back from Tommy. I'm worried about him, and it's not like I can just pop by his foster home to find out what's going on. To top it all off, I have Eastside goons tracking my movements.

Our last dress rehearsal goes smoothly and this time my shorts stay on. Great news for my sore vagina, bad news for Vin's raging monster. I don't think we'll ever be in that bed without him being like a steel rod, it flatters and scares me all at once. Trust me, I love his penis and the sex—I've never had such great sex before—but he's intense and my lady bits are in a permanent state of ouch. She's also a floozy who perks up whenever the beanstalk is close by.

I ask Vin to swing by Adri's to pick her up because it's our tradition to get ready together for every party and this one is no different.

"My bitch!" she squeals, coming down her driveway.

"My ho!" I squeal back, hopping out of the Hummer.

We collide in a heap of arms and legs as Vin's laughter rumbles from inside the Hummer. I don't think I've ever been this happy in my life, and even though a shot of guilt hits me in the chest, I know my mother would agree. I was never given the chance to just be a kid, to go to parties, or scream into the arms of my best friend. All of this is too good to be true.

Adri slides into the backseat as her eyes meet Vin's in the rearview mirror and her voice drops a few octaves to mutter, "Vincent."

"Hey, Adri. I like the new pink highlights," he responds, and we both look at him with shocked expressions. "What? I do. They suit her." He shrugs.

She squeals again and throws her arms around him and the driver's seat, gripping him in a fierce hug. "My Vin is back."

He awkwardly pats her arm and gives me a sidelong look. "I'm trying to let shit go. I've been getting good advice from my girl."

She sits back with a smile on her face as we pull out of her driveway, and I link my hand with his. He looks at me softly and I mouth a thank you. It's a good start. Now I can only hope things go as well with his brother.

Vin drops us off, making us promise to be ready in an hour. *So not happening.* We walk inside, finding my aunt and uncle in the kitchen, and whatever they've made smells divine. The hunger in our stomachs rumbles, forcing us to head to the kitchen instead of my room. Vin's going to be extra pissed.

"Girls! Aunt Debbie made beef sliders!" Uncle Scott exclaims in greeting.

"Hey, baby girl." My aunt kisses my cheek. "Have some food. Hello, Adrianna! Gosh, your hair looks fantastic!" Aunt Debbie grabs some of Adri's new pink-highlighted hair in her hand to get a closer look.

"Thank you, Aunt Debbie." Adri beams.

We devour some food with the family, both of us being lectured on alcohol and drugs before the party and I once again soak it all in. My mother worked too much to lecture me about safety, and in all honesty, she probably thought I could teach her a thing or two. It's nice to have people care about where I'm going and who I'm seeing.

Finally, I'm seated in front of my vanity, doing my hair and makeup while Adri changes behind me, using my fancy mirror to check all her angles. We do our makeup, both in nudes, and I take my hair out of the rollers, leaving it big and bouncy.

"Em!" *Shit, the beanstalk is here.* Tell me why my floozy pussy is perking up? *Bitch, simmer down and relax.*

"Yeah! We're almost done!" I yell back and rush to pull on the dress Adri picked out for me.

"He just walks into your house screaming for you?" Adri laughs as she gives herself another once-over in the mirror.

"Pretty much," I huff.

Vin is chilling with my aunt in the kitchen when we eventually go downstairs. She's feeding him sliders while his raspy laugh has me gripping the doorframe. Will I always be this obsessed with him?

"Hey!" I call out when I catch my bearings and walk into the kitchen. "She's married, you know?"

"Unfortunately." He pouts as he stuffs the rest of his food into his mouth and gets up from his chair.

"You kids have fun tonight. Your uncle and I are so excited to see the performance tomorrow!" Aunt Debbie exclaims, then smiles as tears collect in her eyes. "We're so proud of you both."

I open my mouth to thank her, but it's not enough. "Aunt and Uncle is such a mouthful to say. How about we try Ma and Dad? I had a mom, so I hope you don't mind Ma?" I ramble a bit to get it all out as Vin wraps an arm around my waist. "I know my adoption has been finalized."

Aunt Debbie cries—full-out sobbing—as Uncle Scott and Adri run into the kitchen with worried expressions on their faces. I want to go to her, but I'm stunned by my own tears as they begin to slide down my cheeks. I now have two loving parents who would do anything for me, they deserve to be called as such. "What is it?" Uncle Scott's panicky voice cuts through the emotion.

"Ember wants to call us Ma and Dad," she forces out between hiccups as Adri gasps from the doorway.

"Ember,"—Uncle Scott turns to gather me in his arms—"we would be so incredibly honored." He wraps me up in a hug as his calming scent washes over me.

"We better get going." I hug them both then turn to grab Vin's hand. "See you later, Ma and Dad."

"I never thought I'd hear that," Ma says to Dad as we move to the front door. It'll take some getting used to, but it feels right.

We pull up to the school and go through the exterior entrance into the theater. Danny pulled his magic with the ambient lighting and its glow is low and soft. The stage is set up with tables of different alcohol and snacks as everyone chills around the theater. A commotion at the entrance behind us grabs our attention and I turn to find Shay arguing with a drama student.

"What's going on?" I ask Vin as he gently shoulders between me and Adri to head toward the door.

"Probably Marlana and her crew wanting in. They've come every other year," he explains in passing. "I'll go tell them to get lost."

"Let them in. More entertainment, the better." He turns to look at me over his shoulder, his brows cinched together in confusion.

"I don't understand women," he mutters as he walks toward the door.

"Tonight just got interesting." Adri rubs her hands together as her face brims with excitement.

"Why?"

Vin crowds the doorway, his wide frame blocking Shay from my view.

"Because that bitch has been here every year with Vin. You think she's going to enjoy seeing you in her place?" Adri cackles as I roll my eyes. You would think Marlana would get over it already. It's been months since she's had anything to do with Vin, but then I put myself in her place and groan. I would be the same fucking way.

I shrug and drag Adri over to the alcohol. I just want to drink and chill out, even if it means dealing with some extra drama tonight. Flamingo Head can try her darnedest, but I won't let her get to me. Adri and I take three consecutive shots of tequila, then grab a beer each.

"Oh, wow!" Adri breathes out, her voice filled with shock. "This should be good."

I turn around while I'm sipping my beer only to see the brightest, most obnoxious shade of purple hair. I choke and end up spraying my beer across the stage. "Shit!" I grab some napkins off the table and start wiping the beer off the stage floor.

"That looks about right where you belong." Her whiny voice is like nails on a chalkboard and no amount of counting will stop me from kicking her fucking ass if she keeps it up.

"Listen, you eggplant-looking, radish-eating, Teletubby." Adri sprays her beer too. *Fucking great.* The stage is going to be sticky for our play tomorrow. "Watch your fucking mouth before I decide to really fuck you up."

Marlana's face breaks out into splotches of red as everyone—including her own crew—laughs at my slam on her hair. I've been tame with her for the past few months even though she's tried to sabotage me at every turn. My patience has run out and I won't back down anymore.

"Honestly, the first day I saw you, I knew you would mess everything up. I knew you would screw up my life," she grinds through her teeth as her eyes shine with unshed tears.

I stand up, towering over her on the stage. "You made those choices. Blame yourself."

"You'll get yours, Emberlise," she sneers out my full name as she fists her hands at her sides. Then Eggplant scoffs and walks off, snapping her fingers at her crew of dogs to follow. They do, all except Shay who starts walking up the stairs to the stage.

"Shay!" Anal Ram screams out. "Get over here!"

"I'm good." She waves her off with a shake of her head. "I'm going to chill here."

Marlana halts in her tracks and studies Shay as she comes to stand with us on the stage. Her mouth tightens into a thin line as she narrows her eyes on me before storming off to the back of the theater with the rest of her crew.

"It was never this bad," Shay explains. "Since you moved here and Vin showed interest, she's become unhinged. I love some drama, but I'm warning you, Ember, she has something planned."

"I'm not worried," I say honestly with a shrug. "If Marlana wants to start a war, then she better be willing to get a little dirty." I down the rest of my beer as the band begins to play a song.

"So, welcome to the dark side." Adri holds out her arms to Shay and they embrace. While Adrianna may be a tad too far on the welcoming side, I don't stop her from talking to Shay. My eyes skip back to Marlana in the corner as she leans in to whisper to her friend, her eyes on me the entire time. I can't bring myself to trust Shay completely because this could all be a ploy to put someone inside enemy lines.

My body begins to sway with the beat of the song as the tequila finally warms through my system. I no longer care about the purple-headed menace or the fact that Shay and Adri are giggling while taking more shots. There are only two things occupying my mind right now, one is moving my body in time with the bass and the second is leaning over the first row seats, his green eyes riveted on my form. I close my eyes and let myself get lost in the music, and too soon it's over. I turn to find Adri, but I'm suddenly picked up, bridal style, and moved briskly to a dressing room I know all too well. He kicks the door shut behind him and places me in front of the vanity.

"You know what to do," he growls, undoing his pants. "Leave the shoes on."

My dress falls to the floor, and he groans at my bare skin underneath. His pants and boxers fall to his thighs and his pierced cock stands proudly. I *do* know what to do. I bend over the stool, placing my hands on the vanity top, and spread my legs. "Give me what's mine," I husk smugly. He doesn't keep me waiting and lines himself up to slam into me. The intense burn catches my breath, and he stalls as I drop my chin to my chest with a pained exhale.

"Baby?" His hand wraps around my throat, pulling my face up so we can meet eye to eye in the mirror.

"Just take it slow. Let me adjust." I press back into him, forcing another inch to slide inside me.

He pulls out slowly, then pushes back in with his hand still around my throat and the other playing with my clit. Soon, the pain fades to a dull ache and I'm slick with my juices as pleasure takes over. My moans begin to rattle the mirror in front of me, spurring him on to pick up the pace. His piercing drags along that sensitive spot inside me with each thrust and I free fall into the blanket of bliss as warm liquid runs between my legs.

"I'm getting good at making you squirt, huh?" His cocky grin meets me in the mirror as I struggle to lift my head. "This pussy loves her daddy, huh?" His words send aftershocks throughout my body, making my pussy clamp around him as he tips his face back on a groan, then his cum is warming my insides.

"Gonna be hard to walk." I wince as he pulls out of me,

the ache intensifying as my wet thighs stick together. Vin goes and gets a cloth and meticulously cleans between my legs before helping me back into my dress.

"Ember, I love you." He grasps my chin, forcing me to meet his eyes. Their depths shine with love, making every bit of soreness worth it.

"I love you." I smile and press a kiss to his cheek. Then I turn to smooth out my dress and notice the dressing room door is ajar. "Vin…"

"Yeah?" His zipper is the only noise in the now silent room.

"Didn't you close that door?" I point at it as my heart thunders through my chest.

"I kicked that shit shut." He stomps toward it and swings it open, finding no one on the other side, but that doesn't mean shit.

"Please tell me it could've bounced back open?" I groan as he comes back to me, a contemplative expression on his face.

"Maybe…" His uncertainty doesn't help the situation, but what else can we do about it? What's done is done and if someone got an eyeful of my man's cock plowing into me, well, I hope they have the decency to keep their mouths shut.

"Fuck it. Let's get back out there," I growl as he nods and throws his arm over my shoulder.

The rest of the night is spent in his arms as we dance to the band's renditions of current and old songs. I even spot Adri and Travis dancing a few times, sparking hope that they can work things out. I'm riding an impossible high, as if my body is suspended above everything as I watch my perfect life play out. I should be enjoying every minute, but there's a whisper of a premonition at the back of my mind, telling me nothing this good ever lasts.

Chapter Eighteen

It's performance night and my nerves are frayed. Not for the play, but because I still haven't heard from Tommy. By now, he would've gotten back to me, so there's one of two things that could've happened. One: they sent him on a scout mission to see what drug route the other gang is taking. Or two: something bad happened to him. If it happens to be option two, I'll have to figure out a way to get to New York to find out what's going on.

The school parking lot is filled with drama students as they all make their way inside and I park in my usual spot. Grabbing my bag of cosmetics and hair products, I get out of the car, turning when a horn blasts behind me. A familiar Hummer pulls into the spot beside Shelby and a grin automatically curves along my mouth. I can't see his face through the windshield because of the sun's glare, but I can feel his answering grin. He slowly gets out of the car and my breath catches in my throat. He has a black New York baseball cap on his head, and it's pulled down over his eyes. This may sound like nothing, but my man could never fit a cap over his luscious locs. He turns his back on me to reach in and grab his bag and I can see the fade on the back of his head.

He cut his hair off.

My stomach sinks with a surprising sadness as I realize I never had the chance to run my hands over them one last time.

He turns back to face me, lifting the hat off his head with a smirk on his face, showing me the fade leading up to short curls on top of his head. He's still so unbelievably gorgeous, but I loved those locs.

"Baby, what do you think?" he calls out to me.

I shrug in response, and for some odd reason, my eyes begin to well up. I take a deep breath and start counting down as he walks closer, and by the time he's standing in front of me, I've got a handle on my emotions.

"Why?" I ask, my voice shaking as I run my hand along the short hair on the back of his head.

"I have been twisting my hair for a long while. I needed a change, and I really just needed a fresh start. I don't know." He looks downward, and I can sense the insecurity pouring out of him. I'm such an asshole for my reaction.

"Hey." I grip his chin, forcing those beautiful eyes back to mine. "I love it. I loved your locs too, but this is nice." He nods but looks unconvinced, so I lift myself to my tippy-toes and wrap my arms around his neck. My reaction was something I should have controlled. Of course, he would be insecure with a new hairstyle after all these years and I was so fucking insensitive. I run both hands along his fade and his body racks with a shiver. "I love how you wanted a change and I find you so fucking sexy." I lean in beside his ear and whisper, "I can't wait to sit on your face, grip these curls in my fists, and ride it hard."

He groans and smothers his face into my neck, his hands sliding down over my ass as he pulls me in tight to him. His tongue glides up the column of my throat and dips into my ear, pulling a whimper of want from my mouth. He's working me up so I'm a puddle of need when we find ourselves in that bed inside a packed theater later. How will I convince him that fucking me in front of our parents and spectators is a bad idea when all I can think about is him making me sore all over again?

The curtains close on intermission as I roll out of the bed with Vin, feeling hot and unsatisfied. He grabs my hand and leads us back to our dressing room. It's not really ours, but we've shared and spilled bodily fluids in here, so we've claimed it.

"Ember," Vin says as he's closing the door. "Did you hear from Tommy?"

"No, I'm honestly getting a little pissed off. He's never left me hanging this long before." I sit in front of the vanity and pull out the ponytail in my hair. Act two of the play is darker and filled with melancholy, and Clara is more disheveled than she was in part one.

"Maybe we should take a trip to New York next weekend?" he asks as he comes to stand behind me, his hands rubbing into my shoulders. "All the sunshine and rainbows are done. Ready for the storm of part two?" He grins at me through the mirror and I answer him with one of my own.

"It's my favorite part," I confess as he leans down to kiss the top of my head. He gets called to the stage and blows me a kiss on his way out. I begin changing into my outfit for the next scene when my phone vibrates in my bag. I pull it out and see Tommy's name. *Finally!*

"You're alive, you dick," I growl into the phone.

"Blur... wat... you... whe... you?!" His voice is choppy as it cuts in and out through the speaker.

"Tommy, your piece of shit phone keeps cutting out. Move somewhere else and hurry. I need to get on stage."

"Emb... ple... go... ome!"

"What?!" I roll my eyes and grit my teeth with frustration. "You need to invest in a new phone. Text me, I have to go." I hang up the phone and drop it to the vanity as I finish getting dressed.

A knock sounds on the door a few minutes later. "Ember! You're up!"

"Coming!" My phone goes off again, but Tommy will just have to wait until after the final curtain. It's his turn to have patience.

An hour later, we do our final bows while the audience is going crazy. I finally spot my parents in the audience, and Ma is screaming with tears running down her cheeks as Dad waves and yells my name. Right there in the center aisle, three rows up from the front sits Travis between an older version of himself and a woman with a touch too much makeup on. Vin's eyes land on them and he clenches his jaw as he bows again, then abruptly leaves the stage. I get it. He feels ganged up on and it was wrong of Travis to bring that man here without warning Vin first. I don't care that the fucker is dying, because even though he's dying, he's still a fucker. I hurry after Vin as the curtains close for the last time tonight.

I enter the dressing room as he's throwing shit everywhere, his breathing erratic, and his body as tight as a bowstring with tension. "Let's just go." I kick shit aside to enter the room. "Change and let's get the fuck out of here. You don't have to face that shit, and I will break Travis' jaw tomorrow."

I'm whipping my costume everywhere and digging through the mess Vin made, looking for my clothes. I'm fuming too and wanting to punch holes in shit or people. Yes, I very much want to punch a few people in the face. Travis is such a little bitch for doing this because he has no idea what it's like to be ignored by his father for seventeen years of his life. He should have had some fucking decency.

I realize Vin isn't moving anymore and I turn around to find him watching me with wide eyes. "What?" I ask.

"You're not pissed at me for reacting like this?" His chest is heaving with the exertion as sweat runs down his brow.

"Fuck no!" I shake my head as I pull my sweater

on. "You should've been asked first if you wanted to see the deadbeat."

He inhales deeply and releases it, resting his hands on his waist as he looks around at the mess he made. His inner turmoil is saturating the air around us as I try to put myself in his position, but it's hard to imagine. I mean, if I somehow knew my father was out there in that theater, I'd be pissed as shit wondering why he'd want to see me now, but I would also want to talk to him and figure it all out. Plus, knowing the fact that there is a time limit on doing so would make it even more confusing.

"Tell me what you want us to do, baby." I move to stand in front of him, placing my hands on his stomach.

"Us?" he croaks out as his voice trembles with emotion.

"Yeah, us. For always, whenever you need me," I reassure him.

"I think I should at least look at him," he whispers, sounding like the scared little boy who feared his father's wrath.

"Okay." I nod.

"Will you come with me?" Just as his hand slips into mine to pull me in close, my phone vibrates on the vanity table.

"Yes, of course I will." I pick up my phone and slide it into my pocket, knowing it's Tommy, but he can wait. This is big for Vin, and I want to be there for him.

We finish getting dressed and tidy up the room a little. I'm nervous, not for me, but for Vin. His uncertainty clouds the room and it's funny how in tuned I've become to him. I can sense all his moods and feelings before he even voices them.

His hands reach for me, and I immediately sink into him. I would gladly give all my strength if that's what he needed. His phone vibrates in his pocket, making us pull apart so he can fish it out. "It's your parents," he says, reading the text. "They've been trying to get a hold of you. They're apparently standing with my parents and wanted to give us a heads-up."

"They're gems." I nod. Must be who was blowing up my phone too.

"Let's get it over with," he mutters, grabbing my hand.

He leads us out to the foyer in front of the theater doors where the school has set up a juice bar for mingling parents and teachers. I spot my parents and walk directly toward them, finding them standing with Sharla, who keeps looking around the room nervously. When she spots Vin and me, she rushes over.

"I had no idea he would come. He told me he wanted to see you but didn't mention this," she rambles as she wrings her hands against her chest.

"It's okay, Ma." Vin pulls her in for a quick one-armed hug, his other hand still firmly in mine. "I don't blame you."

"Okay," she says, visibly relaxing. "Do you want to leave?"

"Guys!" my dad booms, interrupting Sharla's question. "That was genuine talent up there. I've never been so proud in my life!"

I rush over to him and Ma and hug them both as their eyes fill with tears. They wear the same look of pride on their faces that my mother had at every show and the thought has tears trickling down my face as they both encase me in their arms.

"Your mother is here too," Ma says. "She's so proud of you."

"Thank you, guys." I sniff as I swipe the tears from my cheeks. "Sorry, I just realized it was my first show without her."

The guilt is eating at me. I've been so busy lately that I haven't given much thought to my mother. The only reason I've been functioning these last few months is because of my need to push down the grief I should've already dealt with. Instead, I tamp it back down. I can't let the grief consume me right now because I still have shit to do.

A throat clears near us and I lift my head from Dad's

chest. "Son." Travis' father steps forward, his face cold as if chiseled from stone and those green eyes blanketed in steel. There isn't an ounce of warmth emanating from this man.

Vin tenses, his jaw clenching. A sure sign of violence.

I move from my parents and stand directly at his side, curling my hand around his. He relaxes slightly and gives my hand a squeeze as I stare into the eyes of a monster. There's no doubt in my mind that this man made every decision concerning his sons, knowing what the outcome would be. It's only when his waning mortality slapped him in the face did he realize where he's headed when he dies.

"This must be your leading lady." He holds out his hand. "My name is Robert. I'm Vincent's—"

"I know who you are," I cut him off and ignore his hand.

We have a little stare down, and I smirk when I see a slight glimmer of anger running through his eyes. Robert is not the remorseful father he's portraying, and I think I might be putting a wrench in whatever plan he has.

He lets his hand drop and gives me a forced grin. "Right." Then he turns to Sharla and says, "Hello, Shar. You look stunning."

"Hello, Robert," she replies coolly as she steps closer to Vin.

"Scott and Deb." He nods to my parents. "This young lady must be your sister's daughter I've been hearing so much about."

"Yes," my dad replies as his jaw flexes, offering no more information.

"Dad," Travis says from behind his father. "We should get you home before you get too tired."

"Yes. Well, that's the plight of the terminally ill." He exhales. "Vincent, please come to dinner this week. We have much to discuss."

I want to roll my eyes, and it takes everything in me to remain still. Robert Greene is nothing like the man he's pretending to be, I can see right through him. When Vin doesn't answer, Travis grabs his dad's arm and leads him back to a beautiful older blonde. That must be Travis' mother. She gives a brief nod to Robert as he strides by her, who shrugs his arm out of Travis' hold.

My phone buzzes again in my pocket, and I release Vin's hand, pulling it out to see the screen. It's Tommy, and I know I can't ignore him further. "Hey, guys? It's Tommy. I'm just going to take this outside." Everyone nods while Vin and his mother are speaking in a heated whisper, so I don't interrupt and head outside.

"Hello?" I answer.

"Ember!" Tommy yells, the sound crashing into my eardrum.

"Yeah, sorry, I had a performance." I hold the phone a little ways away from my ear.

"I don't care!" he cuts me off, his voice frantic. *Rude.* "Where are you?!"

"At my school." I speak slowly, but a buzzing sounds in my ears as my heart picks up. Tommy is never this worked up. "What's going on?"

"You need to leave. Go home." I can hear the sound of a car's engine in the background. "I'm on my way. Fuck!"

"Tommy, chill out—"

"No!" he exclaims. "He's coming!"

"Who?" I begin to pace the entrance of my school as I look out over the filled parking lot.

"Raphael!"

"Let him." I stop pacing and shrug as a smile curves over my mouth. I could end his surveillance quicker face-to-face.

"No, listen!!" he screams, his voice cracking with the pitch.

"I am!"

"That picture you sent me," he's panting heavily. "That's Raphael."

My blood runs cold and I lose all feeling in my fingers as the numbness spreads upward. There's a pit growing heavy in my stomach as I let Tommy's words sink in. Is Raphael my father? Does he even know? It makes sense that my mother followed him to New York. He's a Kingpin there, after all.

"Ember!" Tommy pulls me back to the present.

"Yeah?" I croak out.

"You're in danger. This is why he was so obsessed with tailing you. He knew your mom!"

"Yeah." My voice begins to fade as the buzzing grows louder.

"What am I missing here? Why was he in a picture with your mom?"

"I think he's my father," I say hoarsely, my throat sealing as anxiety worms its way through my stomach.

"Holy shit…"

"Yeah," I whisper.

"Okay, listen. Get to your house and lock up everything. I'm on my way."

I nod and hang up the phone as I continue to stare out at the parking lot. Shit… everything is starting to make sense. I'm stuck, rooted in place by my disbelief. Why would my mother have anything to do with a gangbanger? She was good, sweet, and kind. It just doesn't make sense, but I know Tommy wouldn't mistake who Raphael was. He earns loyalty based on violence and terror, and his men absolutely fear him. He's cunning, ruthless, and from what I've heard, loves getting his hands bloody. His violence teeters on the fine line of psychotic and I'm now realizing where my darkness comes from.

A blacked-out sedan pulls into the parking lot, and I know—I just feel it—it's him. I still make no move to run. He'll get to me, regardless. I need to face this and protect the people I love from danger, and Raphael is the epitome of that.

The passenger side of the car stops in front of me, and the rear door opens, but still, I don't move a muscle and the inside is so pitch-black I see nothing. Finally, a face leans over and materializes through the darkness. His eyes are pools of tar, and his skin is like a rich terra-cotta, a few shades darker than mine.

His full top lip curls up into a sneer. "Hello, daughter." His voice is smooth, like soft velvet beneath the palm of your hand. When I don't answer him, his face transforms into a grin. "You are beautiful, sweetheart." My hands tighten into fists as the front driver and passenger doors open. The darkness is seeping in and the need to touch warm, satiny blood becomes unbearable. "Be careful, don't hurt her," my mobster father calls out as he retreats back inside the dark interior of the car.

"Yes, boys, do be careful." My voice isn't my own, and my vision blends in hues of red. Pure anger comes over me, feeling as hot as the sun itself.

The goon on the driver's side comes around hesitantly when he spots the look on my face, but the passenger side goon is a fucking idiot and only sees a young girl. He grabs my arm and tries to drag me to the rear side door. Big mistake. I catch him off guard when I pull him back toward me and quickly punch him in the nose. A spray of blood hits my face, making me smile as I soak in the violence. A dam is crumbling beneath the weight of my anger and there's no way I can hold it all in. While he's grabbing his nose, I give him a swift kick in the knee, hearing a crack. He's down and crying out in no time. I turn my sights on the driver as he puts his phone back into his pocket. That's when another two cars pull into the parking lot. They're both blacked-out sedans, the same as the one in front of me.

"Darling, as impressive as you are, I just want to talk. Get in the car."

I can't take on all the fucking goons and my family will come looking for me any minute now. I refuse to put them in the middle of this, so I nod and lower myself into the backseat as the driver closes my door and scrapes his passenger off the ground, taking him to another car.

"What do you want?" I ask, still vibrating with anger as I take in his coal-black hair and pristine suit.

"You're my daughter. Do I need to want something to see you?" he asks smoothly.

"It's been almost seventeen years." I scowl at him as he continues to stare at my face. I wonder if he recognizes himself reflected there.

"For fifteen of those, they locked me up," he spits out, his eyes blazing with the rage I imagine is simmering under his skin. Just like mine.

"Daddy goals," I reply, my words dripping with sarcasm.

"I'm sorry." I look at him with shock as he quickly puts a rag over my face. I try to react, but my muscles instantly become heavy. Then darkness quickly takes me under.

Chapter Nineteen

My head is pounding, the dark void slowly fading. How much did I drink last night? I try to remember the last thing I did and I'm met with a wall of fog. I groan and run my hand down my face, my eyes opening as the confusion hits me. Where the fuck am I? Nothing looks familiar in this room.

Sitting up, I do a quick scan around me, noticing there are no windows and absolutely no noise. Then everything floods back in stunning clarity, and I remember the play, seeing Vin's deadbeat dad, and then seeing my own deadbeat sperm donor.

That motherfucker drugged me!

He fucking drugged me!

I bolt up out of the bed and search my pockets, of course, my cell phone is missing. Where the fuck am I? And how long have I been out? My stomach growls incessantly and I realize it must have been a while. I move around the room, opening a door to find an empty closet painted all pink, which kind of reminds me of Marlana's head and it's the only bit of color in this entire room. Everything else is a stark, clinical white. The next door leads to a bathroom, thank God, because these people would have to deal with pee on the floor if there wasn't.

They locked the last door tight, meaning it must be the only way I have in and out of this hell. Why the fuck am I even locked up? *Get your shit together, Ember.* I start pounding on the steel slab, my knuckles singing with a delicious ache.

"Where the fuck am I?! Hello??!! Anyone there?"

No one answers, but someone must be standing right outside the door. Raphael wouldn't go through all this trouble just to have me escape. I continue pounding on the door for another five minutes until I realize there's no sound filtering in here. It's almost like this place is soundproofed.

I give up when my fists begin to throb and fall back on the bed. My family is probably going crazy. Vin is probably attempting to kill someone to find me, but I know it'll be impossible. None of them would ever make the connection to Raphael.

Tommy!

Yes! Tommy said he was on his way to my house. So he will find my parents and Vin and tell them who has me. I exhale with relief as I turn onto my side. Tommy will save me, he always does. I stare at the pink closet and listen to the grumbling in my stomach. How long have I been here? I have no natural light to judge time and no noise to tell me if people are awake. Though, I have a feeling we are back in New York in the underground base.

The Eastside Rampage has a bunker. It's not what you're thinking, it's not small. This compound spans the size of a shopping mall and it's all underground. I've heard it was an old army base before the Rampage claimed it.

I've been here many times because the fight ring is also located here. This is where I used to come once a week and beat the living shit out of men. Why am I here now? And why did Raphael bring me here? Obviously, my questions won't be answered until I see the deadbeat myself.

I don't know how long I've been lying here when the lock turns on the door. I raise my head as two men enter, their bodies wide and muscular. Rampagers through and through. One has a tray of food and the other has a gun trained on me.

"Really?" I snort and point at the gun.

"Here's your breakfast. Raph says to eat it all," the guy holding the tray says as he places it on the small desk in the corner.

"Well, Raph can go fuck himself," I snap, sitting up to watch them act like pussies in front of a teenage girl.

"Here's a change of clothes as well." The other one holding the gun throws a hoodie and track pants onto the bed, and then they both back out of the room, that gun still aimed at my face.

Fucking brainless minions.

I eat everything, because one: I can't be weak if I need to fight my way out of here, and two: I'm fucking starving. I finish the food and go inspect the clothing that was brought. I find a roll of tape in the hoodie pocket, bright pink, my signature color. So, he wants me to fight, and it also confirms I am indeed in the bunker.

I shower and change into the clothes, then tape up my hands. If the fucker wants me to fight, then I'll fight. The only fight he's witnessed of mine that I know of is the one from the night of the fire, and I really want him to see that I can rip his head off if I'm given the chance.

It doesn't take long for someone to come back, and when the door opens, it reveals the driver from the other night. Now that I see him up close, he looks vaguely familiar.

"How do I know you?" I ask as I stand from the bed, flexing my taped-up fists.

"I drove you here?" he says with a touch of sarcasm.

"I know that, but before then. You look familiar." I take a few steps closer to him and have to angle my face upward to look into his eyes. He's about six feet, a little taller, thick, muscled build with thick black hair. His skin tone is similar to mine, a light sepia that could become darker under the sun. His dark eyes narrow on mine, his thick lashes framing the scrutiny.

"I've seen you fight before, but I doubt you ever saw me," he finally replies as he pushes the door open further. He doesn't seem as scared as the others of me escaping, which means my chances of doing so under his guard will be slim.

"Why are you here?" I cross my arms over my chest, refusing to move an inch without answers.

"I'm here because I am the best at combat and *he* wants us to spar. You have a fight tonight." Raph sent him.

I nod because I've already figured this much out. Raphael wants me to fight, and I'd bet there's a lot of money on this, especially if he's made it known I'm his daughter. I wouldn't mind some sparring, I have a lot of pent-up anger I need to work through before I can ever hit the ring again. I can't get in there with emotions clouding my senses.

"What's your name?" I follow him out of the room, watching the way his shoulders bunch as his arms swing with his steps.

"Carmelo, but most call me Carm," he says over his shoulder. I look behind me to map exactly where I am and if I can potentially escape, but my room is at the end of a hall, the corridor ending abruptly by a concrete wall.

"Where are we going?" I turn back to find him watching me curiously, his face filled with a haughty expression.

"To the gym. I'm guessing you'll want to take some aggression out on me after yesterday." His chuckle reverberates around the corridor, the sound bouncing off the concrete walls as it tries to find its own escape.

"Something like that."

I follow him into the concrete gym and release an exhale when I find it empty. The thought of having a bunch of Rampage goons in here, ready to report everything back to Raph would've been a distraction. We warm up together to begin grappling and wrestling on the mat. It takes an hour to release all the wound-up aggression inside of me, and when I turn my head to look at Carm, I find him panting on his back as well.

"You're good," he grunts as he inhales deeply, his eyes on the ceiling.

"You are too," I admit as sweat rolls down my temple.

"Tonight, you're fighting a dirty cop on Raph's payroll. He's as big as me, but not fast. His hits though, are hard, so I would avoid his punch." He brings his hand to his chin, stroking his goatee. "He has a bum right knee. He was shot there about ten years ago."

"Why are you telling me this?" He turns to look at me, his eyes hardening as he takes in my sweaty face.

"Raph wants you to lose. He wants to damage your confidence so you will bend to his will." His jaw clenches with his admission and then he pushes up to his feet, his eyes avoiding mine.

"So? How does telling me this help you?" I sit up and begin to pull the tape off my hands.

"None of it helps me, but I'd hate to see that fighting spirit dim out." I nod my thanks and follow him as he leads me back to my room, neither of us speaking a word. When I get inside, I find another tray of food and a few more sets of clothing. The click of the door has me turning to realize I am once again alone.

I'm standing in a room located just off to the side of the cage and it's the size of my walk-in closet at home. I bounce on the balls of my feet as I wait for my name to be called. I've been here many times before, but this time is different. The energy is dark and foreboding, and my stomach is tight with apprehension. I've heard four sets called so far through the mic, so I'll be the fifth and last fight of the night. Showcase, that's what I am, the showcase. I was only the showcase one other time, and that was the night of the fire.

I'm still trying to figure out Carm in all this mess. I know for a fact he's familiar and I've seen him before, and I'm hoping I might convince him to help me out of here and not just in the ring. My music plays, "Bodies" by Drowning Pool, and I can hear some people screaming and cheering for Blur. The door opens, and I'm ushered out by three goons, because you know, I'm still a prisoner. I pull my hood up over my head and let it cover most of my face, hoping it hides the uncertainty in my eyes.

The guy I'm fighting is already in the ring, and Carm was right, they're about the same size. He's probably a little bigger than Carm though, and his face looks meaner. Stupid dirty cop. I can't wait to feel his blood coating my hands. His face morphs into excitement as I approach the cage, rubbing his hands together like he's in for a treat. So… dirty and likes to beat on young girls. Noted.

I step into the ring and pull off my sweater, revealing a simple pair of yoga pants and a sports bra, leaving my scars on display. The filthy asshole peruses my body like he's about to own it, and the rage inside me begins to boil as I close my eyes and lean against the cage. All the noise around me fades and I let the darkness consume me. I want this to be as enjoyable as possible and I really want to show good ole Dad just what he helped create.

"I have just learned we have a change in rules tonight, ladies and gentlemen." I open my eyes and look at the emcee. He's looking nervously back and forth from the corner of the room to the cage, and I follow his sight to find Raphael with Carm and a few other men. Father dearest is looking like a pig in shit with that grin on his face.

Once the crowd calms down, the emcee continues, "This showcase is going to be different from any other you have seen here in the cage before. Tonight, these two must fight… to the death!"

Are you fucking kidding me?

I'm not a murderer. I've come close to killing people, but I've always drawn the line. I school my features because this pig across from me gets off on girls' fear, I can just see it as he hungrily looks over my face. There's no doubt in my mind that this man will kill me and enjoy it, so I need to pull up my big girl pants and kill this motherfucker first. This isn't a problem because I know every way to kill someone with my bare hands, but it doesn't mean I ever wanted to put them to use.

The emcee is counting down as the pig begins to circle the cage. I close my eyes and concentrate on my breathing, timing my inhales with each number counted. My eyes fly open as his lumbering feet run my way and I stand my ground, letting him throw a punch. At the last second, I twist my body and his fist just skims my nose. Carm was right, his punch is powerful. I grab his forearm, using his momentum, then pull him into the cage, face-first, and punch him hard in the ear. He screeches, and I watch with lust as blood trickles out. He must be hearing a lot of ringing, so I take advantage of his disorientation and punch him in the throat. The crunch of his trachea is so satisfying.

The pig gags, then growls with frustration and starts throwing punches all over the place without focus. I back up just beyond his arms' reach and circle him.

"I am going to kill you, you little bitch." His declaration has my stomach tightening as I let the hot rage bubble through me, the burn hitting every muscle in my body.

I ignore him and concentrate on his weak points. Right now, his ear is bleeding, his throat probably feels on fire, and I remember the knee Carm told me about. Just as he tries to punch at me again, I drop to the mat and punch his right knee, the cartilage molding to my knuckles. He roars in pain then falls to his back, and I roll away as he scrambles to his knees, his breathing sounding a little wheezy. I take this moment to slap his chin with an uppercut, then back up as his back meets the mat again. While he struggles to his feet a second time, I plan my next move.

He turns to look at me with his hands on his knees and the motherfucker smiles with a mouthful of blood. I wait for his next move, and I don't have to wait long. He strikes out with his left hand, and I dodge, but I'm not quick enough to dodge his right as he grabs my throat. He gets a firm grip and uses both hands to squeeze. I send a quick prayer up to whoever is watching over me because Juan and I have gone over this scenario hundreds of times over the years. I let him continue to squeeze and let him enjoy himself for a minute before I go in.

He's so engrossed with his hands on my throat that he doesn't notice my leg coming up to slam into his balls. His eyes widen and he immediately drops his hands before vomiting on the mat. I pummel his face until the warmth of his blood and vomit are dripping off us both. Then, as he's on his knees wobbling back and forth, I step behind him and look my father in the eyes. My arms wrap around his neck and I push and pull at the same time until a loud crack permeates the air as his lifeless body hits the mat. *Dead.*

The noise of the crowd explodes back through me like chaos, and my name is being chanted like a reverent prayer. I grab my sweater off the floor and pull it on over the blood, snapping the hood down over my face. I just played God back there, and it weighs heavily on me. No matter how vile that man was, it wasn't my place to take him out. I wait patiently by the door for the goons to unlock it and lead me back to my room. I'm in desperate need of a shower and food.

When the cage door unlocks, I look up to find Carm. "Brutal," he says with a grin. "Not a scratch on you."

I shoulder past him and head toward my prison cell. Tommy needs to hurry and get here already. I'm afraid of what I will turn into if I'm here for too long.

Demix

Chapter Twenty

Two days pass as I stare the hours away at the ceiling. At least, I think it's been two days. I can't gauge time well in this prison cell, but I can make assumptions through meals, unless they're fucking with that as well. This is my second dinner tray that I've forced myself to eat since killing a man. I force myself because I know I will have to do it again. I'll have to stand in that cage and fight to the death. I've stopped praying for someone to save me and devised a plan of escape. Living with my aunt and uncle has made me grow soft because I began to rely on people to help me—save me. It's time to be the Ember I was before and be my own savior.

The food is similar to cardboard as I swallow it down with water, then I lay on my bed and wait. It shouldn't be much longer now if the previous days' schedule means anything. About an hour later, the key turns in the lock and I'm filled with trepidation but relieved all at once. I need to get out of this small room, but I'm dreading the anticipation I feel about doing it again.

"Let's go," Carm says into the room, his voice hard. I peel my eyes off the ceiling and look at him. When I haven't said anything for a few minutes, he comes in and closes the door behind him. "You have to do it. To survive, you have to do it. So please, get up and let's prepare."

"Why do you care?" My brows crash together as I fold my hands over my stomach, not moving an inch off the bed.

"Because, like I said, I don't want to see your fight dim." His jaw pulses with his aggravation as his eyes narrow on me.

"What difference does it make to you?" I sit up and tip my head, curiosity beating out my anger.

"Nothing I can explain right now. Let's go." I get up and follow him to the gym again, hoping to haul more information out of him. Then I tape my hands, pull my sweater off over my head, and wait. He observes me closely and nods when he's ready to go. We grapple, and today, I beat him more than he does me. The surprise in his features would be laughable if I could push back the darkness.

"Were you holding back before?" he asks, his hands on his knees as he sucks in a breath.

"No." I shrug, barely winded.

"Today is different," he says. "You're fighting differently."

"Last time, I thought I was just fighting in a cage. This time, I'll kill instead." My hands curl into fists at my sides as my heart pounds through my rib cage.

His chin lowers to his sweaty chest and droplets fall from his hair. I'm no longer fighting for show and submission. I'm fighting to kill or be killed. "Tonight is going to be easier. He's a rival gangbanger from Queens. His name is Fringe. I caught him pimping in our territory. Raph wants quick work of him. I don't know his weaknesses, but he hasn't been fed in a few days." I keep listening and reach for my sweater. We're done here. "Wait, can I give you some advice?" he asks, and I nod for him to continue. "Do what you have to do and then erase it. Don't dwell and don't obsess. It's survival, kid, and you're a soldier."

I nod again and wait for him to lead me back to my room

so I can prepare for my next kill.

I'm back in the shitty cramped room outside the cage, waiting for my name to be called once again. I have heard *Blur* being chanted throughout the night and realized I have gained more notoriety by draining a life with my bare hands.

Charming.

The familiar beat of "Bodies" filters through the wooden slab and I stand up, waiting for the door to be unlocked and me being escorted to the cage. It opens, revealing three large goons, and I follow them to the ring, hopping inside with a grin. There's no way in hell I would ever portray the turmoil racking my insides.

My opponent is a large man with pale skin and bright red hair. His face is almost completely covered in tattoos, save for his eyelids and lips. The strange thing is, they're flowers. Yeah, he has many brightly-colored flowers all over his face.

"For every girl I had to kill that stole or tried to run, I got a flower." He runs his finger over the skin of his face and fucking smirks. "I have room for one more," he reveals, pointing at a small open space by his jaw.

I pull my sweater off and shuck it to the corner, then I stand and wait for him to make the first move. I've effectively shut off my emotions and my vision bleeds into hues of red as he stalks toward me. The closer he gets, the wider his grin grows, but I don't move, not a muscle, as he reaches out to grab a handful of my hair. Everything becomes slow motion then as I determine his next moves. I quickly punch the inside of his elbow and move in, bringing myself almost flush with his body, then I stomp down on his foot as he brings his head down with a grunt. His arms encircle me as I rear my head back and smash it into his nose.

The spray of warm blood kisses the back of my neck, and I crouch to face him as his hands fly to his nose. Next, I swing my leg out and kick him off his feet, watching as his back slams into the mat with a loud *thud*. He's turning to get up on all fours when I kick him hard in the kidney and he screams as his back bows off the mat. Then I stomp my foot down on his solar plexus as he struggles to breathe. Standing over his torso with a foot on either side of him, I grab a fistful of his shirt, bringing him up to punch him twice in the temple, making him groggy.

My eyes flick up as I search the crowd for the man responsible for my actions. At the same moment we lock eyes, the heel of my hand connects with my opponent's nose, and it crunches then slides into his skull. He convulses as I watch transfixed when blood and mucus pool around his head. Soon, the seizing stops and he lies lifeless.

That's two on my tally now.

I walk to my sweater—unfazed by the deafening screams of triumph around me—and put it on, pulling my hood up to cover my face. I'm shaking with adrenaline and need to bring myself down with a quick jog in my cell or else my muscles will erupt in painful spasms.

The cage door opens and before I can step out, someone grabs my arm and drags me out of the area. I look up and see the back of Carm's head as he angrily stomps in front of me, forcing me to shuffle along, trying to keep up.

"Wait," I demand, pulling my hand back.

"What?" he snarls, his eyes flaring with anger.

"What is wrong with you?" I throw my arms out as the hood of my sweater falls, revealing my bloodied face. "I'm doing exactly what you told me to."

He releases a long exhale and looks around us before facing me. "How much more can you take?"

"I need the gym." I walk around him and head in that direction. "I need to run off this energy or I may very well kill you too."

"Fine," he grits through his teeth and follows me. "But if you try to run, I will kill you."

"Noted."

We get to the gym and Carm stands against the wall as I run out the adrenaline on a treadmill. He scrutinizes me for a while, then breaks the uncomfortable silence. "I used to be the one who would set up your targets." He scratches at his chin as our eyes clash. "Whoever you intimidated and battered for this gang came from me."

"Interesting," I drawl, my feet pounding into the belt.

"You were the ace up our sleeve. Not one of them knew what you were capable of until it was too late." He walks over to me. "You're his new toy and he won't let you go willingly."

"Already figured that out. Thanks"

"Even if you are his daughter." I turn off the machine and face him. So he knows I'm Raphael's daughter. The fact that more people are in on the knowledge of my parentage is a little disconcerting because I was hoping I would forget it all when I escaped. "He doesn't care about family. He cares only about loyalty." His face crumples with frustration. "Remember that. He will never view you as his daughter or be a loving father."

"I don't care. I'm not proving any loyalty to him. I'm killing these people—whether they are innocent or not—to save myself! I am killing to stay alive, not to prove some warped sense of loyalty!" I fume as I jump off the machine and get in his face.

"You don't get it." He shakes his head then drops his chin to his chest as his hands press to his waist. "He will kill family as well."

I don't answer him. I know Raphael will kill me if I don't comply, and that's why I am doing what I have to do to stay alive. Carm groans in frustration when I keep my mouth shut, and then he leads me back to my room. I'm not connecting the dots he's providing, and I just don't have the time to figure it out, along with deciding how the fuck I'm getting out of here.

"You could just help me escape," I suggest as I follow his brisk lead.

"Did you hear nothing?" He turns on me, his face a mask of anger. "He would kill me without batting an eye. You need to do what you have to do to survive? Well, so do I."

"You didn't choose to be a part of this mob? You were forced?" I ask sarcastically when he turns back around to stride toward my holding cell.

"Something like that," he snaps.

The conversation ends as we approach my room. He quickly unlocks the door and slams it behind me as soon as I clear the threshold, leaving me alone once again. I take a shower, change out of my bloody clothes, and lie on the bed. For the second time, I work to convince myself that I did what I had to. I try my best to be the soldier Carm told me to be and disconnect. It's been so hard not to think about my family, friends, and especially Vin. The shame I feel when I do is incapacitating, and I don't want them to find out the things I had to do here to survive. Vin's green eyes and cocky grin flits through my mind and my breath catches in my chest. I miss him. I miss him so fucking much. The first tear falls down my cheek as I try to count to ten. I can't lose it now, I need to hold it together a little while longer and try to get out of here before I have to kill again.

I've noticed a pattern with the fights. They happen every two days, which means I have roughly forty-eight hours to figure out how to escape this compound. It's obvious Carm won't help me, and my only other option are the goons either bringing my meals or escorting me to the cage. They rotate so I haven't had the same person twice and I realize it's keeping me from forming an alliance with any of them. My only constant is Carm, but how can I convince him? First, I need to get him here before the next fight. Maybe I'll convince him I need another workout to drain the tension before the next fight. It has to work.

The next morning, I wait on my bed for my breakfast to arrive. At least, I think it's morning, I can't be too sure. As soon as the key jingles in the lock, I sit up straighter. One guy enters with my tray and a second guy guards the door. This is my only chance.

"Hey," I begin. "You don't have to answer me. I just need you to tell Carm I need an extra workout session today."

The one holding the tray stares at me and assesses my face, so I keep it neutral and hope he doesn't see the distress hidden in my eyes. Finally, he nods and turns on his heel to leave, the door firmly locking behind him. Now I wait to see if this actually works.

Lunch rolls around, and two more goons show up to deliver the tray. I debate asking them as well, but then decide not to. I don't want to look too eager and alert them to my desperation.

Finally, about an hour after lunch, my door is unlocked and Carm walks in. He looks irritated with his jaw clenched tight. "You beckoned?" he sneers as his knuckles whiten with the grip he has on the door.

"I can't sleep." *Not a lie.* "And I can't get these images of blood out of my head. I need to run it off."

He stands in the doorway, studying me for a few minutes before finally agreeing with a nod. I hop up quickly and put on my hoodie before he changes his mind. "Let's go, Miss Torres." He opens the door wider.

"It's Craven," I snap as I brush by him.

"You're a Torres, regardless of what's on your birth certificate." His words hit the back of my head, making my stomach knot.

"I was raised a Craven—"

"I don't mean your name. I'm talking about the blood in your veins. Fuck, you're every bit a Torres. Look what you're capable of. Was your mother a fighter?" Nausea swirls as he forces me to face the monster inside of me. I don't answer him, and he hums to himself. I have tainted blood too. He's right, this darkness that runs through me—the part of me that loves to make someone bleed—is Torres through and through.

I'm running on the treadmill, trying to figure out how to break the silence and beg him to help me. He is my only hope, but I need him to form a connection with me to do it.

"I don't know who the next fight will be with," he says quietly from his perch at the wall. "It's all really hush-hush."

"Do you think he suspects you of telling me?" My feet thuds on the treadmill as I keep my breathing even.

"No." He drops his chin to his chest as his hand rubs at his temple. "I don't know. I just have a bad feeling."

"How much worse can it get? I'm taking lives when I don't want to, regardless of who it is." I swallow down the lump forming in my throat. This whole situation is crazy, and I miss home. I miss Whitsborough.

"It can always get worse. Trust me."

"I do," I say as I stop the machine and turn to look at him. "Trust you, that is."

"Don't be stupid," he snarls at me and pushes off the wall. "Don't trust anyone here."

"Too late. I know you don't want anything bad to happen to me." I step down off the treadmill to stand in front of him, my chest heaving with my breaths.

"I can't help you this time." He shrugs, his jaw pulsing with restrained emotion.

"You can get me out of here, Carm," I plead with him. "I have a mom and dad who are probably worried about me. I was starting my life over, being a regular teenager—"

"No, I can't," he cuts me off and scrubs his hand down his face. "I have a little brother and Raphael would kill him if he found out I helped you."

This changes everything. I don't want to put anybody else in danger because of me, especially a young kid. I will just have to escape during a meal drop-off.

"Don't fight your way out on a meal drop-off," he warns, watching me closely. What the actual fuck? Is this guy a fucking psychic? Did I say that shit out loud? He chuckles softly and punches my arm lightly. "It's what you were thinking, wasn't it? I mean, that's what I would do. They have orders to kill you if you try it. They are all packing heat."

"Fuck," I exhale. It's a lost cause. I'm stuck here murdering three people on average per week.

"You're not stuck here," he says, a sad smile forming on his mouth.

"Fucking stop, you creep!" I point in his face as he laughs, the sound mirthless.

"Gain his loyalty and he'll ease up. It won't be easy to convince him. I'm sure he'll stage something dramatic and something he knows you will have a hard time choosing him over, but if you want out, choose him."

Fuck, I don't like the sound of this. There are many new things in my life he could use against me. My new family, my boyfriend, and my best friends. Any of them and I would cave because I would always choose them, even over myself. I would always choose them over him.

"Let's go, Blur. You should rest before tomorrow. You're going in blind." His hand lands on my shoulder as I shudder out a breath. It's been a while since I've felt the weight of a sympathetic hand.

I follow him out of the gym and back to my cell, feeling alone and defeated. I can't use Carm to help me out of here, and I have at least twenty guns ready to take me out whenever I leave my prison room. It's time to fake my loyalty to my father.

"Is there any way you can get a message to him?" I ask as we head down the corridor.

"I can." He side-eyes me. "What do you want me to tell him?"

"I need to speak to him. I've killed two people for him, and he can't avoid me forever."

"Okay, I'll tell him a nicer version of that," he says with an eye roll. I walk into my room feeling every ounce of soreness and exhaustion, but sleep will not come easy, especially when it's plagued with blood and death. "Get some rest," he says while closing the door. "I'll come back tomorrow."

I fall on top of the bed and stare at the ceiling until the white becomes out of focus and my breathing levels out. Tomorrow, I will face someone unknown, and that leaves me with a heavy ball of dread in my stomach. I pray to God it's not any of my family or friends.

I'm awoken by the motion of my bed dipping at my feet. I sit up as straight as a bolt and curse myself for sleeping so deeply.

"You look so much like your mother when you sleep," Raphael says wistfully. I don't dare answer him. If he's here, then I need to listen to every word he says without interruption. "I loved your mother from the moment I laid eyes on her. She was pure and so good, her inner light blinded me." He shakes his head and runs his hand over the bedspread. "I grew up on the streets of New York. My family was poor until my father started to change things around for us. Soon I was watching some of the most powerful men bow down to my father and I knew I wanted that respect one day. I started making money at six, just delivering packages on my bike. As a teenager, I was selling dope on the corners until a good friend of mine introduced me to someone in Toronto, Canada. We kept in touch, and he moved our product there. I became high on the ladder here and worked my way to be the next in line to inherit the Eastside Rampage.

Prestigious, I know."

Not exactly what I was thinking, but whatever. He waves my silence to continue.

"I decided one day to take a trip to Toronto and see how my new friend was doing with the distribution, also to look for more potential business. His family lived in Whitsborough, and his younger brother had started at a high school called Precious Blood. Sound familiar?"

Again, I don't answer, but I stare at him expectantly. He grins at me and brushes a lock of hair out of my face, almost lovingly. The touch feels very much like a father's and it makes me long for my uncle who is more a father than this man will ever be.

"That day, when we picked his little brother up, I met the most beautiful girl I had ever seen. She looked like an angel and her laugh was like Heaven's bells. I was immediately in love. I had to have her. So I stayed and courted your mother. Soon she was just as in love with me as I was with her. It was also lucky that her best friend was dating my friend's little brother." My breath catches. He's talking about Robert. He studies my face closely and smiles. "Ahh, so you know Robbie. I hear he's dying these days, but he's been an amazing business partner after taking over for his brother many years ago. See, I had to kill his brother for skimming off the top. Business, you know?"

Fuck, Robert is in business with the Eastside Rampage.

Raphael continues, "I hear he's grooming a son to take over for him. I will have to check in on that. We can't have any loose ends when the old bastard kicks the bucket."

My mouth goes dry. *Travis*.

That motherfucker is grooming Travis.

"Your mother knew nothing about those things. I needed her to stay pure and light. She knew me as Ray and thought I was in Toronto to check out universities. Her parents hated me from the start. They saw through my ruse and tried to break us up, but it was too late. Within three months, your mother was pregnant.

I convinced her to come back to New York with me and not tell her parents about the baby. I told her they would make her abort or force adoption, and she was young and believed every word from my mouth. So she followed me. For the first year, I made sure she didn't work. I took care of her, and she became untraceable." He scratches his chin and carries on, "She got a hold of her parents one day. She was eight months pregnant and desperately missed her family. When they found out she was pregnant and living here with me, they wanted nothing to do with her. Disowned and forgotten. They broke her and she was distraught for the rest of her pregnancy. So naturally, I had them killed," he adds flippantly.

I lose all feeling in my face. If this is true, my grandparents knew about us and they turned their backs. They deliberately kept the information from Aunt Debbie. I'm not so remorseful about their deaths, but it's becoming clearer just how much of a monster the man who sired me is.

"When you were born, my world shifted. A baby girl who looked so much like the woman I adored with eyes like the clearest ocean. You were beautiful and already so full of fire. I knew you would be strong and I spent every day with you for six months until my arrest." He gets up from the bed and starts pacing my small room. "I mean, they arrested me before. Most of the police force is on my payroll, so I wasn't worried. Then I quickly learned it wasn't the police, but the FBI. They had a solid informant, someone who could account for everything I did with proof to back up each accusation. So I went away, but I still had my connections and soon enough, I found out who that informant was. I was patient, my dear. I waited until they released me to strike. I want you to understand this: I will kill anyone who tries to get in my way."

I already knew this. That's why I need him to believe I won't get in the way. I just want to leave and live my own life with my family and friends.

"Who was the informant?" I ask as my throat works on a swallow.

He reaches my bedroom door and opens it slowly,

his back to me. The silence is deafening, and I instantly feel nauseous. His cold, empty eyes turn to look at me over his shoulder as he sneers, "Your mother."

Chapter Twenty-One

The room is destroyed as plaster dust coats the air around me.

I've punched over fifty holes in the walls and ripped everything I could apart.

He killed my mother.

The house fire deemed an accident wasn't a fucking accident.

My fists are a mess and bleeding. Blood is dripping everywhere and my voice is hoarse from screaming through my broken heart. I'm not leaving here until his blood is coating my skin. I am going to kill him and enjoy every second of it. He made a mistake telling me that. If he thought for one second I would be afraid and bend to his will, he was fucking wrong. I am a motherfucking Torres.

My door flies open, and I prepare myself for a fight until I see it's Carm. I don't relax though because fuck everyone here. I can't trust anyone. "What the fuck is going on?" he breathes out as he takes in the state of my room.

"Did you fucking know?" I seethe as my vision pulses in waves.

"Ember." His hands come up, placating me. "What happened?"

"My mother. Did you know?" His eyes widen a fraction before he schools his features and drops his hands. *He knew.*

"Yes," he answers honestly. "I knew."

"Leave," I grind out between my teeth as red begins to saturate through my eyesight. "Leave before I kill you."

"I tried to warn you that he doesn't care! He will kill anyone." My fists clench and blood begins dripping out even more from the multiple cuts. "Fine, I'm leaving." He drops his head and turns. "Clean yourself up. You have a fight in a few hours." Then he's gone.

I suddenly feel the urge to pray for whoever they put in that cage with me tonight because I am going to shred them apart.

My song hits the speakers and I stand, pumping my fists with the energy to kill another. The pain that shoots through them and up my arms reminds me of why I'm here. My bloodlust has become unbearable, and bones crushing beneath my knuckles will be the only relief I find.

The door swings open and I grin as I narrow my eyes on a full-grown beast of a man in front of me. He swallows visibly.

Scared, like a little bitch.

I shove past him and make my way to the cage, ignoring the screaming of my name around me. All I hear is the thumping of my heart in my ears and all I feel is the pain in my fists. I can't wait to be covered in blood.

A man is kneeling in the center as I enter the cage, the door remaining open behind me. He's impossible to recognize because a burlap sack covers his head, but his clothing is similar to what Carm was wearing today, although I didn't get a good look. The stature is the same as well. If Raph thought putting Carm in the ring for me to kill would test my loyalty, then he's a fucking idiot. I would kill him without a second thought. I stalk forward and rip the sack off his head.

My breath lodges in my throat and I fly backward, my back hitting the cage.

"Ember?" He tries to focus his black and swollen eyes on me as he sways on his knees.

Fuck.

This is it. I'm dying tonight, and I'm okay with that. It'll be worth it to save Tommy's life.

"Kill me." I turn to face my father. "Kill me, you son of a bitch!"

"Ember," his broken voice sounds behind me. "Do it. Get out of here. I'm nothing, you hear me?"

"You're everything. Where would I be without you?" My voice is shaky as I turn back around to face the person who taught me that I was worthy of friends.

A gun cocks behind me as I close my eyes and exhale.

"Kill Tommy or I kill you. I have orders." Carm's voice hits the back of my head.

"You knew about this too," I whisper as my voice cracks with emotion.

"No." I can't turn to look at him because my eyes are locked on my best friend.

"I can't kill him. He's my family." I look at Tommy kneeling on the mat, his head hanging as tears coat my cheeks.

"He knows the deal. If you don't kill him, he still dies."

The crowd has quieted down, and you could hear a pin drop in the cavernous space.

"Daughter!" Raphael yells out. "That man has been a traitor to our family. You must kill him, and then you will take your rightful place by my side." Just the thought of that makes me want to kill. I will never be by his side because when I'm through with him, he'll be nothing more than a corpse.

"Do it, Ember," Tommy groans.

"Kill me," I beg Carm. "Because I won't do it, and if you let me out of here, you're dead too." The gun goes off behind me and I wait for the impact.

Nothing.

I look up to find Tommy lying on his stomach with blood pooling around his head. My body stiffens with the sight as ice rushes through my veins, sealing everything within its range. Everything stops as my eyes burn, unblinking at the corpse who was once my closest friend. My fingers curl into fists as a dull beat echoes throughout my chest, slow and steady.

"Get everyone out!" Carm yells to the goons from outside the cage, his voice sounding as if underwater.

I barely register the stomping of people's feet because I'm too mesmerized by the blood flowing toward me. I bend down and dip two fingers into it, bringing them to my forehead, moving down over my eyes, down my cheeks, and then stopping at my chin.

I wear his blood in place of my tears.

I wear his blood like a warrior.

I wear his blood to help me kill our enemies.

As soon as the cage door unlocks, I move with a speed that even the ice in my veins can't slow down. I'm outside with my hands around Carm's throat, earning my nickname Blur. He drops the gun to the ground and holds his hands up. *Fucking little bitch.*

"Do it." His eyes are full of sadness. "I'm sorry, but I couldn't kill you, my little sister." The words absorb into my mind, but I don't care. I punch him in the nose and revel in the quick drip of his blood. Then he drops to his knees, and I follow him, picking up the gun. I cock it and point it at his head. "He's my father too." He looks me in the eye. "He raped my mother and killed her when I was born. There's also—"

I cut him off when I smash the gun against his temple, then he's out cold. If he doesn't die from that, I'll be back to finish the job, but for now, I have a bigger fish to fry. It makes sense now why he looked so familiar. He looks like our piece of shit father. Speaking of…

I look around to find the place empty. Why would they leave me alone? They really don't recognize me as a threat and it's fucking laughable. I look back at Tommy's body and steel my heart.

I'm about to bathe in blood.

Chapter Twenty-two

The hallways are empty as I pass by the bedroom they locked me in and then the gym, turning down the next corridor. They have to be here somewhere. I tighten the hold on the gun in my hand, testing its weight against my palm. It has nine bullets left, and I pray that's all I will need. I'm not the best shot, but I can shoot to kill.

Nine bullets.

The sound of my boots hitting the tiled floor echoes throughout the empty hallways. I could be quieter and sneak up on them, but a part of me wants them to know I'm coming, like a predator hunting my prey.

Nine bullets.

I just keep running that thought through my head because if I even think about Tommy… No, I can't. I will have time to mourn him after. Right now, I'm hunting.

Nine bullets.

Finally, the sound of voices filters from the end of the corridor and I smile in anticipation. If I die here today, then I die.

I've accepted that, but I will not go out without a fight. I turn another corner and find two men on either side of a set of double doors. I automatically slip my hand with the gun behind my back and continue walking forward. They both have their eyes on me, and the one to the right raises his gun.

"Stop!" the one to the left yells out.

"You're honestly going to threaten me with a gun? I'm not even armed." I shake my head with a smile. "I need to speak to my father."

Someone barks out a response from inside the door. The fucking dumbass goon holding the gun turns and sticks his head in to hear what they're saying. So I raise my gun and aim for the back of his skull. I hit him at the base of the neck instead, but meh, close enough.

Eight bullets.

The other goon dives to grab the fallen gun and I shoot him in the head. That one is spot-on.

Seven bullets.

I reach the door, step around the blood, and kick it open. My father is sitting at a large desk, looking annoyingly calm. His hands are steepled in front of his face and he has a look of pride in his eyes.

Seven bullets.

"My dear,"—he drops his hands and opens them wide—"are you going to shoot me?"

I look around the room, looking for any of his minions, but find him alone. He stands from his desk, his arms still open wide.

"Yes." I shoot his left knee and watch as he falls back into his chair, screaming. "But only to make sure you don't run."

Six bullets.

His screams turn into hysterical laughter as his right hand inches toward a drawer on his desk. So I shoot that shoulder, and it's my turn to laugh maniacally as he screams again, his arm dropping like dead weight.

Five bullets.

The blood bubbles out of both wounds, and my heart rate kicks up. Watching him bleed and in pain is euphoric, and a familiar rush comes over me. The edge of my vision thrums with my heartbeat, and the red starts seeping in.

Five bullets.

I feel it.

It moves smoothly, effortlessly.

Through the pain, into darkness. It devours every crack and crevice, filling the voids.

I won't fight it this time.

No.

This time, I will welcome it. My savior.

Five bullets.

Placing the gun on the desk, I look my father dead in the eyes, and what he finds startles him, making me laugh again. It shouldn't. My darkness came from him, after all. It should look familiar.

"I forgive you," he whispers, dropping his chin to his chest.

I chuckle dryly before reaching out and grabbing a handful of his hair, lifting his face to mine. At that moment, a dry flake of Tommy's blood floats off my face and lands on his cheek.

"Thank you. I'm going to need it."

Carm is no longer lying where I left him, and all that's left of Tommy is the puddle of blood in the middle of the cage. I don't have it in me to search for them because my whole body is sore and exhausted. My fist, still clenched around the gun, is throbbing and torn open in several places. My black clothing looks like a dark garnet saturated in blood, and I can only imagine what my face and hair look like.

Four bullets.

Turning away, I leave the cage and Tommy behind me. I have to get out of here and back home. The ice inside me is blocking any feelings of humanity, and I can't seem to make myself care about anything. I always knew if I let the darkness in completely, I would be forever altered, but I can't bring myself to regret it. Raphael deserved every torture he received.

I make it out of the underground compound and step into the bright sunlight. I've been bathing in his blood for at least twelve hours and the sun only serves to brighten the red on my skin.

I wish it could have lasted longer.

Being back in New York is a pain in the ass. Waiting for my family to get here will take a while, and New York police are fucking annoying. The compound is in a desolate and abandoned factory area, so my ass has to walk to the nearest gas station. My clothes are stiff from drying blood and my skin itches where it's flaking off.

The road looks long and never-ending and the gun in my sweater pocket feels like it weighs twenty pounds, but when I spot the gas station on the horizon, I walk a little faster. It's unbelievable, but not one car has passed me this entire time. I walk inside and begin the story I will have to make myself believe for the rest of my life.

Chapter Twenty-Three

She's been home for two weeks. I haven't been able to see her and it's eating at my patience. I understand the legal hurdles to get through, psychological testing and police interviews, but that girl is mine, and I'm not waiting much longer.

She was gone for a little over a week—eight and a half days of fucking torture—and I can't squeeze a single detail out of her parents. They want her to tell me on her own terms and I say fuck that because I am about to lose my shit.

My mother told me they found her in New York, covered in blood, and holding a loaded fucking gun. I still don't know if it was her blood or not. I've spoken to the police and told them about the gang trailing her from New York but fuck this place and the local police. If the trail doesn't end with a box of donuts, they won't fucking follow it.

School's done in two weeks, and it'll be Em's birthday. I want to bring her to our cabin in Muskoka, even invite the prick and Adrianna. She loves them, so I'll tolerate them for her. I will do just about anything for her, and yet here I am, pacing my bedroom like a fucking pussy.

Fuck this.

I grab my leather jacket and open my bedroom door when the sound of my front door opens and then shuts. What the fuck? My mother is at work tonight, so I know it isn't her. I stand at the top of the stairs and look down.

She's standing in the center of my foyer, as if conjured from my very thoughts.

Her hair hangs down her back and covers half of her face. Her skin, like the creamiest mocha, glistens with perspiration like she ran her ass all the way here. She has on a black lace tank top and a pair of the shortest fucking shorts I have ever seen. Her long legs are bare and tempting. She has no fucking shoes on her feet, and her toes are covered in dirt. Where the fuck did she come from without shoes?

"Em?" I slowly descend the stairs, my body coiled as if I'm approaching a wild animal.

Her eyes flick up and I stop in my tracks. Her beautiful, tropical ocean eyes look vacant and void of the warmth I'm used to seeing. *Fuck, where's my baby?*

"Where are your shoes, Em?"

Finally, there's the slightest spark as her plump lips curl up into a cruel smirk and she chuckles, the sound making my dick so hard it hurts. "That's the first thing you want to ask me?" she sneers, her body remaining still. "After three weeks?"

"Yeah, baby. You could've cut yourself and got an infection. That shit can kill you." My hand glides along the banister as a chill runs along the back of my neck, sending goose bumps along my skin.

"I'm not afraid to die." She shrugs like it's nothing, as if her very life isn't now intricately woven with mine. I walk down and stand on the last stair in front of her. Her head is tipped back, her hair hanging around her shoulders. Standing this close, each feature is revealed in clarity. Her face is pale and her eyes are bloodshot, heavy bags darkening the space underneath. She isn't sleeping.

I step down the final stair and she suddenly throws herself into my arms, wrapping her toned legs around my waist. I let out a loud moan when my hands grip her ass. Her ass is so round and so fucking plump. All I can imagine is me fucking her from behind as it slaps off my stomach. Her fingers run up the back of my head, sending tingles straight to my cock.

"I'm going to need you to fuck me, Vin," she growls as she leans in to bite my bottom lip. "Fuck me so hard and make it hurt."

I'm pretty sure I'm about to blow my fucking load. I'm going to do what she says because if I'm whipped, you better believe it's going to be fucking pussy whipped.

I carry her back to my room and throw her on my bed. Then I'm down to my boxers in no time and sliding her shorts off to join the rest of my clothes on the floor. She doesn't have any panties on either and I groan as I drop my face down to her pussy. My mouth waters instantly as I inhale her scent, and I look up to find her watching me, perched up on her elbows.

"You gonna eat that shit, baby? Or stare at it?"

I growl and suck her into my mouth, my tongue swiping all the way from her asshole to her clit. Nothing has ever tasted as good as her. *Nothing*. I slide my tongue inside of her, working a rhythm as she moans, her hands grabbing the back of my head, pushing me in closer. I clamp her clit between my teeth and start licking it in quick, tight circles, the hardened nub pulsing. She comes so hard that I have her juices running down my chin. She's always so fucking wet for me.

"Fuck me, Vin," she groans.

I crawl up her body, shedding my boxers and her shirt. Her tits are perfect, not too big but still plump, her nipples the color of dusty rose. They harden in front of my face, and I grab one in my mouth, biting down hard, then sucking away the pain.

Her pussy presses up against my hips, making her impatience clear. Fuck, I'm impatient too. It's been too long since I've had her. I line myself up to her sweet heat and look her in the eyes, the cold emptiness now replaced by raw hunger.

I'm going to fucking feed her every inch of this cock. I slam into her, knowing it's going to hurt and not giving a shit. She asked for pain and that's what she's going to get. She takes it without a whimper because my girl is a fucking sadist. I work up a punishing rhythm and she moans, her slickness coating my thighs. My balls begin to tingle and I won't be able to go too much longer. Pulling her right leg up over my shoulder, I reach my hand down to her asshole, slicking my fingers through the juices pooling between her ass cheeks. I play with her asshole a bit and then slowly sink two fingers inside.

"Holy fuck," she groans as the tight ring of muscle clenches around them.

I pump my fingers in and out of her ass as her pussy tightens around my dick. She's almost there, but I'm not able to hold on anymore. "I can't wait until I'm slamming my dick into this tight ass." That does the trick, and she explodes around me with a scream. My girl is fucking nasty and I love it. I thrust in as far as I can and come so hard as stars explode behind my eyelids.

Epilogue

I've become good at faking life. Each day, I pretend to be normal. I'm pretty sure Vin sees through it most days though, but I'm grateful that he lets me be. I wouldn't know where to start or how much of the truth to reveal to him otherwise. Our sex has become a rough volley for dominance, and he doesn't say anything, just gives me what I need. And I need it… It's the only time I *feel*. There are two different situations in which I feel anything. The first is sex with Vin, and the second is my recurring nightmares. So I ride his dick multiple times a day, and the soreness is welcomed because at least there's something. Then I pass out and have nightmares filled with blood, gore, and torture. Flashbacks that will haunt me forever.

School is done for the year. I didn't have to return because of my circumstances and finished my exams online. I did well, but I no longer care about that or most things. I'm empty inside and I can't muster an ounce of emotion for anything. The worry is evident in my parents' eyes, but I'm sure they're really putting their faith in the therapist they've found for me. Trust me, it's not working. I no longer function normally, and I probably never will. I'll grieve for the girl I once was when I find the time to let myself go.

There is an open investigation into my incident with the

local police department and the New York police department. I didn't divulge any information regarding the Rampage or about Raphael because my revenge was for me alone. I claimed I was taken from the school parking lot, drugged, then woke up on the street in New York, covered in blood and holding a gun. So, for now, I'm safe.

As for the fact that I have a half brother out there, I don't give a shit. Carm can be dead for all I care. Anyone connected to Raphael is less than shit under my shoe. I really don't have a fuck to give.

The sun is beating down on my skin and the warmth seeps into my muscles. My body is constantly aching due to lack of sleep, but Vin has swept me off to his cottage in Muskoka for a long weekend of relaxation for my birthday, so I'm trying my best to be grateful. He's invited Travis and Adri too, and that's fine, although I haven't seen them since I was taken. I just can't bring myself to care. They can sense the distance between us, even though I text them every day. Again, not a single fuck to give.

Vin went into town to grab some alcohol and food about ten minutes ago, and being here alone is nice, peaceful. I stand and brush the beach sand from my ass and walk back inside the cabin. I haven't run in a while and suddenly, the urge is overwhelming. The twists and turns of the dirt roads are quiet and solitary and they call out for my pounding footsteps. I put on a pair of shorts over my red bikini bottom and head out to the road.

About fifteen minutes into the run, the sound of a car approaches me from behind and it slows down to match my pace. Looking up from the road, I find a blacked-out sedan, identical to the ones that snatched me from my school. I wait for the pounding of my heart and the twisting of my stomach, but come up empty. The rear window rolls down and Carm's face appears. I stare into his eyes, willing myself to grow angry at his survival, but all I feel is a blankness.

"We need to talk, Ember." His voice is like a dull roar in my ears, the words a mash of inflection.

"About?" My hands curl around my waist as I raise a brow.

"Can you get in the car? It'll be easier. We can even park on the side. I won't take you anywhere." His assurances mean nothing to me. *He means nothing to me.*

"You think I'm afraid of you?" I step closer to the car and stare him down. "I will never let that happen to me again. I would kill you without a second thought."

"I know." He nods. "Please?"

I open the rear door and climb in. Two men sit in the front, the driver's face reflected in the rearview mirror, and I commit it to memory. I can't see the passenger since he is facing the window, but I take in his dark brown hair with rich mahogany highlights, not unlike my own. His shoulders are wide set, filling the small space with ease.

"You killed our father," Carm states. It's not a question, although I answer him anyway.

"Yes." I wait for a reaction, anything that can potentially detonate the sleeping bomb inside of me, but he's yet another disappointment.

"I am now head of the Eastside Rampage." He inclines his head as his jaw tics with words he'd rather not say.

"Congrats." I give him a slow clap.

"Yeah." He runs his hand over his face as he exhales. "You're my only sister, Ember. I'm not going to leave you alone."

"You're going to regret that when you're dead," I promise as his eyes widen with my declaration.

The guy in the front passenger seat snorts, his shoulders moving slightly with the sound. Is he laughing?

"What's so fucking funny?" I snarl at the back of his head.

He turns his face to look at me, and suddenly my world tips as I become lightheaded, my body coated in ice. Light turquoise eyes with a beauty mark under the right one stares back at me.

"Hello, twin."

Carry on for a sneak peek into the next book Into Darkness in the Whitsborough Chronicles Series!

PROLOGUE

"I forgive you," he whispers, dropping his chin to his chest.

I chuckle dryly, reaching out and grabbing a handful of his hair, lifting his face to mine. At that moment, a dry flake of Tommy's blood floats off my face and lands on his cheek.

"Thank you, I'm going to need it." I jam my forefinger into the gunshot wound at his shoulder and revel in his screams. His blood pumping out around my fingers and down my arm like a warm, soothing bath. "I doubt my mother forgave you for taking her from me." I grab his chin, smearing it with his blood. "We were all each other had."

"She ... knew it ... was going to happen." He's panting and his leg wound is losing a lot of blood. I can't have him dying too soon, I'm just getting started. I look around his office and find a fancy-looking Burberry scarf wrapped around a wooden coat stand. That'll do.

I apply the makeshift tourniquet around his leg and look into his eyes. "Thank you, my daughter."

I laugh and slap him hard across the face, the sound

bouncing around the room like a cacophony of mocking laughter. Finally, the meek mask he's been wearing drops and his eyes become cold. "There you are, Father." I grin. "It's finally nice to meet you."

"My son will come looking for me," he says between blood-coated teeth.

"Carm?" I put my finger to my nose, tapping lightly, as I look to the ceiling in thought. "I killed him." The words tumble out of me with complete nonchalance as I shrug.

The alarm in his eyes sends me into another round of manic laughter. "Your mother would not want this," he pants out as his eyelids grow heavy.

Just the mention of her from his mouth sends me into a red void and what little restraint I had on my anger is suddenly gone. I punch him in the face and his nose buckles under my knuckles as his yell of pain awakens a hunger.

"We're going to have so much fun," I say as I reach out and tweak his crushed nose.

His answering whine of pain makes me giggle.

For all book updates and social platforms, check out my website

ABOUT C.A. RENE

C.A. Rene lives in Toronto, Canada with her family, where most of the year varies from chilly to frigid. Most days you'll find her wrapped in her many blankets in bed while reading or writing her next dark, twisted story.
Her stories boast of inclusivity and refusal to be conformed in any small box. Writing across genres is a hobby and drinking wine is a must… Or coffee … with a splash of Baileys.

Also by C.A. Rene

<u>The Whitsborough Chronicles</u>

Through the Pain

Into Darkness

Finding the Light

To Redemption

<u>The Whitsborough Progenies</u>

Ivy's Venom

Carmelo's Malice

Saxon's Distortion

Gabriel's Deception

<u>Desecrated Duet</u>

Desecrated Flesh

Desecrated Essence

<u>The Reaped Series</u>

The Reaper Incarnate

Hunting the Reaper

Claiming the Reaper

<u>Hail Mary Duet</u>

Blue 42

Red Zone

<u>Fusion Core</u>

Tension

Release

<u>Steel Dragons MC</u>

Dragon Slayer

Dragon Strife

Dragon Scorch

<u>Hell's March MC Duet</u>

Hell's Viper

TBA

<u>Second Chance Standalones</u>

Fighting the Tide